HALFHYDE AND THE CHAIN GANGS

BY THE SAME AUTHOR:

HALFHYDE AND THE CHAIN GANGS

Philip McCutchan

St. Martin's Press
New York

Library of Congress Cataloging in Publication Data

McCutchan, Philip, 1920-
    Halfhyde and the chain gangs.

    I. Title.
PR6063.A167H28   1986   823'.914   85-25051
ISBN 0-312-35662-5

First published in Great Britain by Weidenfeld and Nicolson Ltd.
First U.S. Edition
10 9 8 7 6 5 4 3 2 1

HALFHYDE AND THE CHAIN GANGS

ONE

There was, Halfhyde found as he stepped down from the train at the high-level platform of the station near the Town Hall, much nostalgia in his return to Portsmouth. Portsmouth was all navy, the streets would as ever swarm with bluejackets, tough, bearded men with a swaggering walk and the very feel and smell of the sea about them as they roistered in and out of the many hundreds of public houses that adorned the port. Though Halfhyde's many initial regrets at having left Her Majesty's Fleet had by now been submerged by the happy thought that he owned and sailed his own ship under the Red Ensign of the Merchant Service, the nostalgia was strong, as strong as the damp smell of blue serge sweated into by a naval draft from Chatham that had been on his train out of Waterloo. As he went down the steps to street level he was submerged by the mass of ratings under the charge of a petty officer second class, a man heavily tattooed as to the backs of his hands. The draft was met by the naval patrol, gaitered seamen under a ship's corporal who mustered and checked the men before they were fallen in to march to the barracks, while their kitbags and hammocks continued by another train of bare vans to the barracks' siding on the line that ran into the dockyard.

Halfhyde watched the men march off in column of fours. The town's traffic was held up for them by a policeman with a bulging stomach and side-whiskers, the tight neck of his tunic seizing him by the neck so hard that rolls of flesh overhung it. There was a bluejackets' band to head the files: such was good for recruiting, and there was talk of war in the air, had been for some while now. Brother Boer was getting uppish again, and might have to be taught a sound lesson, given a sound thrashing for his impudence. If it came, it looked like being a land war rather than a naval one, but all the same the fleet was making ready, and new battleships and cruisers were being commissioned continually.

The men marched away, the band playing 'Goodbye, Dolly Gray'. More nostalgia, the sound of songs of war . . . Halfhyde shrugged, turned his back and sent a porter to get him a cab. He had no gear with him, he intended returning to London that same day en route for Liverpool, but he was not going to have his father-in-law, if indeed Sir John Willard still regarded himself as such, imagining that he was too penurious to afford one-and-sixpence. It had been Halfhyde's sense of duty that had impelled him to seek audience with Sir John, nothing else; he did not look forward to the interview and hoped he would be spared a meeting with the unfortunate Mildred.

The porter came back, touching his cap. 'Cab's awaiting, sir.'

'Thank you.' Halfhyde handed the man tuppence, which was gratefully received. The cap was touched again, and the porter led the way to the cab. The scraggy horse was whipped awake and behind the clopping hooves Halfhyde looked out at the Town Hall square, was taken past the Theatre Royal and on past Government House to turn right further along past the back of the military barracks, then left again into the High Street of Old Portsmouth, past the George Hotel with its memories of Lord Nelson, to stop outside the residence of Vice-Admiral Sir John Willard.

Halfhyde got out, looked back at the cabby. 'You'll kindly wait,' he said. 'I shall not be long.'

* * *

Standing with his back to the fireplace in his study, Sir John's face was grim. He snapped, 'Master of a gun-runner to the damn Irish rebels!'

'Not so, sir. Well you know it! My crew and I were instrumental in preventing the arms reaching the rebels – as was fully reported in the newspapers—'

'Which was why you asked to see me, no doubt. Because I would know you were in this country. Had it not been for that—'

'I would not have come, sir. That's true. But in the circumstances, a sense of decency—'

'Hah!'

'Hah notwithstanding, sir, I demand an apology for your accusation of gun-running.' Halfhyde was standing also, and his long jaw was thrust out. There was a hard light in his eye. 'You will apologize at once, sir. As a gentleman—'

'Oh, very well!' the vice-admiral snapped, reddening. 'If it relieves me of your presence the faster, then I apologize. And now pray tell me what you want of me, Halfhyde.' He paused, glaring distastefully. 'I suppose you call yourself *Captain* Halfhyde now.'

'No, sir. I do not call myself Captain Halfhyde. I *am* Captain Halfhyde—'

'We'll not argue the point. Kindly answer my question.'

Halfhyde took a deep breath. 'I want nothing of you, sir. I came merely to express my regrets as to the past . . . and to enquire after Mildred, who is, after all, my wife still.'

'Whom you abandoned.'

'I'm sorry—'

'Sorry indeed! Lady Willard has been far from well since . . . I wish no damned apologies from you, nor anything else—'

'Nevertheless, sir, I do not run from my responsibilities. Despite financial difficulties I shall still maintain my wife so far as I am able to do so. I—'

'You can keep your damn money, Halfhyde. My daughter wishes to have none of it.'

Halfhyde shrugged. 'Well, you're far from a poor man, I'll grant, sir. All the same—'

'Must I repeat it? My daughter will accept nothing from you, d'you hear me?' Sir John's colour was rising dangerously towards apoplexy. 'Your money is tainted and such as you've already given her will be returned – there was mention in the newspapers of a woman aboard that ship of yours—'

'Yes. A passenger.'

Sir John glowered. 'You expect me to believe that!'

'Perhaps not a passenger only,' Halfhyde admitted. 'I am a man, sir, and I have the needs of a man. When one's wife—'

'What you call needs . . . my daughter no doubt regards

3

them as *disgusting*.'

Halfhyde smile frigidly. 'You sound as though you agree, sir. In which case I find myself very surprised, not to say astonished, that your daughter was born at all—'

'I regard this conversation as degrading, Halfhyde – and highly improper. If you have no more to say, I'd be obliged if you would kindly remove yourself from my house – and not return again.'

Halfhyde gave an ironic bow. 'As you say, of course, sir. May I, as a final request, ask how Mildred is? I am not without some regard for my wife, and I wish her nothing but well, and wish for her happiness. If—'

'My daughter has her interests. She has her horse. She stands in no need of sympathy from you.' Sir John tugged at a bell ribbon, his mouth clamped shut. He said nothing further; when his manservant entered the study, he merely gestured towards Halfhyde, who was at once shown out with no godspeed from Sir John Willard. He re-entered the cab, directing the cabby back to the railway station, his face grim. As he had tried to show, he was not without remorse for a marriage that he should never have entered upon in the first place. That was not entirely his fault, though he had often blamed himself. Lady Willard, scenting a suitable suitor in a lieutenant of the Royal Navy, as Halfhyde had then been, for an unattractive wallflower, had been pressing. She knew well enough there would be no other aspirants. A feeling of pity for Mildred, allied to an excess of whisky taken one night, had done the rest. What little remained of joy in the marriage had evaporated under those very interests of Mildred as mentioned by her father: she was never happy away from straw, horse dung and the hunting field – or the race track. Her face was itself equine, so was her posterior, which rose and fell when she walked, like the buttocks of a horse being gently led around a ring. She lacked only a tail. And bed was far from being her favourite place. She was as cold as a winter's night in Halfhyde's native Wensleydale in the North Riding, as unresponsive as Aysgarth Falls when in the grip of ice. When Victoria Penn had come into his life unbidden, across the world in Sydney, Halfhyde had more than welcomed the thaw into the hot sun of summer and – so far as his anxieties in regard to the gun-running Porteous Higgins had allowed – had enjoyed

4

the soft nights beneath the Pacific stars as the *Taronga Park* had steamed with her clanking engine towards the Chilean port of Puerto Montt.

Going back now to London, Halfhyde's mind switched from thoughts of Mildred to more fruitful ones: the future. No cavils had emerged from the authorities as to his claim for the refitting of the *Taronga Park*, her engine-room shattered by fire-axes when half-way across the South Atlantic as a result of Porteous Higgins' seizure of the ship. Halfhyde had performed a good service for the government by upsetting Higgins' plans for arms supply to the Irish rebels; and the government had been unusually grateful. But the refit had been a long one; only a few days before, Halfhyde had brought his ship from Queenstown to Liverpool in search of a cargo – and a crew. More than half his original crew, men in the pay of Porteous Higgins, had jumped ship in Queenstown, taking Higgins' bounty with them, and they had appeared to have made good their escape. Others had died, killed at sea by Higgins or his confederate Gaboon. Halfhyde's first mate, Perry, had died in Chile. So now there was much to be done and as ever the future held financial uncertainty. The obtaining of a cargo was the essential factor; Halfhyde was prepared to take a cargo for any of the world's ports, and on arrival hope to find another to carry him on again to anywhere else.

In the meantime, however, he had something else to do: a call upon the Admiralty the following morning. With the country moving towards war, he could not stand aside, nor might he be allowed to. He was still a lieutenant on the unemployed list, a naval officer in retirement liable to recall. For the future conduct of his livelihood he had to know where he stood.

* * *

Halfhyde dined that night, extravagantly, at the Café Royal, accompanied by Victoria Penn who had been waiting for him at Waterloo station. The girl's face had been somewhat strained as she saw him striding along the platform from the Portsmouth train: he might have been cajoled back to Mildred. But he had at once taken her in his arms and lifted her bodily off the ground, crushing her close. They kissed; and she knew then that all was well. In the privacy of a hansom cab they kissed again, and she asked about his day.

'Better forgotten,' he said crisply. 'Though it was not as bad as it might have been. I never set eyes upon the old faggot – Lady Willard. An attack of the vapours, no doubt, at the mere thought of me.'

'And – your wife?'

'She has her horse,' Halfhyde answered, repeating Sir John's words with a grin. 'And what have *you* been doing in my absence, Victoria?'

She said, 'I went along to look at Buckingham Palace.'

'Impressed?'

'Yes,' she said. Victoria Penn, born in the North Riding not so far from Halfhyde's own boyhood home, had been many years in Australia and now thought as an Australian; and there had been nothing in her life, or in Australia, like Buckingham Palace. 'I hoped I might see the Queen, but no. There were a lot of soldiers marching, in red coats and funny hats—'

'Bearskins. They'll not be wearing their red for much longer. This new-fangled khaki as worn in India . . . that'll be what they'll wear in South Africa.' Halfhyde had bought an evening paper at Waterloo. He flourished the pages at Victoria. 'It's all building up.'

'Let's forget it,' she said.

'I doubt if anyone wants to do that. The crowds'll be out soon, cheering their heads off as the troops march off for the railway and the transports.'

'Well, I won't be cheering. Not if you get involved.'

He took her in his arms again, and said no more about the possibilities of war. The cab set them down at Halfhyde's bidding in Birdcage Walk, and they strolled in St James's Park, looking at the ducks on the water and Buckingham Palace looming over the green of the trees. It was a peaceful scene, far removed from the gunfire of a land battle or the stormy heave of deep waters and the gale-torn route to the west coast of South America and Australia round Cape Horn. Nevertheless Halfhyde lost himself in thought around that other cape, the Cape of Good Hope, and the ships that might soon be assembling in Table Bay, the warships and the transports that would take out the regiments to rout the overweening Boers and their leaders,

Smuts, Cronje, Kruger, farmer-generals in slouch hats, shirt-sleeves, waistcoats and bandoliers.

At his side Victoria said, 'Come back to London, love. I'm here, right?'

He smiled down at her. 'I'm sorry.' They walked on, across the Mall and up St James's Street into Piccadilly. From the direction of Piccadilly Circus there came something like uproar: a crowd of people, civilians, soldiers, bluejackets, surged along. They were cheering and shouting and singing patriotic songs: 'Soldiers of the Queen', 'Goodbye, Dolly Gray', even 'The Girl I Left Behind Me', brought across the years from Wellington's armies. The blood-lust was up already. Halfhyde and Victoria were surrounded by the crowd, good-natured, happy, looking forward to stirring news when the British troops were ordered out. A burly bluejacket, a leading stoker by his badges, seized hold of Victoria and planted a smacking kiss before releasing her and moving on, waving his sennit hat in the air, displaying the name of his ship on the ribbon: HMS *Powerful*. Halfhyde drew Victoria out of the seething mass, turning left along Bond Street to thread through lesser thoroughfares for the Café Royal.

After dinner she was pensive. She said, 'That bloody hotel you recommended.'

'What's wrong with it?'

She shrugged. 'Oh, nothing. Just lonely. You could have come there with me. Don't know why you had to go to that Mrs what's-her-name.'

'Mavitty. She's an old friend, a good landlady years ago when I was impoverished on the half-pay list – I've told you before. I owe it to her to make use of her services again. She'd be hurt otherwise.'

'Soft-hearted, aren't you?'

'Not particularly. A sense of duty,' Halfhyde said austerely, 'doesn't come amiss at times.'

'And your wife?'

'I did my best. No man can be expected to cling to an icicle, especially when continually upon a horse. Though I'm far from saying I applaud myself—'

'Look, I wasn't criticizing.'

'I know.' He reached out and laid a hand over hers. 'We shall

7

be back aboard tomorrow evening – have patience, as I must myself.'

'That's all very well. You said you had rooms at Mrs thing's, didn't you? That's not like having just a room in a lodging house, what you do is your—'

'By no means under the good Mrs Mavitty's roof, Victoria. Mrs Mavitty has principles, just like your own namesake in Buckingham Palace. She would be scandalized at such brazenness and would undoubtedly throw us out into the street. She looks upon me as a gentleman, Victoria.'

She glared at him. 'And gentlemen don't f—'

'Not in Mrs Mavitty's house.'

Later he saw her to her hotel, not far off Leicester Square. She was ruffled, so much was obvious. Victoria, Halfhyde thought, had much to learn about English life. In basis it was not so different from New South Wales, where morality also prevailed on the surface. But Victoria Penn had come from the King's Cross district of Sydney, where crime and prostitution prevailed over respectability. To put no finer point on it, she had herself been caught up in prostitution; she had left that, and Porteous Higgins who profited from her activities, behind her with relief. But she was not attuned yet to the outlook of such as Mrs Mavitty who had her good name to consider.

When Halfhyde reached Camden Town Mrs Mavitty had news: Mavitty, a morose, hen-pecked man who escaped as often as possible to the nearest public house, had been informed by a fellow drinker, who had got the word from a friend who worked in a lowly capacity in the War Office, that the British South African colonies had been invaded and that a column of four thousand men under General Symons, part of the Ladysmith garrison in Natal, had come under attack, their camp being heavily shelled by the Boers from Talana Hill. In carrying the hill by assault, his artillery being outranged by the Boers, General Symons had been killed.

'So it's war,' Mrs Mavitty said, standing arms akimbo and wearing a formidable expression. 'Dearie me, sir, all them poor soldiers! But we'll just show that Kruger he can't get away with it, won't we, sir? Mind, Mavitty does get things wrong sometimes . . .'

TWO

Mavitty had got nothing wrong. Halfhyde confirmed his veracity from the next morning's newspapers. The correspondents in South Africa had lost no time in sending their cables to London. The country was at war. Outside in the streets the population was going mad, it seemed. Throngs were everywhere, cheering their heads off. Making his way to the Admiralty, Halfhyde found the Mall packed. Speaking to a policeman, he was told that the gates of Buckingham Palace were virtually under siege, with the invisible Queen Victoria being cheered to the echo.

Once inside the Admiralty building, Halfhyde kicked his heels for an hour past the time of his appointment before being taken to the presence of a captain RN wearing a uniform frock-coat agleam with brass buttons and gold-thread stripes. The captain, by name Grant-Pellew, seemed to be in a sour mood.

'Lieutenant St Vincent Halfhyde,' he said, shuffling a file of documents. 'Mixed record, what? Some good, some bad – like the curate's egg. Excellent seaman, no coward, but impetuous. And constantly fell foul of senior officers. Inclined to dispute orders – I don't like that. Does anyone?' The question was rhetorical. 'I see that you were often right but that's no excuse and don't quote Lord Nelson at me. Well, what is it you're asking?'

'Orders, sir. As a lieutenant on the unemployed list—'

'Yes, yes.'

'I am at my country's disposal, sir, that's understood. But for purposes of my own affairs—'

'Your own damn affairs have nothing to do with it, Halfhyde.

9

Her Majesty does not concern herself with the personal affairs of her officers and men.'

'Quite, sir. But I think I am in a different position from most people in that I own and command a ship of my own. If I am to return to the fleet, I shall have a number of dispositions to make in regard to my ship and my crew. All I ask is to be informed of what is expected of me – and informed in good time.'

'Really. Well, you have a nerve, I'll say that, Halfhyde. You will be informed in *our* good time, not yours.' Captain Grant-Pellew drummed his fingers on the top of an immense desk. 'The *Taronga Park* ... oh, you did well enough there by all accounts. The man Higgins. Where's your ship now?'

'In the Mersey, sir, awaiting a cargo.'

'Yes, I see. Well, I can give you no firm decision, Halfhyde. War is war. If a need arises for your services you will be informed. In the meantime you need to earn a living, I suppose. But you must confine yourself to home waters, in case—'

'I'm damned if I shall!' Halfhyde said tartly.

Grant-Pellew got to his feet, his face cold. 'I remind you of your position. You still come under Admiralty orders when required. You will take no foreign cargoes until you receive clearance.'

'My dear sir, I—'

'That is all, Mr Halfhyde. You may go.'

* * *

The train journey to Liverpool was a disagreeable one. Halfhyde was in a seething mood. He had no love for coasting and no love for being inhibited in his movements whilst waiting on the pleasure of the Board of Admiralty. Inaction irked him; and he could soon find himself in sorry financial straits. The *Taronga Park* was a deep-sea vessel, with too much draft to enter small coastal ports not dredged to take foreign-going ships – besides which it was uneconomic to use such a ship for coastal cargoes, ill-paid cargoes even if they could be found. And again, the coastal ships of England already had the monopoly of their own trade, the trade to which they had long been accustomed and in which their masters were well known to shippers and consignees. Halfhyde and the *Taronga Park* would be interlopers.

'Stop bloody worrying about it,' Victoria said crossly. 'It'll settle itself if you don't bloody agitate.'

'If it doesn't, I may find you too much of an expense,' Halfhyde snapped.

'Well, I like that! Know something, do you?'

'What?'

'Half the time, you're a bastard.'

She had said it a little loudly. Eyebrows were raised: they were not alone in the carriage. Halfhyde said, 'Try to remember this isn't Australia, much less the Cross.'

They didn't talk much after that. Halfhyde read the *Morning Post*. Much military movement was expected; the troop trains would be leaving for Southampton where the transports for the Cape would embark them. Some regiments at home and overseas had already had advance orders: the First Battalion The Border Regiment was expected to be among the first to go, standing by to be trooped from the Malta garrison to Table Bay. At home the King's Own Yorkshire Light Infantry and the Royal Scots Greys were under orders to sail, along with a battalion of the Argyll and Sutherland Highlanders, and another of the Royal Munster Fusiliers. The list seemed endless ... Connaught Rangers, Scots Guards, Loyal North Lancashires, Royal Dublin Fusiliers. Plus, it seemed, half the Empire – Canadian, Australian and New Zealand troops all shortly to converge on Table Bay and False Bay to join the local levies from the South African colonies themselves.

Patriotic as he was, Halfhyde could have wished it all to have happened at a more propitious time. Mentally he ran an eye over his bank balance: less than five hundred pounds. No mean sum as it stood, but little enough to run a ship, pay his seamen and meet his port dues, bunkering costs and stores bills. It was just as well Sir John Willard had turned down his offer of continuing help in Mildred's support ...

* * *

It was raining when the train pulled into Lime Street station, a typical dirty Mersey day with soot-blackened damp dripping down the bleak walls of the shipping companies' offices, and sad-looking horses pulling brewers' drays, bread carts and cabs, leaving their droppings to lie in puddles of water. Coming down to the docks the scene was gloomy though busy even at this late hour of the afternoon, the cranes lifting their long necks to hoist the cargo slings and lower them into the holds of the ships at the quays, the dockers grabbing for the crates and bags with their wicked-looking cargo hooks, implements that could easily be turned into weapons and often were. Liverpool was no soft spot; but it was prosperous and Halfhyde hoped against hope that he would share in that prosperity as soon as he could arrange for a cargo.

He paid off the cab at the foot of the *Taronga Park*'s gangway. As he was seen, the watchman emerged from the shelter of a deckhouse: Halfhyde returned the man's salutation absently as he caught Victoria's expression.

'What's the matter, Victoria?' he asked.

The girl shivered. 'Liverpool's the matter, love.'

'You've seen it before.'

'This bloody rain.'

'It rained enough in Queenstown.'

'Sure thing! But I thought we'd left it behind.' She gave another shiver and said, 'Reckon I'm homesick for Sydney. Can't you find a cargo for Sydney?'

Halfhyde laughed. 'If I do, I'll be as happy as you. You know one thing, though: I'll not keep you if you want to go, Victoria. I don't own you. That's always been understood.'

Her eyes softened and she put out a hand to touch his. Then, looking up, she said, 'There's Mr Foster. And it's bloody wet for us as well as him. Let's get aboard, right?'

They climbed the ladder to the after well-deck. Foster, Halfhyde's Second Mate on the run from Sydney for Queenstown, now First Mate in Perry's place, gave Victoria a hand down to the deck as she reached the head of the ladder. Halfhyde asked, 'All well, Mr Foster?'

'Yes, sir.'

'Any word of a cargo?'

'No, sir. I'm sorry.'

Halfhyde shrugged. 'Not your fault. It's early days in any case.' As they walked for'ard to the ship's central island superstructure Halfhyde told Foster about his somewhat inconclusive interview at the Admiralty.

Foster said, 'Well, sir, let's hope you're going to be left in peace.'

'I'm not too sure that I'm a man of peace basically, Mr Foster.' Halfhyde led the way to the saloon. As they sat on a long leather settee beneath the ports, the steward appeared with a pot of tea. Halfhyde went on, 'But the war, now. I've a feeling it should put some cargoes in the way of many ships, not just the *Taronga Park*. There'll be stores to be shipped out to the Cape.'

'They'll likely go aboard the transports, sir.'

'Not all, not all by any means. Tomorrow morning I shall make my rounds of the exporting agencies.' Halfhyde had not forgotten the strictures of Captain Grant-Pellew at the Admiralty; but if he could obtain a war cargo for Table Bay, or Durban, then he would be well prepared to cock a snook at Grant-Pellew.

* * *

Once again, as in Sydney when he had first sought a cargo, it was a case of tramping the streets, waiting upon shippers and agents, an undignified proceeding for a master mariner who owned his own ship. Around Water Street and Goree Street, all the purlieus of the shipping companies and exporters ... Halfhyde sought solace in the Bear's Paw between his abortive calls; the Bear's Paw was a most excellent tavern and there he could exchange yarns and experiences with fellow masters, none of whom, however, held out much hope of a cargo in spite of the war. The *Taronga Park* was old and slow and never mind that there were still many square-riggers at sea, sailing in and out of Liverpool – often enough, with a fair wind behind them, they could make a faster passage than the *Taronga Park*. Besides – and this counted – the *Taronga Park* and her master had attracted a good deal of publicity after the taking of Porteous Higgins and his arms consignment – and then the subsequent trial at which Halfhyde had been the principal witness for the prosecution. But surely that publicity had been good rather than bad?

'Doesn't follow at all,' a shipmaster said in the saloon bar one evening.

'Why not?'

'Because people are funny, Captain.'

'That's no answer,' Halfhyde objected; but on reflection was able to appreciate the point. He and his ship had been a very integral part of a particularly nasty crime on the high seas and mud tended to stick, however unfairly. The *Taronga Park*, he was to discover after almost a fortnight of abortive endeavour, had become a marked ship in the minds of the agents, almost a ship of ill omen – and any seafarer knew just what that meant. Also, Foster's words seemed to be proving correct: government stores and equipment were tending to go aboard the government transports and the requisitioned ships; and so far the Admiralty was showing a total lack of interest in chartering the *Taronga Park*. In the meantime the costs were mounting. Harbour dues had to be met in due course and were far from cheap; Foster and the watchman had to be paid for standing by the ship. And when at last a cargo should come along, he would have to sign a full crew and they would want an advance.

Three weeks later an envelope marked On Her Majesty's Service came addressed to Halfhyde. He opened it with mixed feelings; it was from the Admiralty. It might – though with regrets for his own command accompanying it – bring salvation.

It both did and did not; there was a lack of definition. Halfhyde was not being recalled to the active list of the Fleet. He was being offered a commission as a lieutenant in the Royal Naval Reserve. If he accepted, there was a possibility that his services might be required in connection with the war in South Africa.

'What's that all about, love?' Victoria asked.

Halfhyde gave her a wink. 'Secret orders,' he said.

'Bloody isn't!'

But he didn't tell her; he knew she would try to talk him out of putting his neck in danger of the war. And he intended to accept. He foresaw no danger in any case. The Boers hadn't got a navy and would be most unhandy afloat if they had. He sat at his desk to write a letter in reply and took it ashore himself to post it. Four days later he had a visitor: a card was sent up from the gangway bearing the name of Colonel Bowler, late a prestigious regiment of Light Infantry. Intrigued, Halfhyde left his cabin to meet Colonel Bowler at the gangway: looking down from the master's deck he saw a short, purple-faced man in a morning coat and tall hat, looking oddly out of place in the workaday scene of the Mersey cargo wharves. A white walrus moustache pointed up the whisky complexion, which was not unlike a blood orange. The colonel was striding up and down with an impatient look. Halfhyde went down the ladder, to be met, as the colonel turned, with a direct stare from very blue eyes.

'Captain Halfhyde, I presume?'

'Yes, sir. May I ask your business?'

'In private, Halfhyde, in private.'

Halfhyde gave a formal bow. 'Of course. At your service, sir.' He led the way to his day cabin, more and more intrigued. At closer quarters, Colonel Bowler had a very formidable look: the blood orange was more of a rock than a soft fruit, and the manner was autocratic in the extreme. The body was compact, the bearing was still military although Bowler was obviously retired from the army. In his cabin Halfhyde gestured his visitor to a chair. 'You'll take a drink, sir?'

'Whisky, thank you,' Bowler said. The voice was crisp and authoritative. Halfhyde poured two generous measures: Bowler took his neat.

'Your very good health, Halfhyde.'

'Your health, sir.' They drank, and Bowler looked appreciative of the whisky's quality. Then he announced that he was a busy man and so no doubt was Halfhyde and he would not delay in stating the reason for his visit.

He said, 'I happen to be one of Her Majesty's deputy commissioners for prisons and was until lately governor of Her Majesty's prison at Princetown.'

Halfhyde gave him a sharp look. 'Dartmoor Prison, Colonel?'

'Precisely.'

'And the connection with the *Taronga Park*?'

'Not so much the *Taronga Park*. With yourself, Captain.'

'But I—'

'Please allow me to explain. I shall do so with as much brevity as possible.' Colonel Bowler took another draw at his glass. 'Now: you must understand that what I am about to tell you is, firstly, secret and must not be discussed with anyone else at this stage. Secondly, I do not myself approve of what is going to be done, but that is neither here nor there since I, like yourself, am under the orders of the government – in my case the Home Office and the Prison Commissioners, in yours the Admiralty. I understand you have been appointed to a lieutenant's commission in the reserve—'

'Yes, sir. Formerly I was—'

'A lieutenant RN – yes, this of course I know. It all has a bearing, as you shall see. As has another aspect – your father-in-law—'

'Admiral Willard?'

Bowler looked irritated. 'Who else, my dear fellow – unless you happen to be a bigamist?'

'By no means, sir—'

'Good. Now, Sir John, possibly to your surprise – I have been very fully informed of all the facts pertaining to you – was instrumental in obtaining a certain mission for you when his advice was sought, and indeed, for the furtherance of this mission, made a recommendation to Their Lordships that you should be employed in the reserve.' Bowler finished his whisky, took out a vast red silk handkerchief and blew his nose with a sound like a cavalry trumpet. From the manner in which his gaze swivelled towards the empty glass, Halfhyde understood that a refill would not be refused; and he obliged.

'Thank you, Halfhyde. Now then: here are the facts. A number, in my opinion a dangerously *high* number of what used to be *my* convicts in Dartmoor has along with men from other prisons volunteered for the war in South Africa. They have volunteered to form a labour battalion under military orders for the construction of defences, gun emplacements, trenches and so forth. As I have already indicated, I am opposed to this, but I have been overruled by the Home Secretary – by the Prime Minister as well. It is considered a fine example of patriotism and bravery, you see – which I can't deny it perhaps is. Perhaps. It doesn't take much brain to see that it could be no more than a damned impertinent attempt at a mass break-out either while they are in transit to the ship that'll take them out to the Cape, or even on the high seas. However, the decision's been made.'

'And it's my ship that has been chosen?'

'Not your *ship*, Halfhyde. You as master, yes, to take out the

Dartmoor company. A ship, a sailing ship – a square-rigger – is at this moment being fitted out for the purpose. I'm told you have experience in sail, both in the merchant ships and in the Sail Training Squadron. You are considered a fitting choice—'

'At my father-in-law's suggestion, sir?'

Bowler nodded. 'Largely, yes. But your record at the Admiralty – not wholly admirable, true, since you seem to have made a speciality of being rude to your senior officers, but on the other hand, the *important* hand, Halfhyde, your seamanship is said to have been of the highest order and your experience of command both in the fleet and in the merchant service has stamped authority upon you. There is also your reserve commission to add to your authority as master, the authority of HM Government – you have a thoughtful look, my dear fellow,' Bowler said, breaking off his discourse. 'Why is that, pray?'

Halfhyde answered with honesty. 'Simply because I can't be sure of my father-in-law's motives in recommending me, sir. They may be of the highest – he may, though this I doubt, wish me well. Myself, I am persuaded that he's much more likely to wish me dead, and his daughter free once again.'

Bowler stared back, a hard look, unblinking. 'Admirals in Her Majesty's Fleet don't behave like that, Halfhyde, as you should know.'

'I am glad of your reassurance, Colonel,' Halfhyde said blandly, 'but shall reserve my judgment. Am I to understand that I'm being given an order?'

'It will amount to that,' Bowler answered. 'It will be confirmed to you by the Admiralty within a day or two.'

'And the *Taronga Park*?'

'She remains yours, but will be requisitioned from your ownership shortly to carry stores to Simon's Town. I am authorized to tell you that you will yourself be placed on pay as a lieutenant RNR from the date of your new commission. You will take your uniform with you but will not wear it unless and until a need arises.'

'And that will arise when?'

Bowler said crisply, 'You'll use your judgment. I think you'll know very well when and if the need arises.' He passed the rest of Halfhyde's orders: Halfhyde was to hand over the *Taronga Park* to his First Mate within four days and then travel himself to Devonport dockyard to take command of the fully-rigged ship *Glen Halladale* and to await the draft from Dartmoor Prison. Bowler added, 'They're as rough a bunch of gaolbirds as you'd ever meet in a week's march, Halfhyde, and I don't envy you. They'll be well guarded, of course, and the man in charge, one of the senior warders, is a first-class fellow – ex Sergeant-Major of the Black Watch. He'll use a firm hand, you may be sure.'

'And my crew, sir?'

Bowler said, 'Your officers are appointed already. Your First Mate is a sub-lieutenant of the reserve, a man of much experience of sail in the ships of Iredale and Porter, who're based here in Liverpool as I dare say you know. Your Second and Third Mates are also from the sailing ships. Your fo'c'sle gang you'll choose and sign yourself, as is your right as master. Have you any other questions?'

'For now, sir, no.'

'Then I shall make my way back to London,' Bowler said, getting to his feet. 'If you wish to contact me before you leave Devonport, I am always available at the Board of Prison Commissioners.'

* * *

That night was a time for celebration and celebration meant the Bear's Paw and a number of other hostelries. Neither the time nor the place for a woman: Halfhyde left Victoria Penn in the care of the watchman and went ashore with his First Mate, to whom he had said only that he was being given a naval appointment and must leave the ship to him pending Admiralty requisitioning. The one unresolved matter concerned the girl, Victoria. To her he had said the same as he had said to Foster; and she had reacted badly to possible abandonment. Halfhyde's response had been that she should not cross her bridges; as master he could take her with him if only he could outwit any authority who tried to frustrate the taking of a passenger. But this was simply to break her in gently to a parting: Halfhyde had no intention of exposing her to the possible dangers of his human freight, and could always invent a direct order from the Admiralty or Colonel Bowler. Swinging on his long legs past the clutter of the wharves, he put the matter from his mind. He thought instead about the sudden salvation . . . to be on full pay as a lieutenant and to have the requisition money from the Admiralty – and, as an employed master of the *Glen Halladale*, no running expenses, no crew payments to meet. It would mean plenty of money in his pocket and a nice capital sum when the war in South Africa was over and his ship handed back to him. It would be worth the dangers. What nagged most at him was Sir John Willard: the old fossil, with the old faggot Lady Willard, might well be sniggering up their wealthy sleeves at the thought of the detested St Vincent Halfhyde being attacked at sea by a bunch of thugs out of Dartmoor . . . Bowler had spoken before he went ashore of the dregs of Dartmoor, men who were in for hard labour, some of them lifers, men who were undergoing penal servitude for grievous bodily harm and manslaughter, which he said was an euphemism for unprovable murder. It was only too clear that Bowler was expectant of trouble and had scant belief in the professed patriotism of the convicts. One hundred men clamped below hatches all the way out to South Africa: at the best it would be no bed of roses for those who had to drive the *Glen Halladale* south through wind and weather, and through the mind-deadening lassitude of the Doldrums . . . but tonight was a time to forget his worries and look to a more financially assured future. And to enjoy himself, and Foster too, by drinking deep: in the morning they would both regret it, but Halfhyde wouldn't cloud his pleasure by thinking about the morning.

* * *

'You were disgusting drunk last night,' Victoria said, 'you and your Mr Foster—'

'Don't nag, Victoria.'

'I'm not bloody *nagging*. I'm stating a bloody fact, that's all.'

'All right, you're not nagging. But you're talking.'

'So I mustn't even talk, eh—'

Halfhyde rolled over in the bunk, face to the bulkhead. 'Shut up. You're doing me no good at all.'

'Maybe a cup of coffee will. Here.' She pulled at his shoulder; a green face rolled back towards her and a furred tongue came out to lick at dry lips. Giving a groan of pain, Halfhyde reached unsteadily for the cup.

'That's no good, you'll spill it. Babies have to be treated as babies,' she said. 'Come on, open your bloody mouth and I'll feed you. For Christ's sake,' she said in exasperation as the coffee ran down the stubble of Halfhyde's chin, 'you need a bloody bib and all!'

A little of the coffee went in and some of the dryness left his lips. His head was expanding and contracting like a concertina. It had been a good celebration, but at that moment Halfhyde felt anything but celebratory, expectant of death at any moment. When he closed his eyes the cabin lifted and swayed, rolled and settled again. His stomach lurched and bile rose to the back of his throat. He said hoarsely, 'Go away . . . leave me alone. I'll be all right soon.'

'Bloody likely, I don't think. Look, you've to get up. There's a man to see you.'

'Let him see Foster.'

'Foster,' she said, 'is as bad as you, or worse. *Bloody get up*, love! The bloke looks sort of important.'

This time she was nagging and knew it; but she persisted. Groaning, Halfhyde lifted himself on one elbow and then swung himself dizzily off the bunk. Standing, he lurched; she steadied him. She brought his clothes, ran a wet flannel over his face, clicking her tongue at him. When she had forced him into shirt and trousers and shoes she went to the cabin door and called out.

'Righto, you can come in now and take a look at the wreck of the bloody *Hesperus*.'

She stood aside. A man with the look of the sea about him entered, darting his eyes around the cabin as he removed a bowler hat. 'Lieutenant Halfhyde?' he asked brusquely.

'Captain or lieutenant, what you will, my dear sir. And who are you, pray?' Halfhyde gestured Victoria to leave them.

The man said, 'Lieutenant it shall be while you hold your reserve commission. My card.' He thrust out the small oblong of pasteboard. Halfhyde focused and read: Commander Horatio Mainprice, Royal Navy. Before he could make any response the commander continued, laying a thick envelope headed like previous one On Her Majesty's Service upon Halfhyde's desk as he spoke, 'Your orders from the Admiralty, confirming what you've been told already by Colonel Bowler. Also in the envelope you'll find a formal commission from the Home Secretary authorizing you to embark convicts for South Africa and to take command of a prison ship.'

'Is that what it's to be, sir?'

'What else? What would you call it?'

Halfhyde shrugged. 'I take your point, sir. But it strikes home more sharply when the words are used. I never saw myself as captain of a convict transport, of a slaver—'

'You should choose your terms more appropriately, Half-hyde. The *Glen Halladale* is no slaver, and convicts are not—'

'Yet there is a touch of the Australian convict transports about this, sir. Tell me: are the men to be brought aboard in chains, with balls attached?'

'In chains, yes,' Mainprice said. 'Not with balls. Each man will be linked to his neighbours by chains.'

'Then I take it they are not yet enlisted into the army?'

'No. They will be enlisted and sworn upon arrival in Simon's Town, when you will hand them over to a Colonel Masters on the staff of the army Commander-in-Chief, Sir Redvers Buller. You will obtain a receipt for them . . . and until that time they will be your responsibility alone, Halfhyde. You will be answerable for the full delivery.' Mainprice paused. 'Colonel Bowler, I understand, spoke of the crimes that put these convicts into Dartmoor Prison. They must all be regarded as potentially dangerous.'

'Then why, for heaven's sake,' Halfhyde asked, his temper frayed by stale alcohol's effects, 'let them go to South Africa?'

Mainprice shrugged. 'It is largely a question of Her Majesty, I'm afraid.'

'Her Majesty?'

'Yes. You know the Queen's love for her soldiers . . . she has been much touched, apparently, by the offer of these men to risk their lives against the Boer. Nothing will dissuade her of their unsuitability and a royal command has been issued. She sees only their patriotism and their loyalty to her as sovereign.' Mainprice blew out his cheeks and gave Halfhyde a look that seemed to hold some sympathy. He added, 'If anything goes wrong it may well be that you'll have Her Majesty in person to answer to . . .'

THREE

Commander Mainprice had given Victoria some lofty looks both when she had referred to the wreck of the *Hesperus* and when he had encountered her again upon his departure, but he had commented neither upon the girl's presence aboard nor upon Halfhyde's whisky pallor. He would be a man of the world; and seafarers were never averse to women and drink. Nevertheless, there had been something in his final look when seen over the gangway that said the *Glen Halladale* would welcome neither. Halfhyde was in full agreement with the unspoken stricture. But the girl sensed that the forthcoming barrier between her and Halfhyde was being strengthened by the naval officer's visit.

'What about me?' she asked. 'You're not going to take me, are you? Not aboard a navy ship.'

He knew that the time for honesty had come, and he said, 'I regret it, Victoria, but my hands are tied.'

'That commander?'

'Yes.' It was a lie only in the strictest sense: had Mainprice been asked the question he would have blown sky-high.

'Stuff him, mate!'

He clicked his tongue. 'An unlikely proposition. But you'll not be left in the lurch, Victoria. I shall be back when Their Lordships see fit, and in the meantime you'll be found lodgings—'

'Not in bloody Liverpool I won't.' She was, he believed, close to tears. He could understand; the Merseyside rain was falling still, damp and depressing, and the wharves had a graveyard feel about them even though the stevedores were busy and the winches and derricks and cranes were working, bringing the constant Liverpool clatter to cut through the weather. Not only this; Liverpool had been a disappointment to Victoria. One of her hopes on coming to England had been that in Liverpool she might find some of her long-lost family, the brothers and sisters she had left behind in the orphanage when she'd stowed away to Australia, but she'd found no trace at all. They had been swallowed by time and the ravages of English poverty. In an excess of contrition Halfhyde said she would come with him to Devonport and he would arrange for lodgings for her there or in Plymouth. That cheered her; Halfhyde gave her a glowing account, tongue in cheek, of the joys and beauties of Plymouth and Devon, forebearing to add that the rain fell there as much as in Liverpool. When he returned to England she would meet him there, a happy reunion.

Halfhyde spent that day in making his arrangements with Foster and in preparing a full inventory of stores, equipment and deck gear to be signed by the requisitioning authority. Then in the late afternoon he went ashore to visit a tailor: his RN uniform, which he had carried with him from Mrs Mavitty's on the off-chance of being restored to the active list of the fleet, had now to have its gold stripes altered to the interlaced braid of the Royal Naval Reserve. He sat in the tailor's shop and waited while the work proceeded on his monkey-jacket sleeve. The tailor had objected that the alteration would take time but Halfhyde was adamant: he would wait.

'I am an officer of the naval reserve, required for service by Her Majesty.'

'But—'

'There are no buts, my friend. You'll do as you're told,' Halfhyde said firmly as he sat down, 'and I shall wait if it takes you till midnight.'

The job was finished long before that; with his jacket in a cardboard box beneath his arm, Halfhyde made his way to the Bear's Paw. The saloon bar was crowded with shipmasters and mates; there was much talk of the war in South Africa, much agreement on how speedily the Boer would be brought to his senses by the weight of troops and war material bound for Table Bay. It would all be over by Christmas, though to be sure that was not far ahead; by the time most of the troops had got out there 'Oom Paul' Kruger would be pleading for peace, all ready to lay down arms. Talking, laughing and drinking, Halfhyde became aware of a rat-like man watching him from a doorway behind the bar; as soon as this man realized he had been seen, he vanished. There was probably nothing in it; no reason why there should be, but Liverpool was Liverpool and men in from the world's seas often had much cash in their pockets, and he had been spending freely in the bar for some days past. A sense of caution entered Halfhyde's head and after one more glass of whisky he left the Bear's Paw, taking a look to right and left from the doorway before he emerged.

He didn't see the rat-like man; he came out confidently to lose himself in the passing crowds. Striding out fast towards the docks he told himself he was seeing trouble where none existed. But as the crowds were left behind and he came into the mean streets where stood the shabby tenements occupied by the stevedores and other dock workers, he began to have the feeling he was being followed.

He looked round.

There was a cab: no one on foot. Nevertheless, his instinct had been right. The cab drew past and stopped some dozen yards ahead. Two men got out, well-dressed men, one with a cigar in his fingers. They came down towards him, smiling.

'Captain Halfhyde, I believe.'

Halfhyde stopped. 'Who is addressing me?' he asked.

'I think there is no need for names, Captain Halfhyde.'

'Then you—' Halfhyde broke off. The hands of both men had moved into the flaps of their greatcoats and, half concealed by the heavy capes that flowed from the shoulders, the muzzles of small revolvers stared. 'I think you'll not use those in the street,' Halfhyde said, and began to push past. The men closed in, blocking his path.

One of them said, 'If I were you, I'd not take the risk. There's no one about. We'll be away in seconds, and Liverpool's no stranger to death. But we've no wish to kill you, Captain. Only to talk. Be sensible.'

'To talk . . . about what?'

'Your cargo.'

'The *Taronga Park*?'

There was a smile. 'No, no. Your new ship, in Devonport.'

Halfhyde stiffened. 'What do you know about–'

One of the gun muzzles edged forward. 'Say no more for now. Come with us, then we'll talk – in more privacy than the street.'

Many thoughts went quickly through Halfhyde's mind. It was not hard to make guesses . . . an offer was about to be made. But these men knew his name, his new appointment to government service – they must surely also know his loyalty and his reputation? They must know about Porteous Higgins, must know that he, Halfhyde, had acted with honesty for the Crown – in all conscience, Higgins' trial had had plenty of publicity in the newspapers! They were obviously playing for high stakes, taking an enormous risk; his first feeling was that they were amateurs at chicanery, men with scant knowledge and less experience of the ways of criminals, yet he was well aware that real criminals were involved: his human freight for South Africa. And these men probably believed that every man had his price.

* * *

Next day Halfhyde was in London, back with Mrs Mavitty in his old rooms in Camden Town. In case of loose talk Mrs Mavitty had been sworn to secrecy in regard to his presence, the Queen being mentioned. Mrs Mavitty's mouth would henceforward remain sealed and she would see to it that Mavitty obeyed also: her respect for Her Majesty Queen Victoria was immense, almost awe-inspiring. The Queen had also been invoked to secure accommodation for Victoria Penn, though it must have taken a good deal of Mrs Mavitty's loyalty to accept any connection between the palace and Miss Penn. For safety's sake Halfhyde left Victoria at Mrs Mavitty's when he kept an appointment in the Army and Navy Club in Pall Mall at five o'clock that evening, an appointment arranged by a circumspect call on the telephone, a new-fangled instrument that Colonel Bowler had seemed surprisingly unfamiliar with. He had tended to shout into it as though on parade and there had been a tiresome repetition of 'hullo' and 'are you there'. But in the end the message had penetrated. Halfhyde had stressed both urgency and a need for secrecy; he would meet Colonel Bowler in the quiet of the club's reading room.

Bowler was prompt; he found Halfhyde ensconced in a deep

armchair in a corner by a big window. There was a small table and another armchair close to Halfhyde's.

'What's all this cloak-and-dagger?' Bowler asked, but asked it quietly after sitting down.

'I shall tell you in full, sir. You'd like a drink?'

'Whisky.'

Halfhyde beckoned up a waiter and gave the order. He and Bowler waited in silence until the whisky was brought; the purlieus of the reading room did not lend themselves to idle chatter, though in fact little reading was being done. A handful of elderly gentlemen, generals, admirals, captains were in repose and largely asleep, though one or two were reading *The Times* or the *Morning Post*. When the waiter returned Halfhyde said, 'Thank you. We shall be requiring no more.'

'Very good, sir.'

The waiter bowed himself backwards. Halfhyde, taking another look around, bent close to Colonel Bowler. 'Now, sir. I have a story to tell you, of what happened last night in Liverpool.'

Bowler nodded. 'Go on, Halfhyde.'

Halfhyde told him the facts. He had allowed himself to be taken aboard the cab; as it had driven off, a black silk scarf had been tied around his eyes: he had no idea where he had been taken since the scarf was not removed until he was inside a room, poorly and anonymously furnished with two chairs and a horsehair settee, a sideboard of ornate design and a floor covered with linoleum. Heavy curtains had been drawn across the single window, and the room had been lit by an oil lamp.

'How far,' Bowler asked, 'from where you were picked up?'

Halfhyde shrugged; he didn't find the question very relevant. 'That's hard to say. Perhaps . . . a matter of two or three miles at a guess.'

'Go on.'

'I was offered money, a large sum – ten thousand pounds, or some one hundred years' pay as a lieutenant—'

'Tempting!' Bowler said. 'What did they want?'

'To send gold bullion aboard the *Glen Halladale*, sir.'

'*Gold bullion?*' Bowler looked startled. 'For what purpose?'

'To be collected at Simon's Town – the ultimate purpose was not revealed—'

'Nothing about the convicts?'

'To my surprise, not a thing. No mention, though I assume they knew since they knew so much else.'

'H'm. . .' Bowler pondered, frowning, the glass of whisky disregarded after a first gulp. 'D'you see a connection yourself, Halfhyde?'

'Frankly, no. Gold and convicts . . . they might well like to mix, I don't doubt, but I was surprised – taking into account my view that the men must know about the convicts – that they should wish to entrust gold to such a ship.'

Bowler nodded. 'Exactly! I think they're *intended* to mix, my dear fellow.'

'How?'

Bowler countered by asking a question of his own. 'What is the value of the bullion?'

'One hundred thousand pounds sterling.'

'Goodness gracious, a lot of money. Heavy, too – cased bullion! It would go a long way, to be sure.' Bowler paused, rubbing thoughtfully at his jaw. 'To answer your question about mixing, Halfhyde: the bullion could be intended to finance certain of the convicts – after an escape. Don't you see?'

'Not really. My belief was that the men intended merely to smuggle the gold from the country – evading the excise or the export regulations—'

'No, no. I see a deeper reason, Halfhyde—'

'But these men were gentlemen, sir, I am in no doubt about that. Convicts—'

'Are also sometimes gentlemen, Halfhyde.'

'In Dartmoor?'

Bowler shrugged. 'Oh, it's not unknown.'

'But the second division,' Halfhyde said, in reference to the fact that gentlemen were usually accorded the privilege, when in prison, of being separated from the common people. 'Would not any gentleman be put into the second division, and not sent to Dartmoor?'

'Not so,' Bowler said. 'The second division's only accorded to gentlemen sentenced to *simple imprisonment*. Such niceties do not apply to penal servitude, Halfhyde. Those so sentenced . . . gentlemen or not, they all serve the same. So, you see, there can be gentlemen in Dartmoor Prison.'

'And there are gentlemen among those boarding the *Glen Halladale*?'

Bowler looked at his finger-nails and said, 'Yes. There's one. By name of Archer-Caine. Large-scale fraud, which attracts penal servitude.'

'Then I suggest he's extracted from the army draft, sir.'

Bowler grinned, showing a line of tobacco-stained teeth.

'I think I would reject that, Halfhyde. But tell me first: what was your response to these men's offer?'

Halfhyde gave Bowler a straight look. 'I accepted. I accepted in the interest of eventually bringing the men to justice – if that doesn't sound pompous.'

'Not at all – your simple duty. You've done right. And the money?'

'To be paid in gold sovereigns, half on my taking the bullion aboard, half to be paid in Simon's Town on delivery. Less a sum paid to me last night – a sweetener of one hundred pounds—'

'Which you accepted?'

'Yes—'

'Thus immediately committing yourself to these men?'

'As was intended, sir – yes. It proved to them that I was with them, which was why I took the money without hesitation.'

'Authenticity,' Bowler said. 'Yes. And the one hundred?'

'With me now, sir, and will be handed over to you before you leave here.'

Bowler nodded. 'It'll be held as Exhibit A! Now to the question of Archer-Caine – a possible involvement and our only current line of investigation. The decision won't rest with me, but I shall recommend that he be retained in the draft to board the *Glen Halladale*, for much the same reason as you yourself agreed to these men's demands – if Archer-Caine is involved, then his removal would mean the bottom falls out of the whole thing and no arrests will ever be made – and there could be other attempts. We must bowl it out while we have the chance, Halfhyde.'

'Why not an investigation of Archer-Caine's associates, Colonel?'

'Well, that'll be done, of course, but as I remember from the man's admission to Dartmoor prison, which was as it happens in my time as governor, little had emerged – he had covered his associations well, or they themselves had. Such will take time, too much time.'

'So my orders stand?'

Bowler said, 'Of course.' He paused, looking at the remains of his whisky. 'Is there anything else, Halfhyde?'

'One thing, sir: you spoke of the men's *demands*. That tells me that you suspect pressure on me as well as reward—'

'Naturally! That has to be accepted, a hazard of doing your duty. I take it you're under threat?'

'Yes. For myself I can accept that. But someone else is also threatened: Miss Penn. The gentry in Liverpool indicated that harm could come to her, another means of keeping me within their control—'

'Miss Penn, you said?'

'She was on board the *Taronga Park*.'

'Oh. Yes, yes. The rather – er – the Australian woman I think.'

The tone was lofty, disparaging. Halfhyde felt his hackles rise. He said with deliberation, 'She may not have appeared a person of much consequence to you, sir. But to me she is important and I shall not let her down, nor see her suffer on my account – and yours, and the Queen's. I cannot take her to sea with me. I ask for protection for her.'

Bowler's eyebrows lifted. 'Really? And if I find that not possible?'

'Then, sir, I shall disobey my orders. I shall not take the *Glen Halladale* to sea—'

'The Admiralty—'

'The Admiralty, sir, may have its pound of flesh by way of a court martial.'

'You're prepared to accept that?'

'I am, sir.'

'And the bullion, and the possibility of an escape by Archer-Caine, supported by the gold?'

'I should be sorry and reluctant. But another master can be found. I shall not sail unless provision is made for Miss Penn's safety.' Halfhyde's tone was adamant. He sat up straight in his chair, arms folded across his chest.

Bowler said remindingly, warningly, 'There is the question

of the offer made to you, and your acceptance of it. You have committed yourself – you said as much, though you had no need to say that since it would be obvious. You have the sovereigns on you. I could deny the whole of this conversation, Halfhyde.'

Halfhyde smiled tautly, a grimace of thinned lips. 'But you would not do so, Colonel Bowler. You would not do so.'

'Why not?'

'Because, like me, you are a gentleman. By the same token, I believe you will appreciate that no gentleman can let a lady down.'

'H'm.' Bowler looked away from Halfhyde's eyes, stared down at his well-shod feet. Halfhyde could almost see the colonel's mental processes: gentlemen did not let ladies down, but women were in a different category, and Miss Penn was a woman. Gentlemen had many reservations in regard to ladies: they did not compromise them, for one thing, though house-maids and such were fair game when it came to lechery . . .

'Well, sir?'

'You are a determined man, Halfhyde.'

Halfhyde waited, saying nothing.

'You place me in a quandary. I can see no way of – of accommodating Miss Penn. To place a police guard on her would invite attention – the whole game would be given away. These men of yours – they can't be fools.'

Halfhyde said, 'I told you, in my opinion they're amateurs, unused to what they are now doing.'

'They would still come to know about police interest in Miss Penn.'

'Nevertheless,' Halfhyde said, 'a way must be found.'

Bowler blew out his cheeks and flapped a hand helplessly. Halfhyde saw that his point had been made. He said, 'I have a suggestion, if I may make it?'

'Go ahead, then.'

'The Rear-Admiral Superintendent of the Dockyard at Devonport knows me well, sir. I have served under him more than once in the past. I believe that if you were to take him into your confidence he would be willing to take Miss Penn into his household – perhaps in the guise of a domestic servant, which would satisfy the proprieties. She would be well guarded by the

Navy and her presence there need never be known to outsiders.'

'Well . . .'

Halfhyde pressed. 'It is the answer I seek, sir. It must be done. Further, Miss Penn should not travel to Devonport with me – that would be foolish. I ask that she be taken under a discreet escort by road, direct to the house of the Rear-Admiral Superintendent – that is, of course, if he is willing. For me, I think he will be, on mention of my name.'

Once again Bowler blew out his cheeks. With reluctance he said, 'Very well, Halfhyde. I shall make such arrangements as I can. I shall be in touch later.' He looked up. 'When do you propose to leave for Devonport?'

Halfhyde said, 'I've handed over the *Taronga Park* to my First Mate – earlier than I had intended, owing to recent events. Now I have a crew to sign, and that may take time since I shall be particular as to who I accept. I shall take the Plymouth express from Paddington tomorrow morning.'

'In that case . . .' Bowler reached into a pocket of his waistcoat and drew out a turnip-shaped watch. 'You had better come back to the Commission with me, Halfhyde. You shall use the telephone to Devonport and make the arrangements with the Rear-Admiral yourself.'

* * *

Back again at Mrs Mavitty's Halfhyde found Victoria by the window of his sitting-room, staring out at the street with her chin cupped in her hands. She said, 'Well, thank God you're back. How about some bloody supper, eh?'

'Mrs Mavitty—'

'Oh, no, mate. Oh, no! We're going out. Café Royal, maybe – or—'

'No,' he said firmly, drawing her to him as she stood up all ready to show defiance. 'Mrs Mavitty is a worthy cook and would be hurt—'

'Oh, for God' sake, let her—'

'Victoria, I insist.' Steel had come into his voice; she knew both the tone and the signs. She could go so far and no further. Halfhyde went on, 'There are things we must talk about, things you have to know now, things you'll never breathe a word about to anyone except two people, whom I shall name soon.

31

Do you understand?'

She stared at him, frowning. 'We're not back to the likes of bloody Porteous Higgins, are we?'

'You've come close. But just listen to me and don't interrupt.' He told her as much as was necessary for her to know so that she could accept that she was at risk; and that he intended making certain no harm could come to her.

'How?' she asked, full of suspicion.

He told her of Rear-Admiral Bassinghorn, his old commanding officer, now at Devonport. She was angry. 'Look, I'm not bloody going to be bossed around by a bloody Navy admiral and his old cow of a wife—'

'Victoria—'

'It'd be like being in bloody prison!'

'Rubbish. You'll be as safe as houses, a naval sentry on the gate—'

'And never bloody allowed out of the bloody gate – I know, I can guess! A bloody skivvy, no thank you! And what about my speech, eh?'

He grinned. 'You'll have to drop the bloodies.'

She was dead against it but he was as adamant as he had been with Colonel Bowler. It was the only solution, he said, and she was to accept it. Or go back to Australia where she would be lonely but out of harm's way. She could board a liner of the Pacific Steam Navigation Company out of Liverpool for Valparaiso in Chile, whence she could take another ship for Sydney. She said savagely, 'I've a bloody good mind to.' The evening was wrecked thereafter by bouts of bad temper and raging silences in between. Halfhyde believed that Mrs Mavitty probably had her ear to the keyhole for a disbelieving expression formed on her seamed face as the dinner progressed. That Mr Halfhyde, he'd always been such a gentleman and kindly spoken with it. The woman was a vixen, quite unworthy of him. But in the end Victoria quietened and when they went to bed she didn't refuse him. Well satisfied, they slept. Halfhyde slept very soundly, as he always did, casting off the day's cares. He wasn't aware of the girl getting out of the bed. But when he woke in the morning she had gone.

He looked in the sitting-room and in the bathroom. No Victoria. Her clothing had gone too, as had the basket-work receptacle bound with a leather strap in which she had brought her overnight wear down from Liverpool. Beneath his hairbrushes in the bedroom he found a note, hastily scrawled in pencil and ill spelled. *I am not goin to no bloody old cow in Devenport, right? Dont look for me, you wont find me. Sorry mate.*

No signature; no love offered. But that *sorry mate* was enough. Halfhyde felt a deadness around his heart and an immense regret.

FOUR

The train journey from Paddington to Plymouth was a kind of nightmare: Halfhyde's anxieties about Victoria nagged without cease. Dismissing Mrs Mavitty's excellent breakfast from his thoughts he had sent Mavitty for a cab and had gone at once to the offices of the Prison Commission; but Colonel Bowler had not yet arrived at such an early hour. Sitting on the comfortable cushions of his first-class compartment as the engine of the Great Western Railway bore him towards Plymouth and Devonport, Halfhyde cursed Victoria's impetuosity and his own heavy sleep.

On arrival in Plymouth a little over four hours after pulling out of Paddington he went by cab to call upon the Rear-Admiral – Henry Bassinghorn, under whom he had served as a lieutenant in the old battleship *Viceroy*, again in the *Prince Consort* and the *Lord Cochrane* . . . splendid days of serving the Queen in China, the Mediterranean and the west coast of Africa, days when that appealing urchin Victoria Penn was way ahead in his future. Now she was impacting strongly upon him; and Bassinghorn understood his worries well enough. All that could be done, he said, would be done; and he had news for Halfhyde.

'Word from the Admiralty,' he said. 'Or rather, from Colonel Bowler via the Admiralty. You're to embark your convicts after dark this very evening, and you'll then haul out into the Sound and sail at first light tomorrow, by which time a medical man will have joined you – a Dr Murchison of the prison service, who is unable to arrive in time before you leave the dockyard berth.'

34

Halfhyde nodded but said, 'The devil take it, sir! May I ask how I'm expected to sign a decent crew at such short notice?'

'Oh, that'll be no problem,' Bassinghorn said. 'I've taken the liberty of making a choice for your final selection. Good men, many of them from the fleet – time-expired seamen, some of whom have served under sail in the old times. Naturally, they're little more than a handful – you'll have to take some greenhorns as well. But I believe you'll approve the older hands, Halfhyde.'

Halfhyde said, 'Your choice is my choice, sir. Our views have always coincided as to what makes a good and loyal seaman.' He paused. 'But why the change in my orders, sir? Has this to do with Miss Penn's disappearance? I left word at – '

Bassinghorn shrugged. 'I don't know, my dear Halfhyde, I've not been informed. You, like I myself, must draw your own conclusions . . .'

* * *

Halfhyde believed the conclusions to be obvious and his heart was heavier than ever at the girl's stupid indiscretion. But his spirits as a seaman rose at his first sight of the *Glen Halladale* as his cab entered the dockyard gate at the bottom of Fore Street. The square-rigged ship, her masts already crossed with their yards but the canvas not yet sent aloft to lie furled in the gaskets along those great tapering spars, lay alongside the wall in the naval dockyard at a berth normally reserved for the cruisers of the Channel Squadron. She was clean and trim and shipshape and that spoke well for her First Mate; but a closer and longer look told Halfhyde that this was superficial: the *Glen Halladale* had seen better days – she was old and time-worn, of wood construction in days when wood was giving way to iron. No doubt she was considered good enough for her forthcoming mission; but overall she had a look of expendability, and that was far from encouraging. As Halfhyde's cab was seen on the quay the watchman at the gangway doubled aft to the entry into the officers' accommodation below the poop so that the First Mate could be there to greet the Master.

Halfhyde, as the cabby opened the door for him, got out and climbed to a spotless deck, where he noted that extra lifeboats had been provided on account of the ship's human cargo. The

First Mate saluted. 'Captain Halfhyde, sir?'

'I am.'

'Welcome aboard, sir. The name's Edwards, First Mate.'

'I've been told of you, Mr Edwards, and what I hear is good.'

Edwards, a tubby man with a good-humoured, smiling face, looked pleased. 'Thank you, sir—'

'I believe we shall get along, Mr Edwards. You run a smart ship.' Piercingly, Halfhyde looked aloft. All the rovings, ratlines, footropes and rigging on which men's lives would depend had been recently overhauled. 'Smart but tending, I fancy, to become worn out like an old work-horse?'

'I'm afraid that's true, sir. I've made representations and have been turned down. The dockyard says she's fit for the voyage and that's that.'

Halfhyde nodded; he had had plenty of experience of dockyards and the stubborn inflexibility of the shoreside foremen, and it was much too late to involve Bassinghorn. 'Now, our passengers. It's not a happy thought, to be carrying convicts, but that's by the way. What's their accommodation to be like?'

'Primitive's the word, sir. Very primitive – the hold—'

'Yes, indeed. Is the hold ready, Mr Edwards?'

'Yes, sir. The shoreside gangs were doubled up this morning to finish the job. They've but recently finished and have been sent ashore.'

'Very well, Mr Edwards. The first thing now is a crew. I'm told by the Rear-Admiral that a selection awaits me at the Board of Trade shipping office. My cab will take me there at once, to open the Articles of Agreement.'

* * *

Victoria Penn, her pixie face tear-stained but determined, had in fact no intention of retiring from Halfhyde's life. Though she was still equally determined to act as no skivvy to an admiral's wife, she had taken the train from Paddington to Plymouth, a slow train leaving some hours after the express that had carried Halfhyde. A hard life, all the way along from the early days in Yorkshire when her father's execution for murder had driven the family from the Dales village where they had lived – from there to Liverpool and thence to Australia on her own and a

36

wretched existence under the sway of Porteous Higgins – all this had taught her cunning while failing to kill her spirit. Cunning was to the fore now. She needed a room, and on arrival in Plymouth she found one by enquiring of the cabbies waiting at the railway station. She walked to the given address and found it a seedy place but suitable enough for her purpose. Having paid a deposit to the unwholesome-looking, rapacious landlady, and having given her name as Nancy Smith, she went out again and found some shops and bought some heavy rope, a cheap, turtle-backed trunk of some size, and a packet of luggage labels. Returning in a cab to the lodging-house with her purchases and getting the cabby to carry the trunk up to her bedroom, she wrote out a label, addressing it to Captain Halfhyde aboard the *Glen Halladale*, and then went down to speak again to the landlady, a greasy-haired harridan with but two teeth and pendulous breasts that merged into a gross stomach. She said, 'Here's some money, right?'

She thrust a sovereign at the woman, almost the last of her money, Halfhyde's money. 'My trunk. I'll be going out again soon. I want the trunk delivered to the *Glen Halladale* down in the docks. Can you arrange that? After dark, right?'

'Why after dark, dearie?'

'Not your bloody business. But here's another sovereign for you to keep your trap shut. You'll do that, eh?'

Eyes gleamed beneath the mat of hair. Two sovereigns made a king's ransom. The woman nodded. Victoria went on, 'There'll be another on delivery aboard the ship . . . maybe two more, depending.'

'What on, dearie?'

'Whether you've kept your trap shut. *And* the men who take the trunk to the ship. Same for them, right?'

The landlady assured her it would be done and not a word would be breathed. Her heart thumping with a mixture of fear and anticipation, Victoria went back up the ricketty, un-carpeted stairs to her bedroom. She put the basket-work container into the trunk and then sat and waited for the night to come down over the naval town. She said aloud to herself, 'I'm being bloody silly, I know that.' But she couldn't help herself. There was time yet to back out; but she wasn't going to. Her skin was clammy with the sweat of fear of the unknown, of what might happen to her if she found she couldn't instil another kind of fear in the men who came for the trunk. It would be in a sense an act of faith – in herself, in the porters, in Halfhyde as well, for she had no means of knowing that fate was moving in her favour.

* * *

As the girl waited in her sleazy, depressing bedroom filled with the unwashed body-smell of the bed's previous tenant Halfhyde was returning aboard the *Glen Halladale* and his new crew were following with their sea-bags. Edwards went ashore to sign the articles and was quickly back. Shortly after his return he reported to Halfhyde that the ship's carpenter, by name Bracegirdle, had carried out an inspection of the hold arrangements and had expressed dissatisfaction with the bunk construction: poor shore workmanship, he'd said, a job botched by too much haste to get ready; but it was too late now to do anything about that. A little after dark the bosun, Bunch, reported a convoy of prison wagons approaching from the dockyard gate. Halfhyde came out on deck with Edwards and Pendleton, the Second Mate. The line of wagons – there were eight of them, each drawn by two horses – stopped with a rattle of harness and a creak of leather alongside the ship and from the leading one a thickset man in the uniform of a prison warder jumped down and marched to the gangway. Stepping aboard, he looked around expectantly and saw the three officers.

'Captain Halfhyde, sir?' he enquired.

'Yes. You are—'

'Name of MacNab, sir, in charge of the prison draft.'

'Once of the Black Watch?'

'Aye, sir. You'll have been told that by Colonel Bowler I don't doubt, sir?'

'Yes. Well, we'll not delay, Mr MacNab, for I have orders to move out into the Sound. As the prisoners come aboard, I want you to point out a man named Archer-Caine.'

'Aye, sir.' MacNab turned about smartly and marched back to the gangway and down to the dockyard wall. He passed his orders quietly and accompanied by the clanking of their chains the prisoners from Dartmoor were herded out of the wagons and fallen in beneath a drizzle that had started with the dark. It was a depressing sight in the light of storm lanterns held by the warders and as the procession started up the gangway Halfhyde caught the dank, acrid prison-smell, as though the convicts had brought an integral part of Dartmoor gaol aboard with them. They were a brutal enough bunch by the look of them, Halfhyde thought as they filed past him, some with their eyes averted, some of them staring boldly at authority as though for two pins they would lift their manacles and smash out the brains of anyone who crossed them. They were of all shapes and sizes, tall, short, cadaverous mostly from the prison diet, with sunken cheeks and haunted eyes; and of all ages, it seemed, from around forty down to twenty: more than forty and they would presumably not have been acceptable to the military even as a pioneer company.

They had not, however, quite the look of dejection that Halfhyde would have expected from men undergoing long periods of penal servitude. That could have been due to thoughts of the future in South Africa, when of necessity they would be given a greater measure of freedom – and the chains would disappear.

Halfhyde had words with ex-Sergeant-Major MacNab, remarking in a low voice on the men's demeanour.

'I take your point, sir,' MacNab said. 'And the reason's not just the change of scene and routine for them. It's as Colonel Bowler will have told you.'

'Possible escape?'

'Aye, sir. It's on the cards. They're as villainous a bunch as you'd find anywhere, sir. It's madness to send them out in my opinion.'

'You expect trouble on the voyage?'

'I do, sir. At any time, sir. But I shall deal with it, never fear. I have a strong presence of warders.' He had; Halfhyde counted no less than twenty of them, as hard-looking as the convicts themselves. Each warder carried a rifle, and each had a heavy truncheon dangling from his belt. MacNab, who was armed with a holstered revolver, went on, 'They'll try something when they believe the time to be right, but they'll not get free of the chains – that is, unless they manage to take a hostage. Which is why I must ask you not to allow any of your men into the hold, sir, for one second of unwariness would lead to trouble.'

'They must be fed, Mr MacNab.'

'The warders will see to that, sir, if you please.'

'And the hold must be kept clean.'

'Safety is more important than cleanliness, sir.'

'Not aboard my ship,' Halfhyde said evenly.

'But—'

'No buts, Mr MacNab. Unclean people in the close confines of a ship can breed disease – as in a barracks ashore. Do you wish to see dysentery, even cholera, break out? Because I do not. So there will be cleanliness, even if it means opening up the hatches and putting the hoses on the holds, once we move into warmer weather south of the equator at all events.'

'Very good, sir,' MacNab said woodenly, his tone making it plain he disagreed and that any trouble coming as a result of over-fastidiousness would be on Halfhyde's head. Then he said out of the corner of his mouth, 'There, sir. There he is. Just stepping off the gangway now, the tall one.'

Halfhyde looked at Archer-Caine: he was certainly tall, a little willowy; there was sensitivity and refinement in the face, and intelligence as well. A gentleman . . . it must be a cruel life inside Dartmoor for a gentleman but Halfhyde's moment of sympathy was brief enough. What a man asked for, he got, and that was that. But it seemed likely enough that Archer-Caine, gentleman, was going to be the one trouble would revolve around, the one who was to be helped on his escape route by the gold bullion – the gold bullion that had not yet come aboard. Halfhyde wondered what would happen if that gold failed to reach the ship before she moved out into Plymouth Sound under her suddenly advanced orders. Such a failure might well put a spanner in the works and confound the plans of the men in Liverpool. There was not long to go now; as the prison wagons had stopped alongside, Pendleton and the bosun had roused out the newly-joined fo'c'sle hands and along the decks they were standing by to take the towing pendants from the dockyard steam tug whose lights could already be seen moving in from the Hamoaze.

Slowly, unaccustomed to the deck of a ship, the convicts moved in single file towards the hatch, and then down the ladder rigged from the main deck to the tween-deck and down again to the bottom of the cargo hold, making heavy weather of the descent as the chains impeded them, rattling and clanking to make a terrible dirge of doom. Archer-Caine stopped for a moment at the hatch-coaming, staring around, looking towards the dockyard gates until he was urged on by one of the warders, who made a lunge with his rifle. As the long line of prison uniforms marked with the broad arrows moved on, Halfhyde's attention was caught by the sound of a cab-horse clopping over the dockyard stone. The cab stopped on the far side of the line of prison wagons and Halfhyde saw, through a gap between two of the wagons, a brand-new trunk being manhandled out; lit by the lamps on the front of the vehicles, the trunk struck him as being of singularly poor quality to contain what he assumed to be the gold . . . he turned to the First Mate.

'Mr Edwards, a delivery, I suspect, for me. It's to go at once to my cabin. Kindly tell off some hands – it will be heavy.'

* * *

The landlady had secured the services of a street loafer willing to make some money in return for helping the cabby to carry the trunk down the stairs. Winks and nudges and a finger held to the lips had told both men the job was something they didn't open their mouths about. They went up the stairs to the girl's room. She got into the trunk; while waiting for someone to carry her down, she had used a hatpin and a steel poker from the fireplace and had laboriously made a hole in the side of the trunk, a hole that she had widened out into an aperture a little more than an inch in diameter.

The men stared. She looked back at them disdainfully and said, 'Right. Here's the key to the lock. Use it, and shove the key through the hole to me afterwards. And rope the trunk up.'

'If that's what you want, missus.'

'It's what I want. Then take me to the *Glen Halladale* in the docks. It's on the bloody label, all right? And don't worry, you'll get paid – on delivery, through the hole. And don't say a bloody word 'cept you've been told to deliver a trunk. And nothing said afterwards or you'll get trouble, right? I got connections and don't forget it.'

The men shrugged; it wouldn't be their worry, nor their

discomfort. They carried out the girl's instructions; she was carried downstairs and put aboard the cab and trundled off into the dockyard, passed through without question by the policeman at the gate. When the cab stopped and once again the men laid hold of the trunk, fingers were thrust through the hole, clutching two sovereigns. These were grabbed and quickly transferred to tattered clothing and the two men left the trunk to the ship's crew. Victoria was lifted and carried aboard: she was no weight to speak of in the hands of the seamen. By the time the trunk had been carried below to the Master's cabin the convict embarkation was complete and already the dockyard steam tug was lying off.

Halfhyde passed his orders: 'Stand by to take the tug's lines. Stand by springs, headropes and sternropes. Mr Edwards, see the hatch covers securely in place and battened down.' He turned to the senior warder. 'Mr MacNab, I wish a strong guard placed along the tween-deck, at least until we haul out from the Sound at tomorrow's dawn.'

FIVE

Halfhyde paced the poop as the steam tub hauled his silent ship up into the Hamoaze and made the turn around Devil's Point to enter the Sound. The rain continued, an unpleasant soak blown into the faces of the men on deck by a light on- shore wind; behind them as they came slowly past the Hoe, high above them on their port side, the lights of Plymouth Town were seen as friendly beacons bidding farewell to yet another ship bound away on the Empire's duty. Halfhyde's thoughts went back across the centuries: from here Sir Francis Drake had sailed to chase the Spanish Armada up the Channel, sailed to drive those stately galleons to disorder and destruction; from the Barbican by Sutton Harbour the Pilgrim Fathers had sailed aboard the *Mayflower* in 1620; from the Sound so many names famed in England's history had sailed: Frobisher, Humphrey Gilbert, Raleigh on their adventurous foreign voyages . . .

Halfhyde felt a chill in his stomach: to be taking convicts to South Africa could scarcely rank with the glorious adventures of the past. Inglorious rather, and sordid – as sordid as his holds would soon be once the sea's unkind motion got to grips with the equilibrium of the gaolbirds beneath his hatches.

Already there was a lurch in the deck as the *Glen Halladale* met the surge of the ocean coming in around the ends of the breakwater not very far ahead. There was a rattle from the blocks as the spider's-web of ropes slatted against the masts, and a creak of woodwork. On the fo'c'sle the First Mate was standing by to let go the anchor; as the ship approached her overnight anchorage, Halfhyde took up a megaphone and called ahead to the steam tug. There was an answering shout

43

across the water and Halfhyde passed the order to Edwards to let go the tow. As the heavy rope slid away from the bitts, splashed into the water and was swiftly hauled back aboard the tug, Halfhyde passed the word to let go the anchor. With a farewell wave from her master, the steam tug turned away and made back towards the dockyard.

When the *Glen Halladale* was lying safely at her anchor, Halfhyde went below to his cabin. And the trunk.

* * *

He had been startled to hear his name called from an apparently empty cabin, shaken to the core to recognize the muffled voice as Victoria Penn's.

'What the devil!'

'Here, for God's sake.'

'What—'

'In the bloody trunk, mate. Get me out, will you?'

Fury overtook him. He swore savagely, fists clenched. He advanced on the trunk, gave it a kick. From inside the girl said, 'Don't bloody do that to me!'

'What do you think you're doing, Victoria?'

'Getting myself on board.'

'Not for long.'

'We've sailed, haven't we?'

'No,' he almost shouted. 'We're at anchor in the Sound! I'll have you sent back.'

'Well,' the voice said reasonably enough through the hole, 'you'll have to get me out first, right? Cut the bloody rope. I'll pass the key through.'

He began to unfasten the rope, obviously knotted by a landlubber. She said, 'Hurry up, I'm suffocating. Cut it, do.'

'Seamen never cut rope.'

He took his time. She began to get hysterical: she would never have lasted the course if it had gone on much longer. When the lid of the trunk was lifted she was pale and tear-streaked. Halfhyde bent and took her in the arms and thumped her down on a chair.

'Now,' he said, his face hard and forbidding.

'Now what?'

'Tell me about it. Tell me why you've been such a

confounded fool, Victoria, and what you expected I'd do when I found you. Come on!'

'Well—'

'For a start, you didn't know when I was sailing – did you? You could have had a long wait – or you'd have been found while we were alongside, and sent packing. So why?'

Damply she said, 'I was just hoping, that's all. Hoping to persuade you. Look, I've nowhere to bloody go, have I—'

'You said you'd go back to Australia.'

'No, I never did. *You* said that.' She was indignant. 'If I didn't go to this bloody admiral—'

'Which is where you *will* go, now. Surely you knew that was where I'd send you, as soon as you came out of that trunk?'

'I said, I was hoping to persuade you. If I couldn't . . . well, then I reckon I'd have had to give in. It was just a try. You can't blame me for that. I reckon you ought to see it proves one thing, anyway.'

'What?'

She said, 'Proves I bloody *love* you. Look, we've been together a long while now, all the way from Sydney via bloody Ireland.' She looked up at him like a small, hunted animal, trusting and faithful . . . he clenched his fists again, beat them against his forehead as he paced the cabin. She had him by the short hairs and he knew it; so did she. There was something between them; he was unable, now, to find it in himself to send her away. All that trouble, all the risk of incarceration in a trunk because she just couldn't take being parted, with the fear that he might never come back for her and she would be alone and starving. And then there was the threat to her safety ashore. The men in Liverpool might find a way, doubtful though that was if she were in naval hands. Perhaps she would be as safe here with him as anywhere else . . . perhaps.

She clinched it for him as he wavered. She said in a voice full of determination, 'If you send me back, I'll finish myself off. Cut a vein – or something.'

'That's blackmail, Victoria.'

'Yes. But I'll do it. I mean that. Can't you see I'm bloody unhappy, mate?'

He said, 'We shall sleep on it, Victoria. There will be time at dawn to put you back ashore – if I so decide.' He picked her up

45

again and laid her on the bunk. He knew he was beaten: he cursed himself for growing soft. He was remembering that note she'd left at Mrs Mavitty's. *Sorry mate*. She was an outcast with no hope in life beyond himself; he couldn't let her down, whatever havoc his softness might play with his future, however much her presence aboard might add to his worries for the current voyage.

* * *

Below in the foul conditions immediately above the bilges, lying in the tiered wooden bunks hastily constructed for their use but not for their comfort, the draft from Dartmoor prison had largely reacted to the rolling of the ship as the restless water, the surge of the Channel around the long sea defences, lifted and dropped. Already the air was heavy with odour; little freshness penetrated the hold. The chains clanked against the bunks and the uprights to which they had been fixed. Once they were in the hold the party had been split up into sections, each section separately chained and bunked down in its own tier and the ends of the chains secured to ring-bolts at the extremity of each tier. Two armed warders, together with one carrying a storm lantern, patrolled the deck between the tiers, feeling ill themselves. No one was going to enjoy this voyage. It would grow worse as the days at sea passed. The convicts, men already made half-way into savages by the grim, harsh routine of the Moor would become more dangerous, more inclined to lash out at authority the moment they saw a chance. The sanction against this would be a cancellation of their forthcoming enlistment into the labour battalion, a return to the Moor and an exacting punishment that would worsen their lot and extend the sentence among the mists and chills and back-breaking work at Princetown.

It was a sanction that might not hold. Like Bowler, like MacNab, all the warders expected an escape attempt and there was no knowing when this might come. Nerves were on edge; and rifles and truncheons were ready and would be used at the drop of a hat to nip anything in the bud. The atmosphere was already on a knife-edge as the *Glen Halladale* rolled, sluggish at her anchor. Archer-Caine, a slim figure in the prison clothing, lying on a bunk, was watchful but quiet, speaking to no one

46

though most of his fellow convicts spoke in low tones to one another when patrolling warders were out of earshot. Archer-Caine had always contrived to keep himself to himself inside Dartmoor Prison, not a hard thing to do since talking was never permitted though often indulged in when the stone-breaking picks were being wielded out in the open air. In a curious way this had given him a kind of authority, a kind of leadership; he was a gentleman and everyone knew it. The opinion of common men that the gentry had the brains and intelligence had not been weakened by the rise of socialism. The common men might rail, but they still respected.

* * *

There was another worry for Halfhyde in the trunk: he had expected the gold bullion and had found only Victoria Penn. What had happened to the gold? It was clear that the men who had made the offer had had no knowledge of the earlier sailing time of the *Glen Halladale*. What would they do now? Halfhyde was glad enough to be relieved of the extra anxiety that the gold would bring, though he had no illusions that its absence from his ship would lessen the likelihood of trouble from the convicts at some stage. But when the news went through to Liverpool that the *Glen Halladale* had left Devonport there would be consternation and it might well be thought – and with justification as it happened – that he, Halfhyde, had informed the authorities. And there had been the threat that if he did that, his life would be of no future account. . .

Well, he could take what came. It would be far from the first time that he had faced danger. He had good officers and, he believed, a reliable crew. Whatever happened on the voyage would be met. He spared a thought for Archer-Caine, in his unaccustomed chains below: if Archer-Caine was truly in-volved with the bullion, then he too might be doubtful as to whether or not it had reached the ship in time for the suddenly advanced sailing. Doubt might prove an inhibitor of plans and of violence . . . Halfhyde, who had been walking the darkness of the poop restlessly, decided to clear his mind of one matter at once, rather than wait for morning. He went below to his cabin and, finding it empty, knocked on the door of the spare cabin across the alleyway and aft of the First Mate's cabin. Victoria called to him to come in.

'Well?' she asked as he entered.

He said, 'You can remain aboard, Victoria.'

Her face showed her relief. She said. 'You've brought me back to life, love—'

'Good. You'll obey orders, my orders. Understood?'

'I always have,' she said. 'Of course it's understood. And you needn't go on about the dangers. I've taken it all in. I reckon we're going to be all right. You're the sort who *makes* things all right.'

He gave a tight bow, ironically. 'Thank you for the compliment. I shall try to deserve it, you may be sure. Sleep well, Victoria – and keep your cabin door locked at night.' He turned away, but not before he'd seen the look of disappointment in the girl's face. He was sorry for that, sorry also for his own desires that were not to be fulfilled; but until this mission was completed, until the *Glen Halladale* was safely arrived in Simon's Town, he intended all his actions to be correct in every particular. It would be a voyage of much uneasiness, of constant watchfulness and tension, and he did not intend to have it said among the afterguard and in the fo'c'sle, and especially among the warders and their charges, that the Master was living in dalliance with a woman, enjoying comforts and privileges denied to all on board except himself. Convicts were convicts by their own failings, but as human cargo – literally – they had to be a different consideration from an inanimate one. So he went alone to his cabin and turned in early; tomorrow would be a full day, with a brand-new crew to shake down and teach to rely on each other as they trod the swaying footropes to let go the canvas from the yards, or hauled down hard on the braces to trim the sails. An eagle eye must be kept on every man from the poop until the Master was certain of that man's capabilities and his nerve aloft.

At six bells in the morning watch next day he was woken in accordance with his orders by the steward, a short, rotund man named Humper. 'A blustery day, sir. And a boat coming off, sir.'

Halfhyde was awake on the instant. 'Where from, Humper?'

'Looks like the dockyard, sir. That's according to the watch.'

'I'll be on deck instantly.' Halfhyde pulled on his jacket and trousers over his nightshirt and thrust his feet into a pair of seaboots. He went up the companion ladder from the after end of the saloon alleyway to the poop hatch, and found the Second Mate watching through a telescope as the single light of a small boat was seen making out through an increasing sea. The wind was blowing strongly from the south-west and sending spray over the breakwater, just visible now as a watery dawn began to cut through the last of the night. Down in the waist, Halfhyde saw the bosun standing by with another man, tending a jump-ladder. As the boat came closer, visible now as more than a steaming-light, Halfhyde saw that it was a naval steam picquet-boat with a bell-mouthed brass funnel; a midshipman stood in the sternsheets, with a petty officer second class at the wheel. So this was not to be the gold, as he had half suspected it might be – there could be ways of avoiding the attentions of the Customs or other prying persons, though it would have been a risky business. As the picquet-boat came alongside and was borne off by the boathooks of the bowman and sternsheetsman, being swayed now and again against the fenders put over by the bosun, the midshipman jumped for the rope rungs of the ladder, clung on, climbed nimbly aboard and doubled aft to the poop.

'Captain Halfhyde, sir?'

'Yes.'

'A despatch, sir.' The young officer reached inside his oilskin and brought out a manilla envelope, sealed with red wax. Ripping it open, Halfhyde saw that it was from the Rear-Admiral Superintendent, who reported that there had been no word of Victoria Penn; not surprisingly! And there was a message for Halfhyde from Colonel Bowler. Investigations by Scotland Yard had not as yet turned up any names associated with Archer-Caine that could in any way be linked with the bullion. If anything should come to light, a cable would be sent to the *Glen Halladale* to meet her in South Africa. Bowler asked if the gold had been put aboard before sailing. If it had not been, he wrote, then he fancied it was possible it might be sent out aboard a steamship to overtake the *Glen Halladale* and swing it across at sea. All ports in the United Kingdom would be under surveillance but if found the shipment would not be interfered with – Bowler still wished to make a full catch of everyone involved, it seemed. The furthest he would go in the meantime would be to put a watch on those involved in any such shipment and see to it that they were brought to book in due course.

Halfhyde went down to the saloon with the midshipman; Humper provided steaming hot tea laced with whisky while Halfhyde wrote his reply to the Rear-Admiral, indicating the presence aboard of Victoria Penn. He confirmed to Bowler that the bullion was not aboard. As soon as the midshipman had climbed back into his heaving picquet-boat with the letters, and had turned away to head back into Devonport dockyard, Halfhyde had all hands turned out to weigh anchor and stand by to make sail.

* * *

The noise below along the convict deck was turning the cargo-empty hold into a drum. The rush of feet up top, the slap and bang of heavy deck gear, of blocks and tackles, the racket from for'ard of the steam-driven windlass as it hove in the anchor for bringing to the cathead, the shouts of the mates and the bosun as the hands were driven aloft in the makings of a full gale that would test them, so early in the voyage, to the limit, the sound of the sea swishing past the hull . . . all this made a kind of bedlam and one that was utterly unfamiliar to the chained gangs still in their bunks. They were docile so far, many of them too ill to be anything else, lying with heads dangling down to the deck, mouths a-gush with last night's supper, a frugal meal of corned beef and haricot beans washed down with water. Slushy, as the cook aboard a windjammer was always known, had thought it a repast too good for convicts. 'Last the buggers'll get o' such high living,' he'd remarked to his mate as the beans were dished out from a ladle and slices of corned beef were laid on top by grimy hands. 'Now on, it'll be bleedin' cracker hash and like it.' Cracker hash was a mixture of stew and crushed ship's biscuit; burgoo, a sort of porridge, was the alternative. In any event, little by now remained in the stomachs. MacNab had gone below himself as the *Glen Halladale* had got under way and was standing at the fore end of the hold, clutching a stanchion as the decks heeled hard over to the weight of the wind once the canvas had been shaken free of the gaskets. The watch on the convicts was being changed now;

as the fresh men came down, the warders going off watch made their report and started the climb of the ladder leading up to the tween-deck hatch.

That was when the first trouble came.

The *Glen Halladale*, coming now around the bulk of the breakwater, the last link with the land, met the full force of the south-westerly. As Halfhyde ordered the braces to be hauled round to start the tack into the wind, the ship gave a heavy lurch and, below in the hold, one of the just off-duty warders missed his footing as he reached the opened hatch, and fell clear to the deck of the main hold some twenty feet below, his rifle falling behind him. As MacNab and the duty warders ran to his assistance, joined by the second off-watch man who had not yet climbed up, there was a rising murmur from the convicts, a sound of naked hate that overlaid the thunder of the seas against the ship's side and the noises from the deck above. As MacNab passed along the aisle between the tiers of bunks, a thick, hairy forearm was lifted sharply, and heavy links of chain caught the senior warder a blow behind the ear. In a moment the owner of the arm was out of his bunk, dragging his chain and his neighbours towards MacNab and grabbing for the revolver in the holster.

'Right, now, Mister MacNab!'

MacNab, flat on the deck and groggy from the blow, stared up at the man, who flourished the revolver in his face. The man called out to the warders, 'You bastards have a care. Do as I say or MacNab dies.'

The three guards looked back at him. On the deck, the injured man groaned. The man with the gun called, 'All of you drop your rifles. One of you's to come over and get MacNab's keys. Then release the padlocks. And do it fast.'

* * *

The revolver shot came clear through the whine of the wind and the general clatter along the spray-filled deck. Hearing it, Halfhyde shouted for the bosun to call out the off-duty warders from the half-deck, which, taking turns for use of the twelve bunks, they were using as their accommodation since the *Glen Halladale* was carrying no apprentices; but they too had heard the shot and were already tumbling out with their rifles and making for the tween-deck.

Halfhyde used his megaphone and called aloft to the main upper topsail yard: 'Mr Edwards! Down to the poop, if you please, at once. Take charge of the ship.'

Without waiting for the First Mate to slide down the halliards, Halfhyde took the poop ladder at the rush, making for the tween-deck and the hatch into the hold. Looking down with the warders he saw a man he believed to be Archer-Caine holding his right arm, which was pouring blood; MacNab was lying on the deck, with a convict bending over him. A number of others clustered around. Halfhyde shouted, 'Below there! We have you covered. I give you thirty seconds to get back to your bunks and away from the warders. After that, fire will be opened on any man who has not obeyed.'

For a moment there was silence, then shouts of derision came up from the hold. One of the convicts, louder than the rest, called up, 'You'll never do that and you know it—'

'Try me,' Halfhyde called back coolly. 'This is a ship at sea and you have committed an act of mutiny. As Master, I am entitled to shoot you.'

He waited, and began counting the seconds. He saw the man he thought was Archer-Caine lift himself on an elbow and speak to the man holding MacNab's revolver. Halfhyde reached the count of thirty and called down again. 'The time's up. I shall give the order . . . and remember, we're barely out from Plymouth Sound. I can have every living man back in Dartmoor Prison before the forenoon's out.' He waited a few moments longer. 'See sense,' he called down. 'Some of you will die, the rest will face charges of complicity.'

The man with the gun, the obvious leader, got slowly to his feet, his face twisted with fury. 'All right, mister,' he shouted. 'You win for now. Don't let it go to your head.'

'Nor yours either, if you think you'll do anything like this again. Meanwhile, I'm obliged for the early warning. Mr MacNab, are you fit to climb to the tween-deck?'

'I am, sir,' MacNab answered.

'Then come up, and we shall confer as to the future.'

'Aye, sir.' MacNab paused. 'Can we have the doctor sent down, sir? There's one of my warders, and the man Archer-Caine, both injured.'

'Very well,' Halfhyde answered. The medical man promised from the prison service had embarked from a boat during the night; Halfhyde had not yet had an opportunity of meeting him. 'Remain where you are then, until the doctor's been down. And I'll send you some extra warders while he's there.' He gestured at two of the prison staff, and they went down the ladder. Another went for the doctor, who appeared after some five minutes carrying a black Gladstone bag – a shambling man with a blotchy face and trembling hands, and one, it seemed, not inclined to hurry as Halfhyde remarked acidly.

'I'm sorry, Captain. I got here as fast as I could. I'm not accustomed to ships, you know.' Dr Murchison put out a hand to steady himself; his advance towards the tween-deck hatch had been more of a crab-wise lurch along the heeling deck. Like the injured warder, he almost lost his footing as he reached tentatively for the rungs of the ladder. He went down slowly, his body close against the rungs, like a limpet, making heavy weather of the Gladstone bag. Halfhyde looked sour: the doctor was an old man, all of sixty, at the end of his career and he looked what Victoria would have called a no-hoper. He left an aura of whisky behind him. His examination was slow, as though his wits had deserted him. Climbing back to the tween-deck he was helped from the ladder by Halfhyde and a warder.

'Well?' Halfhyde asked.

'The warder's dead, I'm afraid. A broken back, such a tragedy at the start of the voyage, Captain—'

'And the prisoner?'

'A bullet through the arm, the fleshy part, not serious if it's kept clean.'

'You've bandaged, Doctor?'

'Yes. But he should be brought up . . . infection can get in and the wound can become septic.' The doctor looked almost septic himself. 'The air in the hold, you see – the vomit and so on.'

Halfhyde nodded. 'Thank you, Doctor. I shall have words with MacNab.'

The doctor drew a hand across his forehead, wiping away beads of sweat. It was hot below, hot from overcrowding and the emanations of the packed bodies, an atmosphere that smote strongly up through the open hatch, which was bad enough – to live in such a stench must be sheer misery ... the doctor shambled away again, holding tight to the handrail running along the bulkhead, his bag banging against his thigh as he went. A couple of minutes later MacNab climbed the ladder, his revolver back now in its holster. His face was grim as he came over the hatch coaming and met Halfhyde's stare.

'I'm sorry, sir,' he said. 'So early in the voyage—'

'Yes. A timely warning at all events. We know what to expect, at least! What's the name of the ringleader, the one who was threatening you?'

'Carling, sir.'

'His offence?'

'Manslaughter—'

'And sentence?'

'Penal servitude for life, sir.'

Halfhyde nodded. 'Nothing to lose. And a violent man, obviously—'

'Aye, he's that and always has been,' MacNab said. 'I shall have a special eye kept, as indeed was the intention from the start—'

'But not kept open wide enough, Mr MacNab. Now it will be kept, like Carling, in a different place. The man's to be moved at once and locked into the fore peak, in isolation. He'll cause no harm there.'

'It'll split the guard, sir.'

Halfhyde said, 'I'll not permit him to act as ringleader again – and as to the guard, he'll not get out of the forepeak and a guard will not be necessary. I'll have the place prepared and will let you know when he's to be moved. Now there's another point: Archer-Caine, who's also to be moved by request of the doctor. How did he come to be shot – presumably by Carling?'

'Yes, by Carling, sir. Archer-Caine had opposed him, telling him he was a fool and would get no support from any man of common sense.'

'There was some talk between them, I fancy, after the shooting?'

MacNab nodded. 'Aye, sir, there was. Archer-Caine did talk sense into him in the end ... though it was you and my warders, with the rifles, that ended the matter.'

Halfhyde gave a short laugh. 'I don't doubt it! I wonder only

54

that Carling could ever have expected success!'

'There's little enough intelligence in Carling,' MacNab said. 'Or in most of the others either.'

'And Archer-Caine . . .'

'A gentleman, sir.'

'So I'm told. The fact does not always go hand in hand with intelligence, Mr MacNab – but that's not what I was going on to ask about. What's your own impression of Archer-Caine, and how has he behaved in Dartmoor prison?'

MacNab pursed his lips. 'He's behaved well, sir. But it's hard to form an impression . . . he's a solitary man, so far as that's possible when they're working together during the set hours. I remember one thing, sir: when he was checked in, and when he was interviewed by the Governor—'

'Colonel Bowler?'

'Aye, Colonel Bowler, sir, it was then. Archer-Caine insisted on his innocence of the charge – of course, many of them do that, it's far from unusual . . .'

'But?'

MacNab met his stare. 'Sir?'

Halfhyde said, 'Your tone seemed to me to indicate that you felt some reservation – in the particular case of Archer-Caine. Am I right, Mr MacNab?'

MacNab rubbed a hand across his chin, frowning. Then he said, 'Aye, sir, to me it had the ring of sincerity, but I can't say more than that.'

'And Colonel Bowler?'

'He'd not listen, sir, except insofar as it was his duty to do so—'

'In one ear and out of the other?'

'Aye, sir, very perfunctory. He'd listened to so many, all saying the same thing – the first-timers, that is. They don't bother with it afterwards, but a lot of the first-timers like to get it off their chests.'

Halfhyde nodded. 'A kind of reflex action,' he murmured. 'The need to make a point, perhaps, to show that Dartmoor's not their normal habitat! Would I be right in assuming the innocence protesters are mostly from what I would call the non-criminal classes?'

'Aye, you would, sir. The others have led harder lives, sir, and accept the facts, take what's their due. But Archer-Caine . . . well, I don't know, sir. But I can say this, that he was of use to us all this morning.'

'Will he suffer from the other convicts now?'

'That will not be allowed to happen, sir. Though I can't say what the end will be, when the draft comes under the military at the Cape and they have a greater degree of freedom, such as is bound to be the case when working as a labour battalion under attack from the Boers.'

Halfhyde was about to comment on the vigilance of sergeant-majors and NCOs when the ship gave an extra heavy lurch; there was a sharp crack like the discharge of light artillery, followed by the thunder of a weight of water crashing down on the fo'c'sle-head to rush aft and sweep men off their legs. As some of that water found its way below to the tween-deck Halfhyde heard the shout from Edwards on the poop carrying clear above the sounds of the weather: 'All hands! All hands on deck!'

He ran for the ladder to the upper deck.

SIX

There was a scene of chaos: the fore upper topsail and lower topsail had carried away, the canvas ripping out from the boltropes under the onslaught of a sudden shift of wind and an increase in its strength. Halfhyde estimated it as well over full gale force; and some of the green hands that he had been forced to sign in Devonport to make up a full crew had shown devilish clumsiness that could not be circumvented in time by the experienced men. The upper topsail had gone altogether; the lower topsail, held by two corners still, was flapping in great strips, giving a series of reports like rifle fire and whipping dangerously close to the men on the footropes as they waited for new canvas to be sent aloft. On the deck itself the port-side brace-winch was useless, its drum wrapped around with fathoms of heavy rope and the bosun seemingly a part of it, his hand thrust into the bird's-nest of cordage, an expression of agony on his face. Halfhyde summed the situation up in a second: the bosun had seen a riding turn coming up and had tried to deal with it, and in so doing his hand had become trapped between the drum and the ever-tightening rope.

'Mr Edwards, the doctor—'

'Already sent for, sir.'

'Good man.' Halfhyde took over, sending the First Mate for'ard to take charge at the foremast. From the poop he kept an eye lifting on the canvas; and looking down again saw the slow, terrified approach of Dr Murchison, who came out from the door leading from the officers' accommodation to the waist, clutching his Gladstone bag and obviously wishing he'd never ventured to sea. He made a staggering rush across the deck to the brace-winch, looking totally at a loss. By this time the rope had been walked back by the hands to the drum of the winch and the turns were coming off. As the bosun's arm became exposed, there was much blood and the hand looked crushed and forever useless.

Meanwhile more seas were dropping aboard, bringing ton after ton of green, foaming water to thunder down on the fo'c'sle and swill aft. There was a continuous overall whine of wind, wind that tugged at the bodies along the yards as they swept in an arc across a lowering sky, holding on desperately to the yards and trying to keep their places on the footropes that swayed beneath. The sailmaker and a number of the hands were bringing up the new canvas for sending aloft when there was a curious sound from below, a kind of slither accompanied by splintering . . . Halfhyde shouted from the poop for the carpenter, who was aloft making a fast examination of the yards, looking for any damage.

'Below, Bracegirdle, below!'

There was an answering shout: 'On my way, sir!'

Bracegirdle slid fast down the halliards and took the deck. He ran for the fore companion-way to the tween-deck and disappeared. He was back within a minute, making haste towards the poop.

'Well, Bracegirdle?'

'It's the convict deck, sir. The hold's a bloody mess. Bunks carried away, sir, and largely smashed.'

'And the men – the prisoners?'

'Under control, sir. All the prison warders are down there, with their rifles.'

Halfhyde nodded. 'Thank you, Bracegirdle. Later we shall go into the question of a repair.' The carpenter turned away and once again swarmed aloft. The replacement sails were going up now and being taken over by the men along the footropes, who fought and battered and hauled them into position in the teeth of the gale's fury. Halfhyde thanked God and Rear-Admiral Bassinghorn for providing him with enough skilled seamen to ensure at least a degree of competence in times of crisis. So many of the commercial windjammers sailed with inexperienced crews, for the newer breed of fo'c'sle hand was largely deserting sail for steam and an increasing proportion of many crews was formed by the apprentices, the youths who were forced to do their qualifying time in sail in order to sit for their masters' certificates, in their turn to desert the sailing ships for steam. As the *Glen Halladale* came gradually under full control Halfhyde's mind turned towards the discomforts and dangers below in the hold. Until a repair could be effected – and it would be a long job for one skilled ship's carpenter and his mate – the Dartmoor draft would have no sleeping billets and that was going to add to the frayed tempers and the difficulties of MacNab and his warders. Yet there was no alternative: there was nowhere else to berth the chain gangs, and that was that. But when he returned to Devonport, Halfhyde would have some harsh words for the shoreside labour that had fitted the bunks in the hold, quoting Bracegirdle's adverse report so soon after joining the ship.

When all was secure aloft, Halfhyde went below to the saloon and found Victoria Penn with Dr Murchison, attending to the bosun. He asked, 'How is it, Bunch?'

'Easier now, sir,' the bosun answered, 'thanks to the lady.' His glance at the doctor was sour. Halfhyde looked at the bandage, which was neatly done but was already showing the seepage of blood. In Bunch's presence he forbore to ask the doctor's prognosis; and for his part Murchison volunteered nothing, watching with pursed lips and shaking hands as Victoria finished the bandaging.

'What about the prisoner, Archer-Caine?' Halfhyde asked.

Murchison said, 'I shall see to him now, Captain, if you'll order him brought up. Where will he be put?'

'Here in the saloon, at any rate for your examination and treatment—'

'A convict, Captain?' Murchison seemed scandalized.

'A human being,' Halfhyde answered shortly. He went to the door of the saloon and shouted for the steward. 'Humper, to the poop and ask Mr Edwards to have the prisoner Archer-Caine brought at once to the saloon.'

* * *

Archer-Caine had been brought up by two warders, the shackles now removed from his wrists. Halfhyde left him to Murchison and Victoria and went to the poop, where the First

59

Mate was watching the sails closely. After the new sails had been sent up, other canvas had been reduced and the ship was scudding along under upper and lower topsails only, tacking into the wind and coming about smartly enough under Edwards' orders as he altered the tack. With such a weight of wind there were two hands on the wheel, having a hard job to keep the ship's head pointing where it should be. One was an experienced old-timer, an ex-naval leading seaman named Patcham, one of those who had done time in the Sail Training Squadron, the other being one of the green hands now learning some of the tricks of his trade. Halfhyde paced the poop, a stiff climb from port to starboard when on one tack, from starboard to port when on the other as the ship laid over to the wind. It was an invigorating day, and Halfhyde relished being back under sail as he had been in the *Aysgarth Falls* en route for Australia after leaving the Queen's service a year or so earlier. A clean life, with no dirty black smoke to pollute the air, no sounds except the natural ones of wind and water together with the creak of rigging and woodwork and the slap of ropes against masts and canvas or the dragging of heavy blocks along the deck . . .

The steward came up the ladder from the after accommodation. 'Doctor's finished, sir, and asks what's to happen to the prisoner.'

'I'll come down, Humper.' Halfhyde went below, bending his tall, angular frame under the companion-way cover as his feet took the treads of the ladder. In the saloon Murchison said, 'He'll be all right, Captain. No more than a flesh wound. But he should still not go back to the hold.'

'Very well, Doctor.' Halfhyde glanced at the two warders: rifles were an unwelcome sight when held against a wounded man who had been of some service to authority, but Halfhyde realized the necessity. There was another necessity as well: he must not be seen by the other prisoners to favour a man said to be a gentleman. Archer-Caine must not, for his own sake, be made too overtly comfortable in the meantime. And in that lay a dilemma: the after accommodation and the half-deck were the only habitable parts of the ship other than the fo'c's'le mess where the hands lived – and currently the half-deck was in the possession of the prison staff. Coming to a decision Halfhyde said, 'He'll be put in a section of the tween-deck, with a mattress provided, and a guard to be arranged by Mr MacNab. But first I wish a word with him myself. In privacy. If you don't mind, Dr Murchison?' he added tartly as the doctor looked surprised and disinclined to leave.

'As you say, Captain.' Murchison moved for the door, followed by the girl. The warders stayed, grim-faced behind the ready rifles.

'I said, in private,' Halfhyde said.

'Begging your pardon, sir. The orders from—'

'Aboard my ship, it's my orders that will be first obeyed.'

The warder was dogged. 'The routine of Her Majesty's prisons, sir—'

'Calls for prisoners never to be left unguarded – yes, I understand that.' Halfhyde, standing with his arms behind his back, body lifting and falling gently on the balls of his feet, stared the man out. 'I am well able to take care of myself, the more so against a wounded man. You will leave the saloon and return only when I call for you.'

'It's very irregular, sir.'

Halfhyde's lips thinned in a cold grin. 'I am an irregular man. And one who is to be obeyed on the instant. Your name?'

The warder's look was hostile. He said, 'Sharp's the name—'

'And sharp's my word. Kindly leave me, both of you.'

The warders went out; the atmosphere was frigid with their disapproval. Halfhyde shrugged it away. He refused to consider the *Glen Halladale* as a prison ship and never mind her particular cargo; neither MacNab nor the distant Colonel Bowler commanded her and Halfhyde meant to run things his own way. And Archer-Caine might be very well worth talking to as man to man. There was still the problem of the bullion shipment and a careless word might be made to drop that would give a pointer to matters that, up to the time of the *Glen Halladale*'s sailing, seemed to have remained a closed book to Bowler and the Whitehall authorities.

* * *

'In my saloon,' Halfhyde said, 'you're a free man. For now you may be easy.'

'It's very decent of you, Captain,' Archer-Caine said. At

Halfhyde's bidding he had remained seated on the buttoned leather settee that ran below the two scuttles on the ship's port side; Halfhyde, wishing to put the man as much as possible at his ease, had sat in a chair at the table set beneath an oil lamp a-swing at the end of a chain secured to the deckhead. 'It's some relief, to get away from your hold, I do confess.'

'And your companions – and the warders?'

'Yes. I've no wish to state complaints behind anyone's back – that's not in my nature – but Sharp's the worst of the lot.'

Halfhyde nodded. 'Sadistic?'

'Very.'

'Towards you in particular – because you're a gentleman?'

'No, I'd not say that. The man's impartial enough . . . a bastard to all without distinction.'

'So the prisoners would take a chance against him – if it came to a break-out?'

Archer-Caine nodded. 'I've no doubt they'd kill him, no doubt at all. But I don't believe you need fear another break-out, Captain. Once out at sea, they'd be foolish to try it, since we're all in your hands and only you and your men can bring us to a landfall.'

MacNab hadn't seemed to subscribe to this view; and Halfhyde fancied that many of the convicts would lack the intelligence to place circumspection above the sheer desire to hit out against authority. But all he said was, 'And afterwards – in South Africa?'

'I can't say. I doubt it, however. Once under military discipline the odds against it would be heavy and dangerous.'

'Not in action. When there is confusion—'

'Oh, yes, there could be a chance then.'

'And you think they'd take it?' Halfhyde asked.

Archer-Caine said, 'Yes, I do.'

'And your action in that event?'

'I'd never act against my own side in action, Captain.'

Halfhyde nodded. 'No. I believe that.' He didn't press the point. Archer-Caine's eyes were level, steady – honest, Halfhyde would have said. The man had an air of quietness, of confidence . . . in his own innocence, some sort of faith that one day he would be vindicated? Or a confidence that, with the aid of the bullion, he would be able to set himself up again if only he could escape, perhaps acquire a new identity in a new land? There were many imponderables and little light. Halfhyde was much tempted to probe Archer-Caine openly about the bullion shipment that was as yet conspicuous by its absence, but this he resisted. He had no brief from Colonel Bowler to speak of it to anyone, let alone the man who was expected to benefit from it.

He got to his feet and took a turn up and down the saloon. He was aware of the convict's eyes following him. He felt no fear at presenting his unprotected back to the man, though he would have hesitated to do so to any of the other convicts. Desperation tended towards desperate methods, often ill-thought-out, and a sudden pounce across the cabin at an unarmed man might be considered productive insofar as it might gain a hostage of the Master. But Halfhyde felt a curious trust of Archer-Caine, and not, he believed, simply because the prisoner had already acted in defence of the warders. He stopped in his perambulation and swung round suddenly. He asked, 'Is there anything you wish to discuss with me, Archer-Caine?'

Archer-Caine inclined his head. 'Thank you, Captain. There is not.'

'I understand you represented to Colonel Bowler, when he was governor at Dartmoor, that you were wrongly convicted?'

'MacNab told you this?'

'Yes.'

'MacNab's a good man, as warders go. He's fair if hard – he has to be hard. I've often had a feeling he believes me.'

'That you're innocent? And are you, Archer-Caine?'

'Yes,' he answered directly. 'That I swear before God. But I fear I shall never prove it, Captain. There is too much at stake . . . too much against me, too many people who have an interest in seeing that I'm not allowed my liberty.'

'I see.' Halfhyde sat down again and faced Archer-Caine across the saloon. The sound of the wind's fury came down from the poop; seas swept constantly across the ports, bringing a dapple of light and dark alternately to run across the broad arrows of Archer-Caine's prison garb, across the rough stubble of the convict's cheeks. There was something in the face that said Archer-Caine wanted to talk, wanted desperately to talk to someone, anyone who might listen sympathetically; and Halfhyde decided to draw him out. 'You may talk freely,' he said. 'I've already told you to consider yourself free here in my saloon. What you say will not be repeated to MacNab, you have my word on that.'

There was a faint smile on Archer-Caine's face. 'It doesn't matter to me if you tell MacNab. I've no need to fear the spread of truth, Captain. I—'

'And Colonel Bowler?'

Archer-Caine said, 'Oh, I've tried to tell Bowler but he wouldn't listen. The military mind . . . a convict's a convict, properly tried before a judge and jury and duly sentenced, and that's that. Bowler's impervious, hide-bound, stiff with prejudice and formality.' He laughed without humour. 'What colonel is not, Captain?'

Halfhyde smiled. 'You might well ask . . . and you might well say the same of admirals. As for me, I've fallen foul of plenty of admirals in the past. It's possible you and I have something in common, Archer-Caine.' He went on to tell the man a little of his own past, of his naval service, of the ups and downs of a tempestuous career afloat and his frequent brushes with his senior officers, of his current commission in the reserve. To some extent, he said, he too had been the victim of those who preferred him to be out of the way.

'But,' Archer-Caine said, 'I doubt if you were ever the victim of false evidence given with intent.'

'No. I tend to bring my misfortunes upon my own head!'

Again Archer-Caine smiled. 'Well, I hope you're not doing so now! Bowler wouldn't approve this conversation if he knew of it – and I appreciate the risks you're running—'

'There is no risk,' Halfhyde interrupted flatly. 'Colonel Bowler runs neither my ship nor my life. Tell me whatever it is you wish to tell me, and I shall judge how, and if, I can be of help to you.'

* * *

Halfhyde glanced at the clock on the saloon bulkhead: the time was passing towards noon. Twice the warders had knocked at the door and put their heads in, to be sent away again with crisp words from the Master. Archer-Caine sat mostly with his head in his hands, hiding haunted eyes. A further probing had been necessary, more encouragement, and then quite suddenly the man had opened up and Halfhyde had simply sat and listened. It was a strange story that he heard, and an alarming one, a terrible indictment of British justice and of British authority and its concept of integrity. He believed two things: that Archer-Caine was speaking nothing but the truth, and that he had hidden nothing. The words had come out under an obvious head of steam as it were, long pent-up, bitter, frustrated, a torrent of self-revelation that could never have been a premeditated prevarication. Everything he said had, to Halfhyde, the ring of truth and utter sincerity; and Halfhyde had been far from unaccustomed in his naval service to the sorting of lies from truth during the interrogation of seamen at the defaulters' table.

Archer-Caine by his own acknowledgement had been a fool, but never a criminal. From his father, already a widower, he had inherited a landed estate in Hampshire. As the only son, the only child in fact, he had been the sole inheritor; but his inheritance was land rather than money. The estate was in a poor way; land values had been falling and the amount he could raise by selling the tenanted farms and cottages had been little enough, falling short of what was needed to run the big house as it should be run, with servants inside and out, and keep it in proper repair. At first Archer-Caine had made an attempt to farm some of the land himself, with the assistance of a bailiff; but his knowledge of farming was nil and he had become the tool of his own bailiff, who had cheated him right, left and centre and let him in for foolish and fruitless speculation. The result had come close to bankruptcy and there had been an enforced sale of the house and the remaining land. It seemed his childhood home had gone for ever.

Then hope had come from an unexpected quarter: Archer-Caine had been offered a directorship of a limited liability company with its head office in the city of London, this offer coming via a solicitor who had once acted for his father. It was not until much later that Archer-Caine had discovered that this solicitor's services had been terminated by his father on account of poor advice and more than a suspicion of dishonesty. By then it was too late. Archer-Caine had accepted the directorship, which brought with it fees of five hundred pounds a year in return for the use of his name, a well-known and respected one in the exclusive circles of Hampshire's landed gentry, with many promises of real money to come, such that would perhaps enable him to buy back his old home and re-establish himself in his proper sphere of life.

He had accepted readily.

Mostly there had been little need for him to attend the company's offices other than for board meetings when he had been lost in a maze of figures and decisions, decisions to which he had agreed, acting from sheer ignorance of business procedures simply as a rubber stamp for his fellow directors' schemes. Broadly he knew that the company's objective, as stated in its articles of association, was the acquisition of farming land while land values were low, this land being held until it could be sold at a large profit, the company being kept afloat in the meantime by the sale of contiguous parcels of pasture for prices beyond their actual current value to the big wholesale butchers who were beginning to emerge and who found it more profitable to own land and start their own beef-cattle herds, thus cutting out the farming middleman. And it was when it dawned at last upon Archer-Caine that he was part of a virtual conspiracy to put the farmers off the land and at the same time to decimate the more impoverished landed estates such as that which had been his own, that he began asking awkward and pointed questions at the meetings of the board. The board, he had discovered early on, was largely composed of dispossessed gentry, in the same boat as himself, from many of the English counties, each being a respected name in his own part of the country.

When he had enlisted the support of the more decent of them against the business element, the seed of trouble had been sown.

'To cut short the rest of it,' he told Halfhyde, 'they felt they had to silence me. To force my resignation from the board was not enough – I had to be discredited. And, very ruthlessly, I was.'

'In what way?'

Archer-Caine said, 'By this time I'd made a fair amount. I lived quietly in rooms in London, not a very fashionable part, and I lived cheaply – always with the object in view, the buying back of the house and grounds if ever it came up for sale again.

Well, it did – it had been bought by a bachelor, a retired major-general, who died. There was an executors' sale and I was able to buy, and I employed the solicitor I've mentioned, the one I thought of as a benefactor who'd been indirectly responsible for getting me the wherewithal in the first place. It was then that everything went wrong . . . I suppose the swine that I was already up against saw their chance. I was accused of having milked the company's funds by making false representations to get cheques made out to me for monies that I was not entitled to. These statements were supported by the clerks in the counting house, who'd been bought and who gave evidence at the trial. The fact that I had comparatively soon bought my own property back lent credence to the lies, and I was unable to refute them – my own evidence, my own bank statements and so forth, were simply brushed aside. Even the solicitor – the one I—'

'Yes.'

'Even he managed by winks and nods – metaphorically – to sway the jury against me when ostensibly appearing as a friendly witness. I hadn't a chance. The judge was hostile from the start – I understand he came from a landed background himself and he detested the company's objectives – he was no friend of theirs, certainly, but much less of mine since he quite plainly believed I'd added crime to ungentlemanly money-making—'

'And so were that much worse for having in a sense added to the depredations on the landed gentry?'

Archer-Caine nodded. 'Yes. A biased judge . . . but it was worse than that. One man in particular, a fellow director, lied till he was blue in the face. Under no circumstances was he going to have any investigation of the company's affairs by letting me be found innocent. His word was accepted without dispute, taken by judge and jury and even by my defending counsel at face value – for such a man could never lie. He was produced by the prosecution as a final witness, and he finished me off. That man,' Archer-Caine said quietly, staring into Halfhyde's intent face, 'can never be fought, and will use his influence until he dies to keep me inside where I'll never be listened to. And that's God's own truth, though it's doubtful, I suppose, if you've believed me this far – let alone the rest.'

67

'I believe you,' Halfhyde said. 'It's a nasty enough story, but it has its precedents. Power, they say, corrupts . . . and that's often proved true. Now – the rest?'

Archer-Caine said steadily, watching Halfhyde's face, 'It's a question of a man's name, a well-known man, a gentleman. If I reveal it—'

'No worse harm can come to you. I think you can only help yourself. The name?'

Archer-Caine took a deep breath. 'Sir Humphrey Tallerman,' he said. 'Her Majesty's Secretary of State at the Home Office. A man with everything to lose if the lies told at the Old Bailey should ever be revealed as such.'

SEVEN

'You'll put your head in a bloody noose, you will,' Victoria said, 'if you don't watch it.' Having come back to the saloon after Archer Caine had been taken away she had told Halfhyde she'd heard everything through the bulkhead that separated the Master's cabin from the saloon. There was, she said, a hole in the woodwork right beside where the convict had been sitting, looking as though it had been gnawed out by a rat on a previous voyage.

'Very handy for eavesdroppers,' Halfhyde had snapped at her. 'No doubt you applied your pretty little ear, my girl—'

'No doubt at all,' she answered cheerfully, giving him a lop-sided, urchin grin. 'And *just* as bloody well if you ask me. You need bloody saving from yourself, mate!'

'So you heard his story, and you don't believe it.'

'I never said that,' she objected. 'But now you've said it, well, I reckon he's a gaolbird with an interest in getting himself out again—'

'Wouldn't you?'

'Sure I would,' she said. 'It's natural. But it doesn't make for truth, right? You're saying you believe him?'

'Yes,' he answered shortly, pacing the cabin, throwing the monosyllable over his shoulder at the girl as she sat curled on the settee.

'Does you credit – I suppose. What are you going to do about it?'

'At this moment I have no idea.'

'But you reckon something'll come . . . look, there's nothing you *can* bloody do and you know it. You raise a stink about this

69

Sir bloke and you'll end up in gaol yourself, mate! That's why I say – watch it. It's not enough, just to have a dislike for bloody injustice, if what he says is true. You got yourself to think about.'

'And you,' Halfhyde said savagely. 'Blast you to hell!'

'Thanks. Just say the word and I'll bloody jump overboard if that's what you want.'

'If I order you to,' Halfhyde said grimly, 'that's exactly what you will do, Victoria. You should never have been such a damned little idiot as to—'

'Don't let's go into all that over again,' she said wearily. 'I'm here, full bloody stop. I only wanted to be with you, mate. And to help where I could . . . don't know how, not really, but . . . well, maybe now I can by stopping you making a sacrifice of yourself for a pommie con. And don't give me any jokes about Australia, either.' She paused, looking at him searchingly across the saloon. 'What about that gold, eh? What was all that?'

'So you heard that too, did you.' Halfhyde's mouth was set hard: there was more jiggery-pokery in the air now. He had decided after all to quiz Archer-Caine about that bullion shipment; and Archer-Caine had, he believed, been honestly astonished that anyone should connect him with a fortune in gold bullion. He knew no one, had no friends or associates, who would or could come up with the sort of money that Halfhyde had mentioned. If that was true, then there were no leads at all to the identity of the shippers, and Bowler would be wasting his time in continuing to look for friends of Archer-Caine. And if it were not Archer-Caine, then who? Surely not any other of the convicts, rough men all of them according to MacNab, and highly unlikely to have powerful connections outside their own seedy spheres? So far the whole thing had been no more than supposition in any case, pure guesswork when it came down to brass tacks: the bullion need not necessarily have any connection with the *Glen Halladale*'s Dartmoor draft; though there could perhaps be a link with the drafts from the other ships bringing out the rest of the labour battalion. Halfhyde knew that a ship was leaving Portsmouth with men from Portsmouth and Winchester gaols, another was bound from the Clyde with men from Barlinnie, and there were others . . . all to converge on Simon's Town. Perhaps the bullion shippers had thought it more expedient to use a ship other than the one in which the eventual recipient of their bounty was travelling – that was, if the convict link was indeed a fact. Halfhyde had begun to believe there was no connection, but Archer-Caine's thoughts were different: he had believed it could be an attempt to drive yet another, and final, nail into his coffin. More lies, and more faked documents to substantiate them . . .

To Victoria Halfhyde said, 'It remains a mystery, and one that doesn't concern you. However, since you've eavesdropped so effectively, I'll have to tell you the facts.' He did so, swearing her to secrecy. She said he would have to tell the First Mate, if it happened that the bullion delivery was made at sea as he fancied it might be. He agreed; but that time, he said, had not yet come.

She asked, 'What about that Bowler, eh?'

'What about him?'

'Could be involved, couldn't he?'

'How?'

She shrugged. 'Oh, I don't know. But you said he came under the Home Office, didn't you? And this Sir. He's Home Office, too.'

'The Home Office,' Halfhyde said heavily, 'is not in the business of supplying bullion to criminals, Victoria.'

'Well,' she said, 'maybe it isn't, but from what I heard this Sir isn't exactly honest – according to the convict bloke, anyway. If that bloke's right, maybe Bowler isn't honest either.'

'My dear girl . . . it was Bowler himself who first suggested a link between the bullion and the convicts—'

'All right, all right! But it's a thought, isn't it?'

'No,' Halfhyde snapped.

'Oh well, I reckon you know best, mate.'

* * *

The south-westerly gale blew itself out as the *Glen Halladale* came down upon Ushant, by which time some progress had been made in the repair to the tiers of bunks in the hold. Bracegirdle and his mate had worked under cover of the warders' rifles throughout, no chances being taken of the chained prisoners making another attempt to secure a hostage. The stench in the hold had become almost unbearable; Halfhyde and Edwards had gone below to inspect, and found their stomachs turning even while they were climbing down the latter. Halfhyde's weather sense had told him that the current calm was temporary and that they would be back in strong winds soon after they were into the Bay of Biscay on passage for Finisterre. Meanwhile they had a little time in hand, enough to deal with the first bout of seasickness and its attendant mess.

He turned to MacNab, who was accompanying the inspection. 'We must clean out, Mr MacNab, while we can.'

'I see the need, sir, of course. But there's little that can be done in safety so far as I can see.'

'We must find a way, Mr MacNab. I'll not have human beings kept in such filth and stench. I shall have the wash-deck hoses connected to the pump, and the hands will swill out while the prisoners are brought up on deck. To have the hold empty will also assist my carpenter.'

'It's a risk, sir—'

'Not too much of one, Mr MacNab. You shall have your warders posted along the deck and in the lower rigging. We shall do the job as fast as possible, for before long there'll be another blow and I'll not want my decks cluttered.'

'There'll be more vomit too, sir,' MacNab pointed out.

'Perhaps, perhaps not. By then they may have got their sea-legs. Kindly see to my orders, Mr MacNab.'

MacNab turned away and with obvious reluctance began passing the word for the convicts to be brought up on deck. Still in their chains, they started the climb. The unpleasant warder, Sharp, was shouting the odds in a hectoring tone, prodding with his rifle to urge the chain-gang on faster as feet were set on the ladder. As the hold began to empty the fo'c'sle hands laid out the wash-deck hoses, leading them down over the lip of the hatch coaming and connecting up to the salt-water pump just aft of the pig pen on the port side. As the last of the convicts came up the ladder, the pump was started by hand power and the water began gushing down, to be swilled across the hold by the brooms and squeegees. On deck the convict draft was fallen in, untidy lines of men grateful enough to breathe fresh air, with the warders watchful behind the rifles. Halfhyde paced the poop, hands behind his back and shoulders braced. It was a curious and unwelcome scene: as when he had first been apprised by Colonel Bowler of his appointment, the old-time convict ships that had taken so-called criminals to a life of exile in Australia came strongly to mind. Those days had been barbarous ones, days when even mere sheep stealers had faced the death penalty and those who took bread to feed starving families had been transported ten thousand miles across stormy seas to face hard labour in the young Australia. By all contemporary accounts those transports had been hell-ships, filthy, stinking, overcrowded with men, women and children in appalling conditions of starvation and disease. The *Glen Halladale* was not going to become like that.

Pacing, his thoughts went back to Colonel Bowler and Victoria Penn's suggestion. It nagged, did that utterance, at the back of his mind. But it was preposterous; Bowler had had a successful military career, he was far from the sort of man to become involved in any dishonesty. Nevertheless there was that somewhat disturbing link, the link of service under the Home Office and Sir Humphrey Tallerman. *Was* Archer-Caine speaking the truth about the Secretary of State? It seemed inconceivable; yet there had been that ring of honesty, and Halfhyde, a cynical man, was never easily deceived. Long sea service had given him a very hard head.

He halted his pacing and turned for'ard, looking down at his passengers. The smell was strong, the prison smell from their clothing and bodies. Presumably nothing would eradicate that short of baths and new uniforms. Preoccupied, Halfhyde was at first unaware that Victoria had come up to the poop from the saloon companion. She moved towards him, body angled to the slope of the deck, her hair blowing out along the remaining wind. Freshly scented, very much a woman. The effect was instantaneous and could be felt almost as a physical force, an emanation from the close-packed men along the deck below the break of the poop. Every eye turned in the girl's direction and there was a rising murmur, harsh, raw: very likely this was the first woman many of the men had seen for years. Halfhyde followed the direction of their eyes, and stiffened angrily when he saw the girl.

'Get below!' he ordered.

'Why? Look, for God's sake—'

'*Get below!*' He moved towards her, threateningly; she backed away from the poop rail, looking scared now. He said, 'Never come out on deck again, Victoria, while the convicts are out of the hold. You should have more sense. What's the point of arousing them?'

She shrugged and turned her back on him, making for the companion-way. Every movement said he was acting like an old woman. She vanished down the ladder; but the harm had been done. The convicts had become restive; the warders were extra watchful now for the first unauthorized movement. Even chained men could turn into a mob; and they outnumbered the combined warders and crew by more than two to one. Halfhyde cursed in impotent fury at the stupidity of the girl's action, but at the same time blamed himself: he should have warned her off before now. From this moment on, all the confined men in the hold were going to have Victoria in mind: the mere sight they'd had of a woman, so close to them, was going to lead to a murderous atmosphere. It would never have been possible to prevent their hearing of a woman's presence – that was bound to come out before long – but seeing was a different matter.

The murmur continued. MacNab came along the chained lines, moving slowly and with deliberation, his hand not far from the butt of his revolver, staring the men in the eye as he passed. They didn't quieten; far from it. The murmur rose higher, more and more menacing. They began to rattle their chains and shout abuse at MacNab and the other warders.

Halfhyde called from the poop, 'Mr MacNab, see the men removed below at once, if you please.'

'Aye, sir.' MacNab, now not far off the break of the poop on the starboard side, looked up briefly as he acknowledged the order. For a split second, no more, his attention was off the prison draft; and in that short space of time one of the men burst through his frustrations, probably acting without conscious thought. A knee came up hard in MacNab's groin, and as he doubled involuntarily the man lifted his length of chain, almost dragging his neighbours off their feet as he did so, and brought the heavy iron cuff down with smashing force on MacNab's head. A second too late, one of the warders, clinging to the shrouds running up to the mainmast crosstrees, opened

74

fire and the man fell, sagging in his chains.

It was a nasty moment, with the safety of the ship itself in the balance. If there was to be a riot by way of a reaction, if the convicts believed they saw a chance . . . Halfhyde, as the prison staff seemed dazed by what had happened, took instant and decisive charge. Cupping his hands, he shouted the length of the ship.

'The *Glen Halladale* is on government service, as you all know. It is also under naval command insofar as I am a lieutenant of the reserve. I shall consider any act against the authority of myself, my officers or your warders an act of mutiny on the high seas. I trust that is well understood by every man among you. Mutineers will be shot and those who live afterwards will be handed over on arrival in Simon's Town, not to the military authorities, but to the naval Commander-in-Chief on the South African station for confinement to the prison hulks to await transport home to stand trial for connivance at mutiny – for which the obligatory sentence is death.' He paused, looking along the ranks of prisoners and warders. 'You will now go quietly below under the orders of your guards. Who is next in seniority after Mr MacNab?'

'I am, sir.' It was Sharp who answered.

'Then take charge until Mr MacNab is fit.'

'I think Mr MacNab is dead, sir.'

Halfhyde looked down at the deck, close beneath the break of the poop. Both men, the convict and the senior warder, lay inert, seemed not have stirred, and there was blood soaking the convict's clothing. Halfhyde said, believing now that both might well be dead, 'Dr Murchison will examine them. Have the prisoner unshackled, and see the rest below at once.'

* * *

Murchison had confirmed Halfhyde's belief: both men were indeed dead, MacNab's neck broken and the convict shot through the heart. At least they would not need to make the long voyage to the Cape with a murderer aboard; but Halfhyde foresaw continuing trouble ahead, trouble that would be far from helped by having Sharp as the senior warder. His tone as he watched the draft being herded down the ladder to the hold had been bullying, unnecessarily crude in its content, calcu-

75

lated to worsen any situation let alone a knife-edge one like this. However, surprisingly enough, the convicts had gone below fairly easily and quietly, possibly subdued by Halfhyde's earlier harangue. Halfhyde was certain that would not last. As the days passed, the conditions and the frustrations would grow worse, would become cumulative in their effect, and it might prove impossible to have the men brought up on deck again – which of itself would worsen the horrible ambience of the hold with possibly dire results. But better, perhaps, to have any trouble confined within the hold – a point that Sharp made after the two bodies had been sewn into canvas, weighted at the feet, and slid from a plank rigged across the bulkwarks in the waist. In Sharp's view they should all be left below to stew in their own filth.

'They're but animals, sir,' he said. The man, Halfhyde thought, had a mouth like a rat-trap, thin and vicious. Refusing to argue with obstinacy and prejudice, he dismissed the warder curtly and went aft to the poop, where the Second Mate, Pendleton, had the watch.

He looked aloft at the set of the sail; the *Glen Halladale* was now moving along again after having her canvas backed to lie stopped as the bodies were put overboard. She was gaining speed fast as the braces were hauled round and was soon scudding along with all sail set now to the royals, taking full advantage of a fair and favourable wind, going ahead with a bone in her teeth, thrusting cleanly through white-capped waves.

'It'll not last, Mr Pendleton,' Halfhyde said. 'Keep a careful watch on the weather and let me know instantly when the wind shifts.'

'Aye, aye, sir.'

'I've a feeling it'll back to the south-west and increase again after we pass Ushant, and suddenly at that. We must lose no time in getting some of the canvas off her when that happens.' Halfhyde turned away and ducked down the companion, making for his cabin. As he reached the door, Victoria came out from the saloon, and he turned.

She said, 'I know what you're going to say. Before you say it, I'm going to say I'm sorry.'

His expression was forbidding. There was a lot he would

have liked to tell her: that her stupidity had killed MacNab, that she had made the voyage harder and more hazardous for every soul on board, not least because MacNab's death had left Sharp in charge of the convicts with all that that implied . . . but he found he hadn't the heart to do so. He could see that she had been crying; and she was obviously filled with self blame. She went on, 'I'll live like a bloody nun. Promise!'

He shook his head. 'That won't be necessary. Just stay below whenever the convicts are on deck, that's all I ask. Now we'll say no more about it.'

She gave him a look of gratitude and moved a step towards him; but he was still angry and he turned away into his cabin and shut the door. He stood staring through the port above his bunk: the problems were mounting. Today's incident would have to be written-up in the ship's log, which would in due course have to be made available to the Board of Trade and possibly, in the circumstances of the voyage, to the Admiralty. Certainly a full and separate report would have to be made to the Prison Commissioners in London where it would be scrutinized by Colonel Bowler, who was going to have many things to say about the presence aboard of a woman. Halfhyde glared through the port, frowning, bracing his shoulders . . . when all was said and done he was the Master and no one from shore commanded him or his ship. Still, it would have been better had none of it happened. Two men dead who should never have died – three, with the warder who had fallen into the hold – that was an indictment of any ship's master.

And how many more would die before this voyage was over and done with? By now the hold would be smouldering with hate and probably also with lust. And there was still the problem of the gold. If it failed to materialize from an overtaking steamer, what sort of trouble waited for the ship in South Africa, trouble from the consignees who might not have been informed that the bullion had missed the ship in Devonport? The mails could at times be slow enough and if the gold had indeed been put aboard a steamer, and the steamer failed to pick up the *Glen Halladale* in the immensity of the seas between the English Channel and the Cape of Good Hope . . . well, then, it might be many days or even weeks before the shippers themselves knew that. But if the needle did prove too small in the haystack might not the steamer take the shipment on to the consignees? In fact that could have been the actual intention from the time the *Glen Halladale* had sailed without it.

He was perhaps worrying over nothing. But it would still be Bowler's worry.

* * *

As Halfhyde had predicted, the wind backed not long after they had left Ushant away on the port quarter and were heading down to cross the Bay of Biscay. Also as he had predicted, the shift came suddenly on the wings of a heavy squall and Pendleton got the hands aloft only just in time. To Halfhyde's order the royals and topgallants were sent down from all three masts and the upper and lower topsails were reefed down. The courses were furled along their yards and with that bare minimum of canvas the ship was tacked into what soon became a heavy gale, a stronger blow now than they had met in the Channel on departure. With the onset of night the job was made the worse. Dr Murchison was kept busy attending to cuts, torn fingernails, hands raw from rope burns . . . minor injuries mostly and ones that aboard a normal windjammer without the luxury of a medical man would have been left to mend themselves. The more serious ones would have been attended by the steward or perhaps referred eventually to the Master and the ultimate medical authority of a handbook known as the *Ship Captain's Medical Guide*. A case of the survival of the fittest . . . his mind busy with his ship, Halfhyde spared a thought for the chain-gangs below. With the hold battened right down for bad weather – and for what could prove to be for the whole duration of the passage of the bay – the atmosphere would soon be thick to the point of being almost unbreathable; and the ship was lifting and falling again in a stomach-jerking motion as she took the increasing waves that swept beneath her bottom-sheathing from fo'c'sle to poop and every now and again came over to swill the length of the ship and remove the last traces of the blood that had spattered up towards the poop and over the sail locker when the convict had fallen to the warder's rifle.

Once the ship was riding steadily Halfhyde left the poop to his First Mate and went below to the tween-deck to take a look at Archer-Caine. A mattress had been provided as ordered, and the man seemed as comfortable as possible in the prevailing conditions, wedged and roped down so that he wouldn't shift and do further damage to his wounded arm. The guard of two warders on the tween-deck hatch, looking seasick and shivering in the damp, close atmosphere as the seas penetrated in rivulets from the deck above, had added Archer-Caine to their responsibilities and he was secure enough. Halfhyde went to the saloon for a delayed meal and was joined by Victoria and Dr Murchison. The meal was frugal: bully beef from tins. Without appetite, Halfhyde ate the bully beef amidst a cold fug and the creak of woodwork and the rattle of blocks on deck as the ship laboured her way through the gale. Murchison ate nothing; and after a matter of minutes of the meal's arrival got up with a muttered apology and hastily left the saloon.

'Gone to puke his guts up,' Victoria said unnecessarily.

Halfhyde snapped, 'Choose a better topic, Victoria.'

She shrugged. 'All right, all right. Sorry I spoke.'

'So am I.'

'Temper!'

Halfhyde glared across the table but forebore to respond. Dr Murchison did not reappear and was soon heard lurching along the alleyway towards his cabin. The sound of the gale, strumming at the standing and running rigging, came down into the saloon like the music of a vast and devilish string orchestra. Over the saloon table the oil lamp stayed steady in its gimbals as the deckhead lay over hard to port. Halfhyde listened to the shriek of the gale and the surge of water past the ship's sides. Not enough surge: in the prevailing conditions under bare masts they were not making a good speed at all and with all his heart he was wishing this voyage finished and the convicts discharged to their military destiny. Gloom and menace seemed to have pervaded the ship from the main truck to the bilges . . . it was as though they were sailing to destruction with nothing to be done about it, a ship without hope. Halfhyde gave himself a mental shake: he had never before felt the imminence of defeat, never before allowed himself to be pulled down by any seafaring problem. And he would not be this time. Much of it lay in the mind, and he was perhaps exaggerating, seeing doom where none existed.

He was aware of the girl's scrutiny, her look of concern. He knew she loved him and he had perhaps been harsh. He smiled at her and she said, 'What's bothering you, mate? I mean, it's not like you to sit there like a bloody grampus, and we're not dead yet, I reckon.' She gave a sudden gesture, flinging the fair hair away from her eyes, then looked at him with a hint of demureness. 'You know what you need, mate,' she said.

'Yes.'

'Well, then!'

He knew he had only to say the word. Perhaps it was only his stubbornness that refused to let him say it; but there was his duty as well. Already the men in their chains had seen the girl and that was bad enough; they could think their own thoughts but if he, Halfhyde, held fast to his celibacy until the hold was emptied on arrival, then they would have no confirmation. He refused to exacerbate matters any further than had already been done. It had always been his principle that a commanding officer should give himself no favours beyond those accorded his men or beyond those legitimately conferred by rank and position. In his view Victoria Penn was not one of the latter.

She read his thoughts: she'd always been able to do that. She said, 'You're bloody inconsistent, aren't you? What about the *Taronga Park*, eh?'

That didn't take much remembrance: he thought again of the nights beneath the Pacific moon as the old *Taronga Park* had thrust through placid waters from Sydney. He said, 'That was different—'

'That's just what men always say when they've been caught out.'

'I'm referring to the fact we're carrying convicts,' he said acidly. 'The happenings aboard the *Taronga Park* . . . we were thrown together, Victoria. In a sense I was no longer in command, full command, thanks to Porteous Higgins.'

'Excuses,' she said witheringly. 'Bloody eyewash I call that.' She got quickly to her feet and went out of the saloon and a moment later he heard the slam of her cabin door. He sat for a while in gloomy thought; increased sounds along the deck, and the heel of the ship to starboard, told him that the *Glen Halladale* was being put over on the opposite tack. From the scuttles the curtains leaned inwards and stayed there as though starched to lie at an angle. The water-bottle slid in its coaster across the tablecloth towards him. Then he heard Edwards' shout down the companion from the poop.

'Captain, sir! Would you please come up on deck? We seem to have a steamer keeping company astern.'

Halfhyde lost no time. He went fast up the ladder, out into the full force of the gale. No more than four or five cables'-lengths off the starboard quarter he picked up the steaming lights of a sizeable vessel, the red port light, with no green visible, indicating that her course was parallel with his own, the two white masthead lights indicating that she was a steam vessel. Edwards reported that she had come up from astern and had then, apparently, reduced speed. Halfhyde brought up his telescope. The ship herself was little more than a blur in the dark, spray-filled night, a moving patch of greater darkness. He asked, 'What do you make of her, Edwards?'

'Hard to say, sir. She could overtake us easily enough if she wished, but she looks as though she's staying put. It's eerie, sir.' The First Mate's voice was tight. 'What can she want of us, sir?'

Halfhyde closed his telescope with a snap. He said, 'I've an idea she may want to put some cargo aboard us, Mr Edwards—'

'In this weather, sir?'

'By no means, but the weather will moderate in time. If she's still with us then . . .' Halfhyde left the sentence unfinished. He had not yet taken Edwards into his confidence in regard to the bullion shipment; Bowler had wanted full secrecy and such was clearly sensible. No shipmaster playing the part of an acceptor of bribes would spread the word too far, and authenticity was Bowler's watchword. Besides, it would bring trouble if the nature of a bullion cargo put aboard at sea should reach the flapping ears of the convicts . . . but then Edwards could be trusted. To Halfhyde, trust between a master and his next senior officer was of more concern than strict obedience to Bowler's desires. But he decided to say nothing until the steamer showed its colours.

In the meantime, acting in obedience to some unformulated sixth sense, he remained on the poop with his First Mate.

EIGHT

Halfhyde stood by the mizzen weather shrouds, holding on against the cant of the ship in the gale's grip, staring out towards the steamer's lights. She was holding her position, keeping station like a man-o'-war. Halfhyde felt an intense irritation: aboard a sailing ship he would have preferred all the sea-room he could get, although it was true that if he happened to fall off the wind the steamer would have enough manoeuvrability to stand clear. There had been no message, though it could be assumed that a steamship would have a signal lamp. The lack of any contact increased the impression of eeriness, the feel of being shadowed by a footpad waiting his chance to pounce.

At eight bells the watches changed. Pendleton came up to relieve the First Mate, and the starboard watch of the hands turned out from below to take over from the port watch. Still the unknown ship remained in company, and Halfhyde remained on the poop. An hour or so after the watch had changed over, the new senior warder, Sharp, climbed the starboard ladder from the waist and spoke to Pendleton. The Second Mate reported to Halfhyde. He asked, 'Will you have a word with Sharp, sir?'

'What's the trouble, Mr Pendleton?'

Sharp had already come across, walking stiffly against the slope of the deck. He answered for the Second Mate. 'The trouble is that my warders report unrest in the hold, sir.'

'What sort of unrest?'

'Not easy to define, sir, unless you know prison life as I do. Yourself, you might never notice it.'

'Try to tell me, then.'

Sharp said, 'It's like a kind of murmur without a voice given to it. Something running through all the prisoners, communicated by some sort of – of *spirit* force is all I can find to call it—'

'Something psychic?'

'I dare say, sir, yes. You get it in prisons. No one can say how it starts, or why. But when it happens, you know beyond a doubt that something's up.'

'And that means certain trouble?'

'In my experience, yes.'

Halfhyde nodded. 'I see. And this time? What d'you think it's due to? I assume that when there's detectable unrest, it has a cause?'

'Yes, sir. That's what I said – you can't say why, not till something more emerges. Then it can be dealt with.'

'How do you deal with it, in a general way?'

Sharp said, 'Why, in a general way, sir, we isolate a ringleader or two . . . and we ask questions.'

Halfhyde looked back once again towards the shadowing steamer, still visible only as to its lights. The wind was increasing now and the sea's broken surface was spume-covered as the tops of the waves were blown off by the gale; there was a carpet of whiteness, only dimly seen, between the two ships. He asked, 'How long has this unrest been observed?'

'Perhaps for the last hour, sir. Maybe a little longer.'

Halfhyde nodded. The steamer had been in company for some three hours now, give or take a little. It could have taken a couple of hours, perhaps, for word of it to reach the hold – possibly at the change of the warders' watches, which were not following those of the ship's routine. At any rate Halfhyde fancied he could see a connection, though the nature of such a connection if it existed remained obscure enough. If one or more of the convicts knew about the bullion, he or they would presumably have been under the impression it had come aboard before the *Glen Halladale* had sailed.

Sharp was fidgeting. 'What do you wish done, Captain? If you ask for my advice—'

'Before I ask for that, Mr Sharp, I propose to inspect the men myself.

Sharp stared. 'Inspect them, sir? Inmates of Her Majesty's prisons, sir, are not ships' companies—'

'Thank you, Mr Sharp, I am aware of that, but I shall still inspect them, and the inspection may help me to arrive at a conclusion. Then, if necessary in my opinion, I shall seek your advice. For your part you must remember that a sailing ship at sea is not one of Her Majesty's prisons.'

There was an angry mutter from the senior warder, a mutter that Halfhyde disregarded. Followed by Sharp, he went down the ladder to the waist and descended by the booby hatch to the tween deck. In the light of a lantern held by one of the tween-deck guards Halfhyde saw that Archer-Caine was asleep, or at any rate appeared to be. Making on for the hatch, Sharp took down another lantern from the racks, lit it and approached the ladder leading into the hold. He went down first, lighting the way. The lantern's fingers of light probed, casting shadows, flickering off the repaired bunks, off the floor of the hold already foul again, off the faces of the convicts, off the chains and wristbands.

With Sharp, Halfhyde moved along the narrow gangways between the lines of tiered bunks, cruelly short in the interest of saving space, no bunk large enough for a man to lie full stretch if he were more than five feet in height.

Every man was awake.

Reflecting the lantern's beams, eyes stared back at Halfhyde and Sharp, like so many cats caught in the moon. But for the heavy breathing – the hard drawing of breaths in the horrible, stinking fug, cold and damp – there was no sound beyond their own slow footsteps. Halfhyde felt the tension, the restlessness reported by the senior warder; he believed he would have felt it even if the report hadn't been made. In a sense a prison was not so far removed from the lower deck of a warship at sea; there was the same constriction, the same loss of liberty, and even the discomforts were similar. So were the mental emanations from the seamen when they believed they had a grievance: an experienced officer could smell out mutiny long before it happened.

There was a similar feeling in the air now, a more frustrated one since chained convicts could never storm the upper deck to mount an attack on the afterguard, but it was nevertheless like tinder. And the spark could come at any moment.

Halfhyde moved on. As he reached the end of the line he saw

that not every man was in fact awake: in two of the bunks, the occupants were turned away from the lantern's probing, humped and anonymous beneath a single coarse blanket each, heavy boots stuck out at the ends of the bunks. Halfhyde's glance lingered but he made no comment; he turned away and nodded at Sharp: his inspection was complete. With the senior warder he climbed back to the tween deck. Sharp asked, 'Well, sir?'

'I agree there is a restlessness,' Halfhyde said. 'As to why, I fancy my guess is as good as yours!'

'And your guess, sir?'

Halfhyde said, 'We shall go back to the poop, Mr Sharp, before we discuss the matter further.' They walked aft along the tween deck and emerged through the booby hatch to the waist and the buffeting of the gale. As they climbed to the poop Halfhyde saw that, as he had expected, the steamer was still in her station on the starboard quarter. He pointed her out by lifting his telescope. 'You'll have seen the steamer,' he said to Sharp. 'I believe it's a report of that that has disturbed the prisoners.'

'Why so?' Sharp asked plainly puzzled.

Halfhyde shrugged. 'There could be many reasons, I imagine. The prisoners may believe her to be a warship – and it's possible she is, although I doubt it. But if they believe that . . . well, the mere presence of a naval escort would damp down any hope of making a break, would it not?'

'Yes, it would that,' Sharp answered sourly. 'In my view it's what we should have had from the start —'

'But we did not and we must make the best of it,' Halfhyde said. 'In the meantime there's something more pressing. Tell me, Mr Sharp: did you notice anything odd about the bunks, below in the hold?'

'I did not . . . no.'

'Then you should have done,' Halfhyde said acidly, 'and so should the warders on watch. Two of the bunks showed no reaction to the lantern's light during my inspection. The only two out of a hundred . . . I'd willingly stake a year's pay that those two bunks contain only boots and clothing beneath the blankets.'

There was an exclamation from Sharp. 'Impossible, quite

impossible! Where would the two men have gone?'

'One way would be up the hatch,' Halfhyde said, 'which we know they've in fact not done. But that's not the only way of leaving the hold, though the escape route, I would agree, leads only to greater constriction and a kind of captivity, but—'

Sharp interrupted, 'It's wild talk, sir – with respect. How did they get out of the chains, how did they fail to be seen by the guards—'

'That we shall find out when they're apprehended, but I suggest there may have been an incomplete personal search for metal files and such, or even the nefarious duplicating of keys in Dartmoor – and as for the guards, there are dark corners in my hold, the darkest being the part from which the escape was made. How's that, Mr Sharp, for the guesses of an amateur – but one with experience of defaulting seamen with ingenious minds?'

Sharp was silent: prison workshops could produce handy tools for escape and had been known to do so in the past, and there were ways of concealing small objects so as to get men past the closest scrutiny. Avoiding Halfhyde's question he asked, 'Where is this place they might escape to, then?'

'Beneath the hold,' Halfhyde answered. 'Sailing ships have no inner bottom plating secured to the tops of the floors to cover the space between the deck of the hold and the top of the outer bottoms. There are only planks, Mr Sharp, laid fore and aft over the limbers – the spaces between the floors, aboard a windjammer – and these planks are removable for the purposes of cleaning and drying.'

'You think the men could have lifted a plank?'

'I do indeed. It would make little enough noise of its own during the gale. Now: the next count of the men will be made, as I understand your routine, when breakfast is dished out at seven bells in the morning watch – which means we have until then at most before something happens. The two men will know that at seven bells they'll be found to be missing.'

'Yes – and with no hope of being able to get further,' Sharp said with a trace of sarcasm. It was obvious he didn't believe any of Halfhyde's prognostications. 'What should we do, sir, at breakfast time?'

'It's a question of what we do *before* then,' Halfhyde said. 'Meanwhile we have the advantage of knowing that something is about to be attempted. I'm surprised only that it didn't take place while I was in the hold. You must call out all your warders, Mr Sharp, and have then placed along the tween deck ready for what may happen. For my money, I repeat, I see a strong connection with that steamer out there, so close upon our tail. I—'

'If I may make a suggestion, sir,' Sharp broke in, 'it would be that we bring the convicts up from below and make an armed search of the place you—'

'Not in the dark hours. I shall not risk that. And to try to carry out a search while the men are in the bunks would be equally risky. Now that we're forewarned, I see no difficulty – the two men can't get away with much now. If nothing has happened by the time the galley is ready with breakfast, Mr Sharp, you will attend the muster with a full guard of your warders – and at that time, when we have the dawn, I shall clear the holds for a search. But I have a strong feeling we shall not have to wait as long as that.'

* * *

Halfhyde remained on deck. His nerves were taut and he felt no tiredness. He was alert for anything that might happen; and reflection was diluting his belief that there was a direct connection with the missing gold shipment. Even though the *Glen Halladale*'s speed had been reduced by the gale there would have scarcely been time for her to be overtaken from a home port – even by a steamer. And there was another aspect that gave him cause for thought: he had been very easily picked up. Too easily. Had he been distantly shadowed from the start? It was possible; a steamer's smoke would of course be seen, but there were any number of steamships in the Channel at any one time and smoke would not be unduly remarked. And his expected courses, subject always to the exigencies of weather and so on as the voyage progressed, had been indicated both to the Admiralty and to the Prison Commissioners. Again Colonel Bowler nagged . . . but it was fruitless to speculate in that direction and Halfhyde dismissed Victoria Penn's ridiculous notions from his mind.

He paced the poop, uselessly thinking, keeping an eye on the canvas and the wind's direction. He felt as though there were an infernal device beneath his feet, a bomb placed beneath his hold all ready to rend the ship asunder. He was convinced those bunks had held no men and he knew there was only that one place where they could be, but he had to wait for the dawn. When at long last that dawn came up in wetness and howling wind his telescope showed him the following ship more clearly: she was no warship. She was a rakish-looking vessel, long and low, painted black with buff upperworks, with a platform bridge before a buff-coloured funnel, tall and thin. Her stem was clipper-shaped with a long bowsprit above some gilded scroll-work becoming visible in the dim, watery light and the general overcast.

She had the definite look of a private steam yacht, some rich man's toy.

Edwards, back again on watch, was looking across at the vessel with Halfhyde. As he had asked earlier, Halfhyde asked again, 'What do you make of her, Mr Edwards?'

Edwards said, 'Somehow she has the look of a pirate, sir!'

'A modern version of Henry Morgan . . . I think we don't move in quite such buccaneering circles in this day and age, Edwards – but I confess I have the same feeling.' Halfhyde paused. 'Now I have another, and it's this: she's closing.'

'She is that, sir. Shall we send up more canvas? She'll take it now.'

Halfhyde looked aloft; there was a little less weight in the wind as the dawn crept up and now he could proceed under shaken-out topsails. But he said, 'No, Mr Edwards, we shall hold our course and canvas for the time being. There may be a message now it's light enough. But the time's come to clear the hold and make a search. Pass the word for Sharp, if you please.'

'Aye, aye, sir.'

'And I'll want all hands on deck as well, Mr Edwards, to stand by for trouble.'

The First Mate aknowledged the order and called for the bosun. Bunch was out of the petty officers' deckhouse within half a minute, somewhat discommoded by his heavily bandaged hand. The shout went up: '*All hands . . . all hands on deck!*' The Second Mate came up the ladder from the saloon alleyway; and from the warders' accommodation Sharp appeared, his holstered revolver at his hip.

'Mr Sharp,' Halfhyde called.

'Sir?'

'Muster your warders, Mr Sharp, immediately. I shall accompany you below with two of them as soon as the prison draft's brought out.'

'You're intending to make a search now, sir?'

'I am – at once. Have Archer-Caine taken back to the saloon and then hold the prisoners in the tween deck. Well guarded, Mr Sharp. I don't want them to be seen openly just yet.'

Sharp waved an arm towards the steam yacht, now coming up more closely. 'You mean because of that ship, Captain?'

'Yes. Quickly, now!'

Sharp lost no time; he doubled away towards the booby hatch and disappeared down the companion-way. Within a minute Archer-Caine came up behind an armed warder and went through to the saloon alleyway. Moments later a volley of rifle fire was heard from below, from the tween deck, cutting clear through the racket of the wind.

NINE

Sharp came back up the ladder from the booby hatch a good deal faster than he had gone down; blood poured from his left arm. He shouted up to the poop as he climbed.

'The bastards have broken out, Captain! The guard was taken by surprise – the two men down in the hold – it's been left too long—'

'We'll hold the inquest later, Mr Sharp. What's the situation below, precisely?'

Sharp had reached the poop by this time. Breathing hard, he said, 'They're out of the chains and climbing from the hold – any moment they'll be on deck and running wild—'

Halfhyde cut in, cupping his hands and shouting down to the waist where the seamen were mustering under Edwards and the bosun. 'All hands lay aft immediately – at the double!' He turned to the senior warder. 'Now, Mr Sharp. Your warders are to hold the men in the tween deck and not allow any of them to break out through the companions fore and aft – they must be contained.'

'But—'

'There are no buts aboard my ship, Mr Sharp. You'll get back down and take charge, and take charge effectively, do you understand?'

Sharp gave him a vindictive look but said no more. He went down the ladder towards the booby hatch. As he did so the hands doubled aft to the poop; as more rifle shots were heard from the tween deck Dr Murchison and the steward came up the ladder from the saloon. Halfhyde reached into a pocket and brought out a bunch of keys, which he handed to the steward.

'Below again, Humper. My revolver in my safe. Take it and mount guard on Miss Penn. She's not to leave her cabin. If any convict breaks through into the after accommodation you have my authority to shoot at once.'

'Aye, aye, sir.' Humper ran back for the saloon companion. Halfhyde watched the approaching steam yacht; he had already noted that not only had the name been painted out but that the whole vessel had the look of a recent repainting. Neither the officers on the bridge nor any of the hands visible on the upper deck wore any distinctive uniforms, no rich owner's livery. As Halfhyde watched, one of the men on the yacht's bridge brought up a megaphone and shouted across the narrowing gap of water.

'*Glen Halladale* ahoy!'

Halfhyde called back. 'What's your purpose with me?'

'A transfer between ship and ship, Captain.'

'The weather's not suitable for you to approach me more closely. You must realize that for yourself.'

'If you'll heave to—'

'I shall not heave to,' Halfhyde shouted back. 'It would be lunacy at this moment. I expect the weather to moderate once we're past Cape Finisterre. If you have cargo to be put aboard, then you must wait your moment – and mine.'

'We don't want—'

'You have my answer. You must wait. And I'll thank you to lie farther off and not become a hazard to my ship.' Halfhyde's temper was worsening fast; at any moment there could be a break-out from the tween deck if the warders lost control. He called across angrily: 'I have rifles aboard and if necessary I shall keep you at a safe distance from me by opening fire.'

He lowered his megaphone; before he turned away he had seen a degree of uncertainty aboard the steam yacht, a conference on the vessel's bridge. There was no answer to his threat of rifle fire but the yacht began to fall back. A point had been established; but the trouble remained aboard his own ship, the danger was imminent and immense to every soul in his care. He turned to the First Mate. 'Take over the ship, if you please, Mr Edwards. I'm going below to the tween deck.'

He made for the ladder; as he reached it Edwards said, 'Your pardon, sir. What do you think that yacht means to put aboard us?'

'We shall go into that later, Mr Edwards. In the meantime, the less talk about it, the better.' Halfhyde believed it might, after all, be the gold. He slid down the ladder and made for the booby hatch. Below, the warders seemed to be holding the line, covering the bunched convicts in the tween deck with their rifles. Sharp was looking scared and on edge, tending to hang back behind the cover of his own warders, no doubt knowing only too well what would happen to him personally if he fell into the hands of the convicts. The mood, as was to be expected, was menacing but to some degree uncertain: the prisoners knew that if, with their superior numbers, they charged the thin line of armed warders they could carry them – but with many casualties to the leaders. Halfhyde summed it up fast: it was a clear case of those behind crying forward, and those in front crying back. And back meant down into the hold again. The bosun, coming aft as ordered with the hands, had reported to Halfhyde that he had locked the fore companion-way from the tween deck and bolted the doors down. There would be no escape to the upper deck that way.

Halfhyde raised his voice, calling for silence as he pushed through the line of warders, watchful behind their rifles.

'You'll listen to me,' he said harshly. 'I shall not repeat what I've already told you as to my possession of Her Majesty's commission, but I advise every man among you to bear that in mind while considering his next act.' He paused, running his glance over the assembled, lowering faces. 'Now, for a start I propose a little reconstruction. It did not escape my notice that two of the bunks were empty, with clothing arranged to conceal the emptiness. From that fact it was an easy enough deduction that two of your number had freed themselves from the chains. I ask myself how, and I answer myself that it's likely enough a master key was cut whilst you were in Dartmoor, and secreted away. The two men lifted planks from the floor of the hold and squeezed themselves down into the limbers – to emerge at a propitious moment with the keys to unlock the remainder of the chains, and then to act the innocents, mingling with the rest of you. No doubt word had penetrated to you that there was a steamer lying off and keeping company. Perhaps word had already reached you before embarkation as to that steamer's purpose.'

There was a dead silence now; Halfhyde believed he could have hit some sort of nail on the head, although he had no idea what it might be. He went on, 'Three things will now happen. First: you'll all remain here in the tween deck under guard, and you'll give no trouble. Second: both the hold and all your persons will be thoroughly searched. Third: when that has been done, you will all be questioned, singly, by me. There are things I have every intention of finding out before the ship is off Cape Finisterre. Finally, two words of warning which are to be taken very seriously: none of you will be so foolish as to imagine the same trick can be pulled off again . . . and you have my word on it, supported by my total authority as Master and backed by Her Majesty's commission which in the circumstances and in time of war can override the civil power, that any one of you showing himself on deck will be shot instantly. Mr Sharp?'

'Sir?'

'I want four warders to be stationed from this moment on the poop, with orders to act as I've just stated. Kindly see to that. The rest to remain in the tween deck while the hold is searched.'

* * *

The prison draft had seemed quiescent, overawed for the time being by Halfhyde's decisive manner and authority. It was possible that the two men who had gone down beneath the hold had once been seamen and knew what they were about, and there might well be others who had sailed the seas in their time; but most would be landsmen out of their element aboard a ship and inclined to speculation about stories heard of past days, of keel-haulings and floggings, of men sent aloft in freezing weather to cling for days on end to the foretopmast crosstrees until sometimes they were brought down as stiffened corpses. The discipline of the men-o'-war and the sailing merchant ships had always been iron-hard and unyielding, mercy seldom if ever shown to those who had transgressed authority. Even army discipline, even prison discipline, paled before that of the sea services – and those who had never known it personally perhaps tended to fear it even more when they gave play to their imaginations . . .

Whatever the reasons might be, Halfhyde, accompanied below by the Second Mate, the bosun, the carpenter and two fo'c'sle hands, was given a clear passage through the convicts to the hatch. It was nevertheless a nasty walk and Halfhyde was relieved when he had passed through and swung a leg over the hatch coaming to take the ladder. Each prisoner had seemed to exude the desire to kill, to throttle, to stab; it was like a miasma hanging over the tween deck, almost tangibly, as noticeable as the continuing prison smell that came up from the hold and from the men themselves.

Once down below, the search was painstaking, every nook and cranny being investigated, every chink between the bottom boards, all of which were lifted individually and settled back again. The bunks were stripped and searched, an unpleasant task that took much time. Nothing was left to chance; and the haul, though small, was worth the effort.

The carpenter showed Halfhyde something in his hand. 'The file, sir. Found it nestling between two of the boards, I did, sir.'

'Small but obviously effective,' Halfhyde said.

'It'd not take too long to file through a link, sir, not with that.'

'Let's see what else you can turn up,' Halfhyde said. The search went on. Another file was found, larger than the first one, wedged down between the boards of a bunk, beneath the palliasse, the straw-filled donkey's breakfast. There was no sign of any keys. Satisfied that every inch of the hold had been checked, Halfhyde gave the order for some of the planks to be lifted again and an examination made of the inner bottoms where the two convicts had hidden. 'Check right through,' he said. 'We don't know which section those men were in.'

The carpenter went down with one of the hands to check the first section; the bosun and another hand started on the next contiguous section. It was an awkward and unpleasant task in the confined space and conducted largely in darkness, the only illumination coming from a lantern held above in the hold itself, and there were many corners and angles between the bilges and keelsons; and the stench was foul, with filthy water slopping, water that had gathered from the earlier hosing down and from the internal condensation and had become foetid.

But that, too, proved worth the effort: the search literally struck gold.

* * *

Halfhyde went up from the hold with the Second Mate, back through the closely-guarded convicts, and up to the poop.

'A word, Mr Edwards, in my cabin. Mr Pendleton will take the ship.'

They went down the ladder. The steward was standing guard on Victoria's cabin as ordered, with Halfhyde's revolver held towards the for'ard door from the waist as though he expected splintering woodwork at any moment. Halfhyde reassured him: the convicts, he said, were held at any rate for the time being. He asked about Archer-Caine.

'In the saloon, sir, with a warder.'

'No trouble?'

'None, sir.'

Halfhyde nodded and went into his cabin followed by the First Mate. He gestured to a chair and Edwards sat. Halfhyde said abruptly, 'You asked about that steam yacht's cargo. I have something to tell you, and it is to go no further – no further, that is, in regard to the background. That may sound obscure, but light will break in a moment.' He told Edwards the full facts of his apprehension in the streets of Liverpool, of the offer made and accepted, of his subsequent report to Colonel Bowler of the Prison Commission, of Bowler's belief that in some way the gold bullion had a connection with the convict draft and with Archer-Caine in particular. He went on to tell the First Mate that his own questioning of Archer-Caine had convinced him that Bowler was wrong on that score. Archer-Caine, Halfhyde had believed, knew nothing of any gold shipment made for his benefit.

Edwards asked, 'Are you saying, sir, that the steam yacht is bringing the gold?'

Halfhyde gave a harsh laugh. 'That was my belief, yes, even though in fact I doubted if she could have raised us by the time she did.'

'If she'd left, say, from an Irish port—'

'Yes, that might have been possible. But I know, now, that the gold's not aboard her, Edwards. She has some other purpose . . . she must have, for the gold's already aboard *us* – stowed in wooden cases in the limbers, right beneath the

95

prisoners!'

Edwards stared at him in consternation. As First Mate he was responsible for the loading of all cargo; as First Mate and officer-in-charge until the Master had joined he could be presumed to have known – should have known – everything about anything brought aboard the ship in Devonport. His professional competence was now called in question; and worse than that were the implications that he might have known . . . a deep flush spread across the weather-beaten face and he said, 'I hope, sir, you don't think I'm involved in this?'

Halfhyde shook his head impatiently. 'By no means, Edwards. You have my full trust and I take you for what you are – an honest man.'

'Thank you, sir. But it was up to me to—'

'Up to you to know. Yes. Now – how in your view could that bullion, heavy as the cases are, have been brought aboard without your knowledge?'

Edwards swallowed, shook his head slowly from side to side. 'I don't know, sir. I just don't know.'

'I take it you were not aboard solidly, all the while?'

'No, sir. There were matters needing my attention ashore now and again—'

'And the ship was left to the shore watchman?'

'Yes—'

'Who never made any report?'

'Never, sir.'

'I see. In that case he could have been implicated. On the other hand there was the shore labour, the carpenters who were constructing the bunks. They would have had every opportunity of getting the cases stowed in the limbers, of course – and they might have had ways of bringing them aboard one by one, concealed among the traps of their trade.'

Edwards nodded. 'They would, sir. Their gear was winched aboard from the quay – I'd rigged the—'

'Yes. As soon as we reach Simon's Town I shall send a cable to the Rear-Admiral Superintendent. In the meantime we're left with a problem – two problems: what does the steam yacht want with us, and do the convicts know of the presence of the bullion? As to that, perhaps something will emerge when I question them, which I shall do as soon as their persons have been searched by the warders. At this moment the gold's known to Pendleton and the carpenter, and Bunch and the two fo'c'sle hands – and they'll not talk if they wish ever to be employed at sea again.'

'What do you mean to do with the gold for now, sir?' Edwards asked.

Halfhyde grinned. 'Leave it where it is, that's the best way of concealment – the only way, in fact. Bring it up, and we may as well tell every man aboard.'

'You spoke of a share for yourself, sir—'

'I did. That's there as well, marked personal for the Master. Another problem: when were we expected to find the gold? In the normal course it wouldn't have been found until we lifted the boards after arrival and discharge of the prisoners – and in the meantime, for all I knew, I sailed without it!'

* * *

As Halfhyde and Edwards were taking their noon sights through a patch of clear weather – a lucky break in the clouds that Halfhyde knew was not going to last – the senior warder reported to the poop. A full body search had been made of all the prisoners, who were still being held in the tween deck. Sharp had found what Halfhyde had expected to find: two keys that fitted the locks on the wrist cuffs. These he handed over.

'Where were they found?' Halfhyde asked.

'One in a stocking, sir. The other . . . in a more personal place.'

'Good heavens! A painful extraction?'

'It was not made painless, sir.'

Halfhyde said, 'Well, we don't want them. You may throw them overboard, Mr Sharp.'

'With respect, sir, I think not. They'll be needed as evidence. There'll be an enquiry at Simon's Town.'

'Very well, then, but have them kept securely – my safe will be the best place. Hand them to the steward, Mr Sharp, if you please. Anything else?'

Sharp said, 'Another file, sir. Nothing more.' He paused, his mouth twitching. 'I think there was slackness somewhere on the Moor, sir. I'll not say where my suspicions lie, it would not be fitting.'

Halfhyde gave him a hard look. 'I trust you're not attempting to lay blame on the dead, Mr Sharp. As a former sergeant-major of the Black Watch, there would have been no slackness of any kind in MacNab.'

'If you say so, sir.' Sharp lifted a ferret-like nose in the air.

'I do. Now – take those keys to the steward. When you've done that I wish the prisoners to be brought singly to my cabin for questioning. Two warders are to be on guard outside the door, but I shall have no one inside.'

Sharp didn't like that but Halfhyde was coldly adamant: he would not have Sharp there; with the senior warder present no convict was going to open his mouth about anything. Halfhyde didn't expect much in any case but was determined to give himself the best possible chance. Sharp went below with the keys, looking offended. When he came back to the poop he asked in a formal manner, 'May I know what sort of questions you'll be asking, Captain?'

Halfhyde said, 'That's between me and each man, Mr Sharp.'

'I think I have a right to know, sir.'

'And I *don't* think you have.'

'In that case I shall—'

'In that case, Mr Sharp, you will lump it. And that ends the matter. I'm going below now. I shall expect the first of the men in five minutes' time.'

He turned on his heel, leaving Sharp fuming, and went down the ladder. Already the sky was covered in heavy overcast again; and the wind was blowing up a little more. A look aloft before leaving the poop had told Halfhyde they could still carry the canvas that was set. The First Mate would know when the moment had come to take off some of the upper sails. The steam yacht was lying off a little farther than before, as though common sense had registered on her bridge, and was taking the weather badly, rising to the wave-crests and then dropping with a nasty lurch into the troughs. There was persistence there all right, intriguing and worrying to any ship's master who was the object of such a strange pursuit. On a sudden impulse Halfhyde went first to the saloon where Archer-Caine sat under guard on the settee.

He asked, 'How's the arm now?'

'Mending, I think, Captain. Painful still . . . and I'm very grateful for your consideration.'

'It can't last for ever,' Halfhyde said, looking down at the prisoner who seemed to contrive a kind of elegance even in his gaol clothing. 'Once Dr Murchison has pronounced you fit enough, you'll rejoin the others.'

'Of course. I understand that.'

Halfhyde turned away and paced the saloon for a while, wondering whether or not he should make any mention of the gold's discovery: there had been the man's earlier denial of all knowledge of the shipment, of any connection with himself . . . Halfhyde decided to keep the facts of its presence aboard to himself for the time being. No useful purpose could be served really by sharing the knowledge with Archer-Caine. He pursued a different tack, asking Archer-Cain if he had heard the rumours about a steam vessel keeping company.

'Yes, I have. In fact I saw her when I was brought here from the tween deck.'

'Any comment?'

A slight smile flickered across the man's face. 'Just a passing thought, that's all.'

'Well?'

Archer-Caine shrugged. 'I doubt if it would be of any interest to you, Captain. You'd not believe my thoughts anyway, I think.'

'Try me,' Halfhyde said. 'I've believed you before.'

'Very well. My fellow directors, that limited liability company—'

'Yes.'

'Two of them, the business rather than the country element, owned steam yachts. That's all.'

Halfhyde met his eye. 'Did you recognize the yacht?'

'No. I never saw either of them, so I wouldn't recognize one in any case. The thought that occurred to me, however, was that there might be some connection.'

'An attempt to cut you out, an attempt to spring you from custody, Archer-Caine?'

Archer-Caine gave a quiet, sardonic laugh. 'No, Captain – not in the way you mean, at all events! Would I have put it into your mind, if I'd been expecting their assistance?'

Halfhyde smiled back. 'I take your point. What, then?' A moment later he ticked over: Archer-Caine had said he would not believe his thoughts. Those thoughts, now obvious enough, were extreme: as he had told Halfhyde earlier, there were gentlemen on the board of the land-grabbing company who were no friends of his, gentlemen whose good names, whose careers, whose freedom depended on him remaining impotent and unbelieved in gaol . . . or dead? Dead from enemy action in South Africa – but that was bound to be one of the imponderables. A man didn't have to die because he was en route for a war zone. He would have a good enough chance of avoiding the Boer bullets and the disease that always struck an expeditionary force in the field, the dysentery, the cholera in India to name but two.

There were more certain ways, much more direct ways. But secretaries of state, directors of companies, did they go so far as murder? It was unthinkable; yet Halfhyde knew the saying that no one was more vicious, more ruthless than a gentleman who had forsaken the mores of his class and had turned to crime.

Archer-Caine saw from his expression that he had arrived at those thoughts. He looked away from Halfhyde and shrugged. He said, 'I told you, Captain, that you'd not believe me.'

'But you believe it yourself?'

'Yes. Oh yes, I do indeed. If that steam yacht is the one I think it may be . . . but I suppose time will tell.'

Halfhyde nodded, but said no more. He left the saloon and went along the alleyway to his cabin. Outside, the first of the prison draft was waiting with a warder. Halfhyde ordered him brought in and the questioning began, the lengthy, frustrating business of trying to prise out a reaction to the mention of bribery without revealing his own knowledge of the bullion's presence aboard and of trying to elicit some information about the presence of the steam yacht that might run counter to the thoughts of Archer-Caine.

He achieved nothing but an aching head, though he was able to make some assessment of the convicts, sorting out the most vicious and desperate from those who might think more than once before creating trouble aboard a ship at sea. As each man was finished with he was taken back to join the chain-gangs; although a number of the men were quickly dealt with as

Halfhyde judged their mental capacities to be scarcely adequate for involvement in anything beyond violence and crime of the bludgeon variety, the interrogation took well into the next day, by which time the ship was not so far off Cape Finisterre and almost clear of the Bay of Biscay. As soon as the weather was fair the steam yacht would doubtless close the *Glen Halladale* again. Archer-Caine's suggestion nagged at Halfhyde until it began to appear the most likely explanation for the yacht's presence.

After the abortive questioning was over and the prisoners were all below again – Sharp had been ordered to return them to the hold from the tween deck, to which on its emptying Archer-Caine had been sent back – Halfhyde was alone in the saloon when Victoria joined him.

'Worried, aren't you?' she asked, frowning in concern for him. 'Bottling it up doesn't bloody help, mate.'

'I'm all right,' he said with a touch of irritation.

'Oh no you're bloody not! I know you, read you like a book.' She sat beside him on the settee, coming close and looking searchingly at his face. Despite himself he found her comforting. She said, 'Don't be such a limey. Bloody relax, let go, why ever not? There's more in life than being the great big captain of a bloody ship.' She paused. 'Worried about that steamer, right?'

'Yes,' he said shortly.

'Well, that's an admission anyway.'

She was persistent and pervasive of his mind. He found himself talking – talking about Archer-Caine and what the man had said; mostly about what he had in fact not put into words: that the steam yacht was there to take him off, probably to his death. Victoria listened, not interrupting. In the end he told her it all; told her the gold had been found beneath the hold. That was when the soothing ceased and she added to his worries.

She gave a whistle and said, 'Oh, my God, mate.'

'What do you mean, Victoria?'

'Don't you *see?*'

Blankly he asked, 'See what?'

'The bloody connection!'

'No.'

'You want your head read, then. Look, whoever's behind

that bloody steamer surely knows you'd never hand a con over, not without a fight. They may not bloody *want* a fight at sea, right? But there's other ways. You've been bribed with gold, you don't know who by – and far as they're concerned you don't know the gold's aboard. But if they pass the word on to the customs blokes or whatever in South Africa ... well, you're going to be bloody found with it hidden away and charged with God knows what, mate!'

TEN

Halfhyde climbed to the poop to clear a buzzing head. The girl had had a point, it was true. He accepted that the crew of the steam yacht would be ready with threats when he refused his co-operation. He could take the sting out of any threat connected with the gold by having it dumped overboard; yet that might not be enough. It was inevitable that there would be talk after arrival in South Africa – talk from the convicts, who could scarcely be kept in ignorance of any dumping of cases of bullion brought up from right beneath them. That would make matters look worse. As he had said to Victoria, however, his report of the bribery to Colonel Bowler was on record and that would clear him and his ship. Bloody likely, she'd said. How did he know that report was on record and not just held within Bowler's head? Bowler was in fee to the Home Office – and he'd do well to remember, she said, that Archer-Caine had implicated the Secretary of State in a vendetta against him . . .

Did he trust Bowler?

Doubts, unworthy ones perhaps, came. The fact that it had been Bowler who had suggested the gold-convict link from the start was probably totally irrelevant, the kind of obvious suggestion that anyone would have been expected to make in the circumstances. Bowler could all along have been making use of a prepared position, exploiting the Queen's own idea of a convict draft to a labour battalion, exploiting it in a diabolical act of chicanery on behalf of his chief the Secretary of State for Home Affairs. Wheels within wheels, pressures, hints from on high . . . no one except the monarch was above the law, but often in theory rather than in practice. Those who made the law were always uniquely placed and power went hand-in-hand with privilege. Almost nothing was impossible to the privileged.

But Bowler came from a good regiment. Would he be able to connive at dirty dealing, at murder, run against the grain of a lifetime's service to the Crown? Halfhyde smiled inwardly, a grim grimace with no humour in it; often enough throughout history men had gone against their own code.

And Archer-Caine?

Was a convict to be believed implicitly? His story could be considered a very tall one and he was able to offer no proof whatsoever. But a kind of proof might come when the steam yacht closed the *Glen Halladale* again.

* * *

At two bells in the middle watch, the midnight to 4 a.m., the wind shifted. Very unexpectedly, very suddenly, it backed to the east, another tearing squall coming off the distant, invisible land mass across the Bay of Biscay; already the Second Mate had noted the falling barometric pressure, a sharp fall, and had called the Master. Halfhyde had ordered the upper topsails to be reefed down hard; and he had reached the poop just as the hands were swarming up the shrouds to the upper yards – just as the squall hit.

It came like an express train, out of the darkness and the blown spume with hammer blows that gave the men no chance. The bosun, Bunch, had reached the footropes and, impeded by his mangled, bandaged hand was making a grab for the main upper topsail yard when the wind took him and hurled him bodily to leeward, smashing him into the maintop as he fell. With a catch of his breath Halfhyde saw him as no more than a blur in the darkness, dropping away to starboard to vanish in the boiling sea. There was nothing to be done about it, not a hope of rescue in the storm's fury. A loss they could ill afford but there was no time to dwell on it. Halfhyde cupped his hands, shouting the men on to the upper topsails, watching the whip of the masts as the whole ship lay over violently to leeward, going so far that the lee rail was under water. Then, under the weight of the wind and the tremendous tug of the straining canvas, something gave. There was no possibility of any saving action:

the maintopmast, lying over with the others at an angle of around sixty degrees, broke away from the maintop, swung violently, dropped in a tangle of rigging and impacted against the mizzen top which came away in its turn and plunged down in another spider's web of ropes towards the poop.

Halfhyde saw it coming and shouted a warning. The heavy weight splintered down across the saloon companion hatch, smashing the woodwork, smashing the saloon skylight so that glass tinkled down, then toppled across the lee bulwarks. One of the smashed spars took the helmsman full in the face, turning it to a bloody pulp and sending the man flying backwards to fetch up behind the teak casing aft of the wheel, which, untended, started to spin like a catherine wheel.

Halfhyde ran for it, flung himself at the spokes, and fought desperately to bring it back. Before he could do so the stern had swung, coming up into the wind, with the mizzen top and yard dragging in the water on the starboard quarter.

Halfhyde saw the First Mate coming aft at the rush to lend a hand at the wheel. He shouted over the tearing fury of the wind, 'We'll have to run before it, Edwards, until this mess is sorted out.'

'Aye, aye, sir.'

In the waist the Second Mate was working desperately with the carpenter and a number of the hands, busy with the axes, cutting away the tangle of gear and broken yards that was threatening the forecourse and maincourse, both straining hard at the boltropes as the wind buffeted, increasing in force and shrieking through the rigging like a thousand banshees. The ship was now lying hard over to starboard under the deadweight of the fallen top hamper, and water was rushing, swilling along the canted deck, sweeping men off their feet as they clung to the lifelines, already rigged fore and aft from the poop to the break of the fo'c'sle. Water was coming green and heavy over the vessel's counter, battering at Halfhyde and Edwards in its passage to drop like thunder from the poop to the waist. Just for'ard of the poop the booby hatch had been smashed in and the seas were dropping down to the tween deck.

Halfhyde shouted out for the carpenter to lay aft. When Bracegirdle reached the poop Halfhyde said, 'Leave the deck gear to the hands. I want a report from below, fast as you can make it.'

'Aye, sir.' The carpenter went down from the poop, making for the undamaged fore companion hatch. He was passed on the way by Sharp, coming aft at a staggering run, holding hard to the lee lifeline and being continually swept off his feet by the unhealthy lurch of the ship.

He called out to Halfhyde from the break of the poop. 'It's all hell in the hold, Captain! Water pouring down—'

'Are you in control, Mr Sharp?'

'Yes, for now anyway—'

'Then clear the hold immediately, and see that you keep control.'

'Bring the prisoners up, do you mean, sir?' Sharp sounded incredulous.

'At once. That's an order. The ship's in danger. They're to be mustered in the tween deck as before, to await further orders. And bring up the man Carling from the fore peak.'

'I can't—'

Halfhyde roared out, 'Get below, Mr Sharp, and do as you're told – immediately!'

As the senior warder disappeared on his mission, two of the fo'c'sle hands were seen making their way aft, sent by Pendleton to take over the wheel, fighting their way along the steeply canted deck. By this time a good deal of the maintopmast wreckage had been cut away and jettisoned over the side, but the top hamper from the mizzen was still lying over and the bulwarks were taking a battering, so was the ship's side as the broken, jagged yards lifted and fell back time and again to smash into the planking. Relieved from the wheel, Halfhyde left the poop and made his way for'ard to take stock of the situation, while Edwards took charge of some hands who had come down from aloft after taking reefs in the courses, and set them to the job of clearing away the tangle from the mizzen top.

The upper deck was a shambles. Halfhyde cursed savagely; it had been an act of God, the fault of no one, but it was a cruel blow to a ship with the particular mission of the *Glen Halladale*. The convicts were the Master's responsibility and he had to have a care for their lives; but they could not be allowed the freedom of the ship and that pre-supposed that they must remain in their chains unless and until the situation worsened –

and that could happen very suddenly. The order for their release would need split-second timing and could still come too late to have them embarked in the boats – all of which, by what amounted in Halfhyde's view to a miracle, had remained virtually undamaged and, from a quick examination, sea-worthy still. But in spite of that, to launch them all from the sharply canted decks might well prove impossible; and the chances were that they would live for only a matter of minutes in the increasing waves.

It hadn't yet come to that; perhaps it never would. But it was a master's duty to look at all the risks and make his plans accordingly. And when Bracegirdle came up from below his report was grim enough.

'There's water coming through the side aft, sir, where the mizzen top took her, and she's shipped a lot of water down the companionways as well – the hold, it's got two feet depth, no less. Otherwise I reckon she's sound – there's no water in the fore peak or anywhere else 'cept the after accommodation . . . water down the companion and skylight—'

'How about the bilges?'

'Filling up, sir. We'll just have to hope the pumps'll keep pace.'

Halfhyde took a deep breath, looking around the decks. The mess would have to wait; the first two priorities were the damage to the ship's side and the keeping going of the pumps full blast until the ship was free of water. He said, 'I don't like the feel of her, Bracegirdle. Too damn sluggish, and wallowing. Get the pumps going right away.'

'Aye, sir.' The carpenter added, 'We're going to be short-handed, sir. Bunch gone and several men injured and sent below to the doctor—'

'I'll see you get all the men you need,' Halfhyde said. The carpenter made his way for'ard as fast as possible, shouting for the hands as he went. Below in the tween deck the prisoners were assembling, brought up from the shambles of the hold, wild-eyed men fearful for their lives, holding on desperately as they came over the hatch coaming to be lined up by warders as scared and sick as themselves. When they were all out and clinging to the handrails, Sharp went aft to report to Halfhyde.

'All up, sir,' he said, shouting above the sound of the gale, his oilskin billowing out from his thick body.

'Any trouble?'

'Not so far, sir.'

Halfhyde gave a grim smile. 'I doubt that there will be, Mr Sharp. To mutiny now would bring them nothing but death by drowning. In the meantime, I'm short-handed and I propose to make full use of every able-bodied man aboard—'

'The convicts?'

'Yes indeed. I—'

'They know nothing of the sea, sir!'

'I'd take a wager you have some ex-seamen among them, Mr Sharp, but it's not important for what I have in mind just now. Any landsman with strong arms and a strong back can help to man the pumps and keep himself and all of us afloat, and that's what's to be done. You'll detail men as required by my carpenter, Mr Sharp, and if I have to, then I'll use your warders as well.'

'Captain, I cannot—'

'Orders, Mr Sharp. There are no passengers aboard a ship in danger – and to keep the pumps working at full pressure is a task that tires men quickly. Everyone will take his trick.'

The senior warder turned away and went back to the tween deck via the fore companion. The *Glen Halladale* laboured on, heavily listed still and seemingly half submerged as the seas raced over her with a sound like thunder. There were now four men at the wheel and Halfhyde was able to hold her before the wind and sea fairly steadily. There was no rest for anyone now; all hands would work right through the night and after that until the ship was safe. The prisoners took their turns at the pumps, keeping them going without a pause.

Towards dawn Halfhyde, fighting his way along the deck for a word with the carpenter, was given hard but not unexpected news: the pumps were not keeping pace. Although temporary repairs had been made to the saloon skylight and companion hatch, and the holes driven into the ship's side by the action of the yards that had gone over had been plugged – the devil's own job in the prevailing conditions – plenty of water was still finding its way below. The ship felt more sluggish than ever; wallowing in the troughs of the waves like a dead duck and then being lifted to the crests as the waves surged beneath her bottom, it was impossible to turn her to head into the wind and sea. Halfhyde's dread was that any increase in the gale might lead to the ship being pooped by some monstrous sea dropping like a thunderbolt over the stern. But he had no option than to run before it until the weather moderated – which it showed no sign at all of doing. It was a question of time now, of how long before the pumps were completely overwhelmed and the ship settled lower and lower until she rode with her upper deck beneath the surface and, finally, went down with all hands.

Of course, there was the yacht: her steaming lights were not at present in view but Halfhyde believed she would not be far away. She could perhaps pick up survivors . . . and if that happened then certain mysteries might well stand revealed, for what comfort that might be in the circumstances. If Archer-Caine's expressed fears were well founded then someone aboard that steam yacht was going to have his quarry handed over on a plate – if Archer-Caine was among the survivors.

With nothing more that could be done on deck, Halfhyde went below to see conditions for himself. He went down through the packed convicts along the tween deck, men waiting their turns at the pumps. He could almost smell their fear over the stench of humanity and bilge-water. They were in an unknown element, at the mercy of wind and water, in a ship that was failing to meet the challenge, a ship that had seen better days, a ship that was good enough for the transport of gaolbirds who would not be missed if they went to the bottom. Halfhyde, looking along the lines of hopeless men, now by his own order freed of their chains, gave them a word of cheer.

'It takes a lot to sink British oak,' he said. 'She'll survive. I have a first-class crew and every man'll do his best for you.'

There was no response. Halfhyde lowered himself over the hatch coaming and his feet found the ladder. Carrying a lantern he went down into the darkness and stepped from the foot of the ladder into swirling water. He moved cautiously away from the ladder, groping for the bunks and their supports. The smell was terrible: dirty water that had gathered up excreta and the contents of seasick stomachs, foetid air breathed a thousand times. Below it all, the gold bullion in its cases. Parts of broken bunks, jagged woodwork, floated on the scummy surface as Halfhyde made such inspection as he could of the ship's side.

He believed that apart from the damage to the side aft the timbers were still sound; if they had not been the depth of water would have increased very much more. Nevertheless there was without doubt a seepage and the most likely source was the tween deck and the fore companionway.

Halfhyde climbed back to the tween deck and went up through the companionway. As he opened the door he was met by a sea that almost threw him back down the ladder, and before he had fought the door shut again a good deal more water had gone down to surge along the tween deck. Shouting for Bracegirdle, he gave orders for the companionway to be sealed down hard.

'The prisoners, sir—'

'They'll be brought up on deck,' Halfhyde said. Holding fast to the lifeline he made his way aft to the poop. Sharp was standing by one of the pumps, supervising a change of convict-power at the handles. Halfhyde passed his orders: all hands on deck for the safety of the ship. He could see that Sharp thought he had taken leave of his senses.

* * *

The dawn came fully up, grey, overcast, dirty, no slackening in the gale's force; still the *Glen Halladale* wallowed and remained afloat. The First Mate reported that the pumps seemed to be just about holding their own now and the ship was no lower in the water. That was cheering news; but there was still no possibility of using the tween deck for the prisoners, who were draped around the waist and fo'c'sle, cold, soaked to the skin and shivering . There was no fight in them; Halfhyde felt no alarm at having them virtually free about his decks. Archer-Caine was lying in the lee of the sail locker, a lifeline hauled up beneath his arms, looking pinched and anxious. The after accommodation was usable up to a point of extreme wetness and discomfort, and between them Victoria Penn and Dr Murchison had done what they could for the injured men, who were lying in the officers' bunks. With the galley flooded and the fires in any case drawn when the gale had struck, the steward was doing his best to provide such fare as was available from the after pantry: cold bully beef and ship's biscuits. It would not go far: it was fortunate that there was little appetite among the convicts.

Soon after dawn Halfhyde's telescope showed him a smudge of smoke astern, very distantly off the starboard quarter.

'The steam yacht, I fancy, Mr Edwards,' he said. 'Still in company, or standing by to pick up the pieces perhaps! The light of day may bring her closer, but we shall see. In the meantime, I've a feeling the wind's dropped a fraction.'

Edwards nodded. 'It has, sir. Scarcely enough, though.'

'Well, it's a good sign at least.' Halfhyde snapped his telescope shut and looked aloft at his masts and yards, bare poles except for the reefed forecourse and maincourse. 'Once we can deal with the trim, we shall come through, if with a reduced spread of canvas. The damage aloft is far from fatal. I'm becoming more concerned with the activities of the steam yacht.'

'With the convicts on deck, sir—'

'Exactly. Some among them might decide to take a chance when there's a distraction in the offing, but I'm not prepared to put them back below until I know the ship's safe.'

'It's a dilemma, sir.'

'Yes! But one that's easily solved. My duty to preserve life comes first. I'm going below to the after accommodation, Mr Edwards, to take stock of the situation there. Call me at once if I'm needed on deck.' Halfhyde turned away and went down the ladder to use the entry from the waist; like the fore companion, the battered poop deck companion hatch had been sealed against the water. With the seas still racing down from the break of the poop before sliding away cross the listed deck, Halfhyde admitted more water to the saloon alleyway as he hauled the door shut behind him. Inside there was more desolation and water swilled up against the canted bulkhead. Halfhyde's own cabin was being used, like the others, for the injured seamen; as he paddled along the alleyway Victoria Penn emerged, looking pale and anxious.

'Well?' she asked.

'It's easing, just a little. We're going to come through.'

'God, I've been dead scared,' she said.

'We all have been, Victoria. You look as if you need some sleep—'

'So do you, mate. Me – well, there's nowhere dry enough.'

He nodded. 'How are the men?'

She said, 'Two of them died. Nothing Murchison could do, he said. I reckon he knows best . . . one had his back broken and the other had some sort of spar through his stomach. Doc had to do some amputations, two arms, two legs. No bloody sight to have to watch, I can tell you. He doped 'em down with rum, but —'

'Yes, I know. Are they all right?'

'Right as they'll ever be, I reckon.'

'Where's Murchison?'

She gave a hard laugh. 'Flat on his bloody back, mate. Took too much of his own medicine – rum. Did the job then went on the bottle. Don't reckon much on him myself.' She paused, eyes troubled as she saw his utter weariness and despondency. 'Sorry about the ship,' she said. She sounded as though she knew the remark was inadequate but it had been sincerely uttered and he took her by the shoulders, held her close for a moment and lightly kissed the top of her head.

'I told you, the ship's going to come through. There'll be a lot of work afterwards for a short-handed crew, but we shall manage.' Halfhyde repeated what he had said to the First Mate. 'I'm more concerned with the company we're still keeping out there.'

'That steamboat?'

'Yes. The ship's still sound and seaworthy but for the time being we've lost our manoeuvrability and stability – and it won't return until I'm able to pump her dry and right the list. In the meantime, if that steam yacht tries any jiggery-pokery we're at a disadvantage.'

'What d'you think she'll do, then?'

He shrugged. 'I don't know yet. We must be ready for anything. I doubt if she'll interfere with us in any way until the weather moderates a good deal more, so the problem's not imminent.'

'How's that?'

He said, 'Well, for one thing, she wouldn't try to board in the sea that's running.'

'You reckon it'll come to that, do you?'

'I don't know. It's a possibility.'

'And if they do?'

'We fight back,' he said. 'I have a prison draft to deliver to the army at Simon's Town. I intend to make the delivery intact.' He left her and walked on along the alleyway for a word with his injured seamen. He found the sailmaker already at work on the two men who had died, sewing them into their canvas shrouds with lead weights at their feet ready for sea burial as soon as the weather moderated sufficiently. Dead in the course of their duty . . . Halfhyde's heart was heavy as he passed on through the slop of water and listened to the sounds of the gale overhead. Always the sea was a hazard, a dangerous way for any man to make a living, and death sailed close astern of every windjammer that fought out across the ocean wastes, but a master always blamed himself when men were lost. And Halfhyde had a strong feeling that before the *Glen Halladale* made port in South Africa many more men would die.

ELEVEN

The plugs and tarpaulins rigged during the night over the damaged side planking had proved effective but not wholly so: water was still coming through in enough quantity to keep the pumps working at full pressure. As Edwards said, they could never have managed without the convicts. But gradually as the day went on and the wind moderated the pumps began to overcome the seepage and the list came off; the ship rode easier in the water and started to lift. It then became possible for Bracegirdle and his mate to effect a more watertight repair that when completed should carry them through to the docking facilities at the Cape. Halfhyde had been considering the idea of diverting around Cape St Vincent to enter the naval dockyard at Gibraltar, but upon receiving the carpenter's report and after making an examination inboard and outboard himself, he believed he could make the passage safely. Much of it, once they had ridden out the current conditions, would be in fair weather. Indeed they would be unlikely to pick up any more storms until they were almost off the Cape.

While Bracegirdle worked on the hull and the broken lower deck entries, the remainder of the hands were set to clearing up the decks and overhauling the rigging, sending up new canvas as the weather moderated still further and squaring off the wreckage of the maintopmast and mizzen top. As the seas, still turbulent, ceased coming over the poop to race for'ard along the decks, the fore companion hatch was opened up again and Halfhyde sent word for the senior warder to lay aft.

'You may take your prisoners below to the tween deck, Mr Sharp. They'll remain there until the hold has been dried out and made more habitable.'

'Very good, sir.'

'They're to remain available for the pumps, of course, in relays, until further orders. And you'll tell them I'm much appreciative of their hard work – they saved the ship, no less, and I noticed no man slacking.'

Sharp said sourly, 'They worked to save themselves, sir, that's all.'

'And so did I – so did all of us. That's the sea, Mr Sharp. Each man is dependent on the next, from the Master to the rawest deckhand. That's a good thing to remember. And now, I suppose, you're going to want your prisoners back in their chains, are you not?'

'It's the regulations,' Sharp said. 'And only sensible in my view, sir.'

'I consider it damnable,' Halfhyde said, 'but the regulations will be observed now the ship is safe. At any moment of danger in the future, they'll be released again.'

Sharp left the poop with a scowl on his pinched, stubborn face and soon after Halfhyde heard him bawling at his warders and the prisoners as the draft was herded down the fore companionway under guard. Sharp's language was foul and provocative: to the senior warder the convicts were nothing more than scum, men who by their crimes had forfeited the right to be considered as human beings, lumps of flesh without feeling. Halfhyde was about to send for the man again and tell him to mind his tongue when there was a shout from Edwards.

'The steam yacht, sir! Looks as if she's closing us.'

Halfhyde swung round. There was no need to use his telescope. The yacht was quite clearly coming in, rolling and pitching heavily in the disturbed sea, her funnel sending up thick clouds of black, greasy smoke. She was still distant, however, and by Halfhyde's calculation would be unlikely to close to within hailing distance in less than an hour. She would have perhaps nine to ten knots of speed; by the patent log streamed astern of the *Glen Halladale*, the windjammer under her reefed courses was making four knots through the water. Halfhyde looked aloft: before much longer he would be able to send up more canvas, and he might be able to keep himself ahead of the yacht if he was given the right wind.

It was a matter of luck and time. Perhaps not too much time now. With his ship out of danger from the sea and back on course Halfhyde recognized that another sort of time had come: the time to call a conference, the time to take more people into his confidence, and to make decisive plans to counter anything the men aboard the steam yacht might have in mind to do against his authority.

* * *

As the conference was called on the poop there was a change in the atmosphere below along the tween deck. The word had spread that once again the steam yacht was in company; this was having its effect on the prisoners, now back in their chains except for those still working at the pumps. Once again the murmurs were running round and there was tension in the air, a vibrancy, an expectation . . . Sharp, who had been called to the conference, reported this to Halfhyde.

Halfhyde asked, 'Can you interpret it?'

'Not exactly, sir.'

'But it clearly links with the steam yacht?'

'I'd say so, yes.'

'Have you any idea as to why, Mr Sharp?'

Sharp pursed his lips and shook his head. 'No, sir, I haven't, not to be precise—'

'But its presence suggests something that's going to operate in their favour?'

'If so, I couldn't say what. It's just that it's giving them some sort of—'

'Hope?'

Sharp nodded. 'I reckon that's maybe it. They see something that might give them their chance.'

'Yes. A diversion – and they take advantage. That's much as I thought.' Halfhyde frowned, looked back towards the steam yacht, closing still and making heavy weather of the waves. Once again, for reasons different from before, he was tempted to run for Gibraltar and its naval and military presence; but that would be a confession of early defeat, and in any case it was only too likely the trouble would come long before he could make the Gibraltar Strait. He must meet it head on and alone. He said, 'Now – the gold, Mr Sharp.' He had told the senior warder the fact of the gold's presence aboard but not the reason for it. 'Has the knowledge of that penetrated the prisoners?'

'Not as far as I know, sir.'

'No extra thrills of excitement, beyond the steamer?'

Sharp didn't think so; if the unidentified men who had been down beneath the hold planking had found the cases, he believed that one of his warders would have become aware. In the prison service, he said, warders quickly developed a sixth sense and some extra current running through the chain gangs would have stood out; but this had not happened. He believed the yacht to be the sole factor.

Halfhyde paced the poop, deep in thought. It was very possible that Archer-Caine had been right enough: his handing over would be demanded; and the demand would be backed by force. Or would it? The men aboard the yacht must be well aware of the presence of the warders' rifles to back the single revolver in the possession of the Master; and it was unlikely that the yacht would carry enough men to outnumber the prison staff. Any such attack could prove suicidal. And during the earlier brush with the steam yacht its crew had backed away from trouble when Halfhyde had told them he would open fire if he had to in order to keep them clear.

There had to be some other factor, but if so then it remained a mystery. In the meantime Halfhyde could do no more than hold to his own theory of a possible attempt at boarding and make his plans accordingly. He stopped his restless pacing and swung round on the First Mate.

'Mr Edwards, we shall do our best to keep running ahead of the yacht, though I fear we'll not succeed. I'll have the lower tops'ls shaken out for a start – the ship can take them now. I've no idea what will develop if the yacht comes close and makes trouble, but whatever she does we shall respond. That's to say that if necessary we shall return any fire – with your rifles, Mr Sharp, on my authority as a lieutenant of the reserve. When you're ordered to do so, you'll send up half your warders to muster on the poop and fo'c'sle. Mr Pendleton, you'll take charge of the hands and stand by for a fight if there's any attempt to board. You'll find Patcham here a first-class second-in-command – he's done it before – even though he's deprived of his cutlass!' Patcham was the ex-naval man who had served in the Sail Training Squadron as a leading seaman and had now been made bosun in the place of Bunch and was attending the conference in his new capacity. Halfhyde laid a hand on his shoulder and said, 'It'll be like the old times, if it comes to that – hands to repel boarders, but this time it'll be no mere exercise!'

'We'll be ready for 'em, sir,' Patcham said happily.

'Bare fists and belaying-pins this time, Patcham.'

'Done that an' all before now, sir.'

'Good!' Halfhyde turned to the senior warder again. 'Mr Sharp, I want Archer-Caine brought aft to the saloon.'

* * *

Further questioning of Archer-Caine brought no fresh information; but the man was certain that the presence of the steam yacht impinged upon himself and no one else. He had heard nothing in the hold or tween deck to indicate that any other of the convicts could be connected with it – and in all conscience, Halfhyde knew, such would be highly unlikely. Archer-Caine was a fairly obvious person, the only one of the prison draft to come close to the circles where there was the money for private yachts.

But was a snatch on the high seas a practical likelihood?

Halfhyde put the question: how would Archer-Caine's enemies get away with it afterwards? 'There'll be a hundred convicts, not to mention myself and my ship's company, who'll testify. How does even a Secretary of State get out from under that?'

Archer-Caine shrugged. 'High places mean low risk – and the yacht's anonymous.'

'But any enquiry's bound to dig hard. It won't be left a mystery, unsolved!'

'I think it could be, Captain. I think it could be . . . with enough pressure applied in those high places. There's nothing so powerful as money, with threats in the background – threats from men who never make them without full assurance that they will be brought off. And no one at home is going to be much concerned about the disappearance of a convict – one less to feed and guard! Besides, they could cover their interest in me to some extent, by taking off not just me but others of the draft.'

'And kill them too?'

Archer-Caine laughed, a grim sound. 'Kill one, kill many. You can hang only once.'

Halfhyde pondered on the gold beneath his hold. Victoria's suggestion – it could come to blackmail against himself. But would not the whole thing smell to heaven, would not the presence of the bullion alone be some proof of the story that would be told in South Africa? Not necessarily; the story itself might well be believed – would have to be believed – but he could still be in much trouble. The rub would lie in the fact of his having been bribed: proof positive of some unsavoury involvement if Bowler denied all knowledge of the meeting in his club in London. But then again, the bullion itself would add to the intriguing mystery and the enquiry would have to probe and find an answer. How were the guilty men to survive that? Were they all lunatics, driven by greed, self-interest and a self-preservative instinct beyond the bounds of sanity to the point where they believed themselves possessed of powers to hold themselves inviolate against the law?

It began to seem so, if Archer-Caine's theories were right. Or perhaps he was the lunatic, inexorably propelled into fantasy by a natural sense of persecution and frustration? Yet there was no doubt – there could be no doubt – that the yacht was there for some nefarious purpose.

Archer-Caine was returned to the tween deck. According to Dr Murchison his arm was healing nicely and when the time came for the prisoners to take up their berths again in the hold, he would be able to rejoin them in their chains. Back on the poop Halfhyde saw that the steam yacht was now within a mile of the *Glen Halladale*, plunging through decreasing seas off the windjammer's starboard quarter.

* * *

By that evening, as a watery sun went down the western sky over a much flatter sea, there was a sense of anti-climax aboard the *Glen Halladale*. Halfhyde, now under a full spread of canvas on the foremast but with a reduced total sail area on account of the damage, was making a fair speed before a fresh wind; and the steam yacht, which had closed more during the forenoon, was matching that speed – but apparently not yet with the intention of overtaking and closing further. She remained in her self-imposed station, keeping her bearing and distance skilfully. It seemed that nothing was going to happen yet. And nothing happened the next day, or the day after that, by which time the two ships were in the latitude of the Gibraltar Strait and again the temptation came to make the turn to port southward of Cape St Vincent and enter Gibraltar Bay. The temptation, however, was brief: the prevailing winds and the earlier run before the gale from the east had taken the ship too far westwards to be able to make the strait before the steam yacht could cut her off and go into whatever action she had in mind. Any such turn on Halfhyde's part would only precipitate trouble, and nothing would be gained by it.

As the weather improved and grew warmer, as the ship came into more southerly latitudes, the drying-out process began below decks; the after accommodation became fully habitable again and the convicts were put back in the foul conditions of the hold. In many ways the higher temperatures made matters worse, increasing the horrible fug that rose up through the tween-deck hatch. Sharp reported to Halfhyde that his warders found it hard to take the stench.

'It's harder for the prisoners, Mr Sharp. Your warders are down there for their watches only. The prisoners are there all the time – and that is what concerns me, the more so when I think of what lies ahead.'

'The yacht, sir?'

'No, not the yacht, Mr Sharp – the Doldrums. Do you know anything of the Doldrums?'

'No, sir, other than by hearsay.'

Halfhyde said, 'A large area of calm, of no wind at all for most of the time. Ships can spend days and even weeks becalmed, waiting for some small breeze to fill their sails and carry them into the Trades. It's a time when tempers grow short, Mr Sharp, and any simmering trouble comes to the surface. Below in the hold it will be little short of hell. Immense heat, and no movement, no shift of air. I shall not condemn them to that, Mr Sharp. When we reach the Doldrums, they will be brought up on deck in batches, and given such air as there is.'

Sharp didn't argue; he could see the sense in Halfhyde's

decision. There were dangerous men amongst the draft and they could be driven to desperate measures. For his part Halfhyde agreed that the chains should remain whilst they were on deck. As a matter of course the warders would be fully alert and watchful.

There was another aspect of the Doldrums, one that worried Halfhyde more than the presence on deck of the chain gangs: when lying becalmed the *Glen Halladale* would be at a strong disadvantage against the steam yacht, to which the lack of wind would bring no problems at all, at least for so long as her bunkers lasted. The question of bunkering itself brought an imminence of attack closer. The yacht's reserves, which had doubtless been topped up to beyond normal capacity for a lengthy voyage, other spaces being taken over to accommodate extra coal, would have been much helped by the slow speed needed to remain in company with a sailing ship – but they would not last for ever. Thus an attack would be likely to come no further south than the Doldrums so as to permit the yacht to break off for bunkering, most probably at one of the French or German coaling ports on the African coast, in Togoland or Cameroon or French Guinea, or even the Belgian Congo, for she would be unlikely to use the British facilities in Sierre Leone – unless the way had been paved for her.

TWELVE

The weather remained fair, with a favourable wind that sent the *Glen Halladale* bowling south towards a half-way point between the Azores and Madeira, a fresh following wind coming from a clear blue sky to carry them down to pick up the north-east Trades, the sort of weather that made a man thankful he had chosen the sea as his profession. The canvas strained from the boltropes, the cleared decks had been scrubbed clean and remained so; and Halfhyde, as the yacht, still in her station, made no move to close further, advanced the promised comfort to the prisoners in the hold, having them brought up on deck in batches of twenty to spend an hour in sunshine and fresh air.

He watched from the poop. Surprisingly, they looked reasonably fit though pale from the lack of air. Murchison, who once the weather had become fair had carried out a daily inspection – cursorily enough in Halfhyde's view – had confirmed no sickness amongst them. No doubt they had been hardened by the rigours of Dartmoor; but the conditions there could scarcely, Halfhyde thought, have been anything like as bad as those in the hold which, in addition to the bunks, contained a row of buckets for toilet purposes, buckets that when the weather had permitted were emptied twice daily by the convicts themselves, two men being released temporarily from their chains for the purpose.

As Halfhyde watched, the steward, Humper, came up from the repaired companionway from the saloon.

'Beg pardon, sir—'

'Yes, Humper?'

'The lady, sir. She'd like a word with you, sir.'

Halfhyde nodded. 'Very well. Mr Pendleton, I shall be below in the saloon.' As the Second Mate acknowledged, Halfhyde turned away and went down the companion ladder. Victoria Penn was in the saloon, kneeling on the leather settee and staring out through the porthole at the blue of the water and the white foam that ran along the ship's side, disturbed and thrown back by the thrust of the winjammer's bow.

'Well, Victoria?'

'I'm bloody lonely, mate.'

Halfhyde grinned. 'There's always Dr Murchison.'

'Dead right there is,' she said witheringly. She lowered her voice, glancing towards the door of the saloon. 'Matter of fact, it's Murchison I wanted to talk to you about.'

'Go on, then.'

'Best shut the door first.'

He moved across and did so. 'All secure,' he said, going back towards the settee.

'Did you know,' she asked, still keeping her voice not far above a whisper and watching his face, 'that he's got a gun?'

Halfhyde's eyebrows went up. 'I did not. How do *you* know?'

'Saw the bloody thing,' she said. 'He had a skinful again last night, went to his cabin, flopped on to his bloody bunk and didn't shut the door. I took a look in. I saw a revolver—'

'You're sure?'

'Look,' she said, 'I've lived in Australia, right? I know a revolver when I see one – there was this butt, showing from under his pillow. I just thought I'd best tell you, mate . . . that's all.'

He said, 'Self-protection, no doubt. The prison service may give a dispensation to medical men sent to sea with convicts.'

'You weren't told that, were you?'

'No,' he admitted.

'I reckon you would have been. Only person aboard a ship allowed a revolver is the Master, right?'

'Normally, yes. This time we have the armed warders . . . I'm not worried about Murchison being armed as such, but on the other hand it's just as well to know. Drink and weapons – they're not good bedmates. I'm glad you told me, Victoria.' Halfhyde paused. 'What do you make of Murchison?'

'A bum, I reckon. Only job he could get – prisons.'

'But he dealt with those amputations.'

'Butcher's work,' she said with a sniff.

'You don't like him.'

'I don't reckon you do either. Me, I'd feel safer if he hadn't got that revolver, mate.'

'Has he been bothering you?'

She grinned. 'Not in the way you mean. Only the fact he's aboard, that's all. As you said – drink and guns don't mix.'

Halfhyde shrugged and went back to the poop, a little disturbed about the fact that to his knowledge the revolver had not appeared before, not even when Murchison had been below in the tween deck or hold carrying out his routine inspections. Of course, it would have been concealed in a pocket but Halfhyde didn't think that had been the case. He would have noticed the distortion of a pocket ... and he would have presumed that if Murchison had felt the need of protection beyond that provided by the armed warders, then the time for it would have been during those occasions when he was in close contact with the chain gangs. And even so, he would have thought it odd for a medical man to carry arms. Such would scarcely help the relationship of doctor to patient – but then the patients were convicts and no doubt Sharp was not the only one who regarded them as less than human.

* * *

The north-east Trades sent the *Glen Halladale* bowling along, well south now of the Azores and heading down towards the dreaded Doldrums together with her attendant steam yacht. By this time Halfhyde had no doubts left that the danger from the yacht was to come in the Doldrums; the moment he lost the wind, the steam yacht would move in. Earlier, he could have run for safety to Madeira, or Horta in the Azores, or Santa Cruz de Tenerife in the Canaries – but Madeira and the Azores were Portuguese and the Canaries Spanish and none of them would have welcomed a shipload of British convicts bound for army service in South Africa, and the yacht would most likely still have been on station when he was forced to take his ship out to sea again.

Pacing the poop restlessly, hour after hour as the ship

dropped south and the area of flat calm loomed, Halfhyde went over and over the facts, and the guesses, and what might well have been the lies: the threat uttered back in Liverpool, his own acceptance for the best of motives of a bribe; the bullion now beneath his hold and his private talk with Colonel Bowler who, if he so wished, was in a position to deny the conversation; the story told to him by Archer-Caine, and the convict's revelations as to Sir Humphrey Tallerman, Secretary of State for Home Affairs, which might well involve Bowler. On the face of it, it was fantastic . . . a case of the bigger the lie the more effective the bluff? But only to fools, and Archer-Caine didn't give the impression of being a fool except perhaps in his ill-fated business dealings, a line of country for which gentlemen had never been well-equipped. The Church, the Law and the Army were still the traditional outlets for those younger sons who did not inherit the great landed estates. With a whimsical smile Halfhyde recalled the rest of the tradition: the fool of the family went to sea . . .

Perhaps he was himself a fool for placing his belief in a man convicted of fraud on so large a scale that he had incurred the punishment of penal servitude. Was it possible for British justice to be so blind or so swayed by men of high position that it convicted an innocent man?

Well, part of the answer was likely to come soon now. Halfhyde was on the poop with the First Mate when the early signs of the Doldrums came with a sudden lessening of the wind that left the sails slatting against the masts. The wind picked up again quickly; but the warning had been given.

Edwards asked, 'Send up the old suit, sir?'

'If you please, Mr Edwards.' The order was passed to the bosun and all hands were brought on deck to start the long job of bringing down the best suit of canvas and sending up the old sails; prudence dictated that in the Doldrums one didn't waste good canvas on the constant friction against the yards as the sails hung limp beneath a windless, burning sky. Along with the job of shifting sail, the standing and running rigging was once more overhauled and some rope replaced after inspection by the First Mate; and by that same evening the wind had gone altogether and the *Glen Halladale* lay motionless in a flat, oily sea. Above them stars shone, hanging close, like lanterns, thickly clustered, to be paled as the moon came up to spread silver light over sea and ship. On deck the air was warm and sultry; below it was like a steam bath, making even breathing difficult.

Astern, the yacht's steaming lights could be seen: she had closed now and was within some six cables'-lengths.

Edwards was watching her. He said, 'She's closing more, sir.'

'So I see.'

'Do you think—'

'I think the time may be right for her, Mr Edwards. Night, and us becalmed, and alone on the sea – there's nothing else but she and us.'

'It's what you forecast, sir.'

Halfhyde smiled in the darkness. 'All men like to be proved right, Mr Edwards, but on this occasion I take leave to be sorry for my apparent accuracy.' He paused. 'I shall make certain assumptions. A full watch throughout the night, and you'll kindly send for the senior warder to lay aft at once.' Lifting his telescope he studied the steam yacht as he waited for Sharp to come aft. So far as he could make out her decks were deserted except for the helmsman and one other man on the bridge, the latter seen as a dim shadow moving backwards and forwards in front of the binnacle. When Sharp turned up Halfhyde told the senior warder he expected trouble at any moment; as soon as the steam yacht was seen to be moving closer, Sharp would be informed by the Officer of the Watch and he was then to muster his warders, or such as were not required in the hold, on the poop and fo'c'sle.

'Do you expect them to move towards us in the darkness, sir?' Sharp asked.

'I'm unable to read their minds, Mr Sharp, and they may delay till daylight comes, but we must be ready at all times from this moment. Myself, I would consider the dark hours to be the most likely – were I in their shoes.' He lifted his telescope again. Still there was no discernible movement of yacht or men. 'How is it below, Mr Sharp?'

'Hot and foul, sir—'

'I mean the prisoners.'

'Oddly quiet, sir.'

'The calm before the storm?'

Sharp said, 'Yes, that's what it feels to me, but I can't say why. True, there'll have been speculation about the yacht and its purpose in remaining with us, but I can't see that the prisoners could hope for much – I mean, I don't believe they can be planning a break-out, here in the middle of the ocean, sir.'

'Earlier, Mr Sharp, you spoke of the yacht possibly giving them their chance.'

'Yes, sir, I did. But I've been thinking about that since, and I don't see what they could expect to achieve except a lot of deaths among themselves.'

'Desperate men, Mr Sharp.'

'Yes, sir, but—'

'A seizure of the ship by the prisoners, and seamen from the yacht to take over would not be stretching imagination too far. If there were to be a break-out simultaneously with some attack from the yacht, we would be hard pressed. You will watch very carefully, Mr Sharp.'

'I'll be doing that all right, sir.'

Halfhyde nodded and the senior warder left the poop to make his way down to the tween-deck hatch. Just after he had gone there was a step on the saloon companion ladder and Victoria appeared; with the convicts below she had the freedom of the poop but just the same she asked permission to join Halfhyde.

'All right for the female sex to show itself at night mate?'

He laughed, but there was little humour in the sound. 'Yes, but stand by to be sent below again.'

'If that yacht moves in?'

'Yes. What state is Dr Murchison in, Victoria?'

'Oh, sober.'

'And the revolver?'

She said, 'I haven't seen it again. He doesn't carry it around, you know that.' She studied him critically, looking close in the darkness relieved by the stars and the moonlight. 'You're worrying yourself sick, aren't you? I know it's tricky, but I don't see what that yacht can do, not really. You've got all those rifles . . .'

'If the prisoners break out,' he said, 'the rifles will be very fully occupied, Victoria.'

'Look, they're all chained up—'

'But their movements are not all that restricted, and they could still take a hostage. A rush against the guards could do the trick, I fancy. Once started, it would be difficult to stop determined men – even with the rifles. Besides, something could have been missed when I had the search made. A file, another duplicate key. When men have something valuable to hide, no search can ever be considered a hundred per cent certain, and ships and their holds have many hiding places.' Halfhyde paced the poop with the girl beside him. 'There's one thing I can do, and if necessary will do – with reluctance.'

'What, mate?'

'Batten down the tween-deck hatch. They'll risk suffocation and I'll not do it with any warders below. If Sharp's men can be got out in time . . .'

'A last resort, eh?'

'Yes. It all depends on the steam yacht now.'

* * *

It was becoming more and more unbearable below as the heat of the sultry night enveloped warders and prisoners. Sweat ran in rivers, the air was thick, the stench could almost be cut with a knife as Sharp climbed down the ladder from the tween deck to make his rounds. With a lantern held high above his head he passed along the tiers, looking at each man. They appeared to be asleep in the main but Sharp sensed wakefulness behind the closed eyelids. The atmosphere was menacing, fraught with the warning of the danger that could come. By this time Halfhyde had passed his orders for the possible battening-down of the hatch; already hands working under ex-Leading Seaman Patcham had rigged the covers half-way across, leaving enough room for the warders to emerge from the ladder into the tween deck, and it would be a simple matter to rig the remaining planks and batten down. If and when the prisoners started any trouble Sharp was under orders to clear the hold of his warders immediately, not using the rifles unless it became inevitable, and as soon as the last of the guards was in the tween deck Patcham and his hands would seal the convicts down. The hold would quickly become a Black Hole of Calcutta and if the covers were not removed in time there could be wholesale suffocation.

Sharp moved on beneath his lantern, all his senses alert and fear sending shivers along his spine. The convicts must know what might happen: the laying of the planks across the hatch would not have been missed in the hold. It was touch and go. If somewhere amongst those men another file or key did in fact lurk . . . Sharp knew his reaction would have to be instantaneous if he and his warders were not to be overwhelmed and the ship given over to lunatic desperation.

He felt the hatred emanating from the men – men who would not hesitate to strike him down, to kill him if they believed they could get away with it. He knew he had not to show his fear by hurrying. To show any trace of fear would give encouragement; but more sweat broke out in the effort to keep his footsteps slow. Then, whilst he was at the furthest point of the hold from the ladder, there was a tremendous clap of thunder overhead, a rising crescendo of sound that seemed to reverberate throughout the ship, and a blinding flash of lightning along the tween deck that for a second or so illuminated the hold and the staring faces in the bunks. At the same time the ship lurched violently, so violently that some of the prisoners were thrown from their bunks to dangle painfully in their chains. Sharp moved fast towards the ladder as the frightening din continued, slipping and sliding on the filth in the narrow gangways, no need now to maintain his pretence. He heard once again the murmur, the rising murmur from the close-set, sweaty bodies, the naked sound of danger as though the terrible clamour from above had ignited a fuse, driving men mad, driving them to a point of no return, some basic and insistent urge to break out before it was too late, before the last hatch covering was slid into place. Sharp never made the ladder. He had not gone far when from an upper bunk a hand came out and laid hold of his lantern; and at the same time his body was seized by a man in the bunk immediately beneath and he was pulled down until a length of chain was looped about his neck and drawn tight. The warder making rounds with him turned back to his assistance, striking out with his rifle butt at the man holding him down.

Sharp tried to speak but the chain tightened and his utterance was lost in a sound of agony and strangulation. Before the warder could use his rifle a thin sliver of steel no bigger than a knitting needle had been slid into his back, angled upwards towards the heart.

As though at some pre-arranged signal the convicts began climbing from their bunks and moving, so far as the chains would permit, towards the warders clustered by the foot of the tween deck ladder. That was when the shooting started but the thudding bullets didn't stop the advance. One of the chain gangs, acting together and using brute force, pulled a ring-bolt right out of one of the wooden hold pillars and the end of the chain came free. There was a concerted rush and the warders broke, going up the ladder as fast as possible.

THIRTEEN

The thunderclap had heralded one of the sudden, vicious squalls that sometimes struck without any warning in the Doldrums. The noise on deck was like an artillery barrage as the thunder rolled and banged and the lightning ran along the masts and yards, vivid fire that had struck right down into the tween deck via the opened companionways. The squall laid the ship right over until her lee rails were almost under; as she righted a little the rain started, sluicing down in buckets, soaking the men on deck within seconds. Edwards went for'ard at the rush, shouting the hands to man the braces and trim the yards. The squall would not last long in all probability and would do little to drive them on their way, but there was danger while it continued. The sea, hitherto so flat and placid, had been whipped up into foam that blew like a blanket across the deck and around the lower masts, penetrating everywhere and making conditions even more unpleasant. Once again the steam yacht was lost to sight astern, her navigation lights invisible in the sudden murk that enveloped both ships, though she was glimpsed now and again as the lightning struck through, plunging about in the wind-whipped seas: while the squall blew, she wouldn't approach. One worry temporarily suspended; but as Halfhyde watched the helm and the straining canvas aloft a man was seen running through the spindrift along the deck, shown up by the lightning as it cut vividly down from the lowering sky. It was one of the warders, a man named Matthews; and he was followed by others of the hold watch. He was yelling something that Halfhyde failed to hear above the shriek of the wind through the rigging until the warder had reached the poop and shouted, 'There's a break-out below, sir—'

'Is the hatch battened down?'

Matthews was breathing like a steam-engine. 'Yes, sir—'

'The warders?'

'We're all out, sir, except for Mr Sharp and one other. The prisoners took them, sir. We hadn't a chance. They just came straight into the rifles . . . there's many of them dead, sir.'

'And no doubt Mr Sharp's dead, too,' Halfhyde said in a harsh voice. 'You'll all come back below with me, and we'll see what's to be done.'

Halfhyde cupped his hands and shouted for'ard to the First Mate, telling him he would be in the tween deck. Then he led the way down the booby hatch and holding fast to the handrail went for'ard as quickly as he could for the hatch into the hold. Patcham was there with two fo'c'sle hands, still driving the chocks down to hold the battens. Clamour was rising from below – shouting, fists banging on the wood, indicating a man at the head of the ladder.

'They'll not get through, sir,' Patcham said.

'I trust not, Patcham, but I want the hatch opened up again, enough to admit me to the ladder.' Halfhyde disregarded Patcham's astonished, concerned look and swung round on the warders. 'You three,' he said. 'Stand by with your rifles aimed down into the hold – cover the ladder – let no one up unless it happens to be Mr Sharp or the other man taken. But you'll not fire unless there's no alternative – is that understood?'

'Yes, sir.'

'Right!' Halfhyde nodded at the bosun. 'Open up, Patcham, and have a care for your safety while you do so.'

* * *

Dr Murchison was in his cabin and the door was locked. There was a glass of whisky with little water in it, slopping in a rack fixed to the cabin bulkhead, and alongside it was a half-empty bottle of John Haig. Murchison's hands were shaking badly and his eyes were bloodshot. He steadied himself against his bunk as the ship lay over to the squall's pounding. The Doldrums . . . Dr Murchison had been there before, many years ago, not long after he had qualified in medicine, and he remembered what it had been like. He bared yellowed teeth in a grimace as he recalled having said once to Halfhyde that he was unused to ships . . . there were a number of aspects of his past that he preferred should remain unspoken of, but in those long ago days he had been an assistant surgeon aboard a sailing man-o'-war, an old line-of-battle ship, the last of Nelson's navy that had survived into the beginnings of the steam-driven ironclads. As now Murchison had been bound for the Cape; and upon arrival there his services had been dispensed with summarily by his captain. There had been no court martial; Dr Murchison had committed no offence beyond his own incapability in his profession – incapability, at any rate, in the Captain's view. There had been an outbreak of dysentery and Dr Murchison, after his medical superior the Surgeon had himself succumbed, had been inadequate to control it and the old line-of-battle ship had eventually arrived in Simon's Town with no more than eighty-six living souls aboard. The unfairness of the Captain's action had rankled very badly indeed and had been the first step in a long line of descent: Dr Murchison took to drink. After drifting for a few weeks he had found a berth as ship's surgeon aboard a passenger ship bound for Western Australia and had been signed off upon arrival in Fremantle because he had passed most of the voyage in his bunk, dead to the world. Thereafter he had drifted again, this time to the state of Victoria and the gold diggings, shallow placers marked by the existence of nuggets of considerable weight found quite near the surface, and he had washed out some pickings that had provided him with a fair sum of money, enough to pay for a steerage passage back to England and an attempt to rescue his medical career before it was too late. He had done some locums for practitioners in Liverpool after his arrival home and had made an effort to keep away from the whisky. Not with much success, though he was seldom too drunk to attend to his patients and recommend poulticing, leeches, or, as appropriate, bottles of medicine dispensed by his employer at threepence a time. When there were no locums to be had, he had set up in business under a pseudonym and on market days in various small towns he had sold useless panaceas to the gullible, tins and bottles of this, that and the other, ointments, lotions, draughts and elixirs all guaranteed to cure any disease known to man. Luck had been with him and his quack activities had never become known to the General Medical Council; but he had eventually made the mistake of visiting a town for the second time and, like a welshing bookie at a race meeting, he had been given the bum's rush out of town and this had destroyed his self-confidence.

Then, almost fifteen years after his original qualification, his life had taken a turn for the better: he had acquired a junior administrative post in the department of the Local Government Board dealing with the Public Health Acts and had thus come under the distant aegis of the Home Office. Ultimately he had retired on a pitifully inadequate income and a few weeks before had been mightily glad to be summoned to a shabby hotel not far from Leicester Square in London where two persons unknown to him, men of obvious distinction nevertheless, had offered·him an official medical appointment in Her Majesty's prison service – a Home Office appointment again, and a very special if temporary one as ship's surgeon aboard a prison ship.

He had been given precise and curious instructions which he had been too needy to query; and threats had been discreetly uttered to ensure his compliance with his orders and his perpetual silence afterwards.

And he had been given a revolver.

Unlocking a drawer beneath his bunk, Dr Murchison brought out the revolver, which was already loaded. His hands shook as he held it. He hoped he would be equal to his part. After a few minutes he replaced the revolver but left the drawer unlocked. His services must surely be required soon: he had a curious premonition that the time was not far off.

* * *

Patcham had obeyed orders with obvious reluctance: the Captain in his view was taking an enormous risk upon himself. As the cover came off and the battens were lifted from the head of the ladder, Matthews and the other two warders closed in with their rifles. A shabby head appeared, a heavily bearded face with angry, pig-like eyes. The man climbed higher, tried to force his way through.

Halfhyde said, 'Stop where you are.'

The man spat, a gob that Halfhyde dodged. 'You'll not shut human beings in a bloody pig stye, you bastard!'

'It's your choice,' Halfhyde said. 'Call it off, send up Mr Sharp and the other warder, and—'

'It's too late now. We're coming out.'

'You know what'll happen. What you're doing is no simple prison break. It's mutiny on the high seas — I'm sick of repeating myself. The warders will shoot to kill.'

'Some of us'll make it. It's one for all and all for one. Some of us are in for life. What life's that, eh? Just you tell me, Captain. Nothing to lose, I haven't.' The words were scarcely out before the man came through the hatch, his big, heavy body launched like a shell from a field gun, one massive hand wielding a length of chain like a flail. As Halfhyde dodged back, two of the warders were hit by the chain and went down with blood pouring from necks and faces; the rifles clattered to the deck. The third warder had his rifle spun from his hand to fetch up against the weather bulkhead, where it was picked up by one of the seamen. Recovering himself, Halfhyde jumped the man, taking him in a strangulation grip round the neck as they both fell to the deck. He dragged the man up and then let go of the neck, and, as the heavy body stood swaying with a look of stupor on the face, gave him a smashing blow to the jaw that sent him staggering backwards, arms flinging about in an attempt to maintain his balance. He tripped over the removed hatch battens and came down on the head of the ladder as another man attempted to climb through. The heavy weight sent the man off the ladder, and both of them crashed down, screaming. More men on the ladder behind them also lost their grip and plunged down to the hold bottom; there were heavy thuds and shouts of anger from below.

Halfhyde knelt by the head of the ladder.

He called down, 'You've not a hope and if you've any sense you'll realize that. I say again, you're aboard a ship at sea and hard rules apply. Seamen know very well that death awaits any man who mutinies. Evidently you have that fact yet to learn. If there is further trouble, each man will be shot as he comes through the hatch.'

He stood up and backed away from the hatch, sickened by the stench rising from the depths of the ship. There was more clamour from below, shouting ... an argument was in progress, some of the convicts in favour of a break-out, others trying to restrain them. For the monent no one else seemed inclined to be the first to climb up. Halfhyde believed that common sense would penetrate; rifles were rifles and death was very final and never mind the understandable lunacy brought about by the horrible conditions and the sheer hopelessness of men committed to penal servitude for their whole lives' span.

He was about to call down again, repeating his demand for the handing over of the two warders – although he believed them both to have been murdered since there had been no suggestion of hostages from the convicts – when he heard the shout from aft, the First Mate's voice carrying clear down to the tween deck through the open booby hatch: '*Captain on the poop!*' He lost no time; leaving orders that the hold was to be battened-down again immediately, he ran for the booby hatch; and as he came out on deck he saw the lights of the steam yacht, coming closer as the squall died and once again left his sails to slat uselessly against the masts. The yacht was now no more than a cable's-length off the *Glen Halladale*'s starboard quarter.

Halfhyde reached the poop. As he stared out across the water, still disturbed from the effect left behind by the recent wind but much flatter than before, he heard the shout through a megaphone.

'*Glen Halladale* ahoy!'

Halfhyde said cripsly, 'Answer her, Mr Edwards. Ask what the devil they want of me.'

Edwards did so. A reply came back: 'You have a certain cargo aboard. That is what is wanted.'

Halfhyde felt the shock of total surprise. The bullion . . . this, he had never expected: it seemed that all his theorizing had been confounded. The yacht moved in closer, obviously intending to lie alongside. Halfhyde laid a hand on the arm of the Second Mate, who had come aft to the poop while the shouted conversation had been in progress. 'Mr Pendleton, see that the warder detachment is mustered fore and aft immediately. Two warders are to remain by the tween deck hatch with their rifles.'

'Aye, aye, sir.' As the Second Mate left the poop to pass the orders, Halfhyde turned to Edwards. Any boarders, he said, would be firmly repelled. With the windjammer lying helpless against the steamer's ability to manoeuvre, the odds were heavily against them, but they could still fight back with good effect. Halfhyde lifted his telescope; he saw three men on the yacht's bridge, obviously conferring together as they had done on the earlier occasion, far to the north, when closing the windjammer . . . by this time the skies had cleared and the stars were giving light enough for the men on the bridge to see the warders mustering on the windjammer's poop and fo'c'sle, and they would be able to see the rifles.

Edwards said, 'They'll be ready to deal with rifles, sir.'

Halfhyde nodded. 'Nevertheless, I have a feeling they may find themselves in the end hoist with their own petard. They're going to find it a daunting task to get the bullion up from beneath the hold – with the whole convict draft on top of it!'

* * *

Below in the hold a terrible vengeance had been taken upon Sharp; as the warder accompanying him on the routine rounds had died with the sliver of steel in his heart, Sharp had felt the chain around his neck tighten further; and then, as the rest of the guards had retreated up the ladder from an impossible situation, he had been literally torn to pieces. In the dim light from his lantern, now hung by the man who had taken it off him to dangle from a cleat in the bulkhead, hordes of prisoners, all now freed from their chains, had seized each arm and leg and had pulled until the limbs came free of their sockets and the senior warder was left to die screaming in a pool of blood. The act had turned the convicts into animals baying for more and more blood – the blood of the warders and of the ship's crew. They were maddened by it; the few voices of reason had made no headway and now those voices were stilled for their own good. Anyone who stood against the mob would be set upon and torn asunder like Sharp. Archer-Caine was keeping his mouth tight shut and had retreated into a corner of the hold beneath a bunk in the hope that he might sink from notice and remain anonymous. For the present he was successful; the single lantern's beams did not reach far and he was currently in darkness. But he doubted if he would ever get out alive, doubted if any of them would. Soon, he believed, the hatch

137

would be opened up and the rifles would be fired again into the mass until every man lay still and quiet. It would be the only possible order for the Master to give, in Archer-Caine's view. If ever they were allowed up, the whole ship would run red with blood. Men were on the ladder, every rung filled, the one at the top battering away at the hatch cover, no lesson learned from recent events; battering and shouting filled the hold with noise that overlaid the snarling, animal sounds from around the bunks, or what was left of them: they had nearly all been torn apart and made into rudimentary weapons, staves to use against anyone foolish enough to try to come down, staves many of which were furnished with long nails at their ends.

* * *

The steam yacht's engines had gone astern to bring her up gently alongside the *Glen Halladale*'s starboard waist. For the time being the warders had been ordered to hold their fire. By this time the dawn was not far off, herald of a day of intense heat and high humidity with no wind to clear it unless another squall with its attendant thunder and lightning should sweep down upon them.

Halfhyde remained on the poop, hands behind his back as the steam yacht touched lightly. From the vessel's bridge a man called across; the voice was that of a gentleman, and he was dressed as such, in a white sharkskin suit with a yachting cap on his head. 'Captain, I would appreciate words with you if I may.'

'Say what you wish,' Halfhyde called back.

'It would be better in private. I ask your permission to come aboard. Or if you prefer, you may come aboard the yacht.' There was a pause and the hint of a threat, very veiled. 'I think you would be wise to agree to one or the other . . . in your own interest.'

Halfhyde looked round his decks, at Edwards and Pendleton on the poop with him, at the armed prison warders fore and aft. He called, 'As you see, I am well prepared for anything you may do against my ship—'

'I don't wish anything against your ship, Captain, I do assure you.' The tone of the voice was perfectly friendly. 'It's only sensible for you to agree . . . isn't it?'

Halfhyde blew out his cheeks in angry bafflement. 'I see no reason why I should talk to you. I have no business with you so far as I know.'

A laugh floated back. 'No? There is a question of a certain cargo, as I've said already. That is very much your business, I believe. Please make up your mind quickly.'

Halfhyde turned away and paced the poop, backwards and forwards, trying to sort matters out in his mind. He would not consider going aboard the yacht; but perhaps no harm would come from allowing the speaker to board his own ship . . . and curiosity nagged, had nagged for very many days past; the mystery was well overdue for solution. He stopped his pacing and turned back towards the yacht. 'Very well,' he said. 'You may come aboard. You only – no one else. And unarmed, if you please.'

'You also, Captain, as to your person.'

'You have my word.'

'A gentleman's agreement, then.' The yacht had drifted off a little way; once again she nudged in. As the two hulls closed, the man jumped lightly across to the windjammer's waist. Halfhyde stared down as he set foot on the poop ladder and came up. He was a strongly built man, tall, and there was an elegance and an air of authority about him, the sort who would not easily be put down. In Halfhyde's mind he failed to fit the picture of skulduggery and attacks upon the high seas: he might be a modern version of the pirates of old but his appearance didn't support the theories that Halfhyde had been developing since the yacht's first contact with the ship.

The man came up to him smiling, extending a hand. 'Captain Halfhyde . . . this is a pleasure.'

'Your name, if you please?'

The man was smiling still when he said easily, 'Well, a name is certainly a useful handle in conversation, Captain. Shall we say the name is Smith?'

'If you wish, by all means use a pseudonym, but the use of it fails to inspire trust to say the least, my dear sir.'

There was a shrug. 'I apologize, but there are certain interests to be protected, as you shall see, Captain Halfhyde. May we, perhaps, go below?'

'As you wish.'

Halfhyde turned and led the way down the companion to the saloon alleyway. Through open cabin doors he had a glimpse of Victoria and of Dr Murchison, the latter sitting slumped in a chair clasping a tumbler of whisky. He went into the saloon, which was empty: he heard the steward, Humper, clattering plates in the pantry across the alleyway. That apart, there was the still silence of the Doldrums, no wind blowing to riffle through the rigging, no breath of air now even to shake the sails against the masts . . . a painted ship upon a painted ocean, and he himself, in some strange way, beginning to feel as alone as the Ancient Mariner.

'Well, Mr Smith?' he asked.

The man coughed. 'May we sit down, Captain?'

Halfhyde nodded. Smith sat down on the settee; Halfhyde remained standing. 'Well?' he said again. 'You wished to talk. You'd better start.'

The man waved a hand in the air, negligently. 'You have all the time in the world – in the Doldrums.'

'A wind can come at any time. If it does, I shall respond to it.'

'Well, perhaps. I dare say you're right – I'm no seaman, of course. But I have one seaman's vice: I appreciate a drink, Captain.'

'Then you'll be disappointed. Tell me what you've come aboard for.'

Smith shrugged. 'Very well. I must, I suppose, accept uncouthness and a lack of hospitality.' He shifted his body forward on the settee and stared at Halfhyde from between hunched shoulders. His tone had changed when he went on, 'Your cargo, Captain. That is what is wanted. You will produce it without argument. And I do not refer to the bullion – I know all about that and in fact I know where it's stowed—'

'So you represent the men in Liverpool – is that it?'

'You might say so, Captain. Not represent them exactly, but we're not unknown to each certainly—'

'You mean you're the principal, Mr Smith?'

Smith nodded. 'Yes, indeed. And the bullion . . . why, that's yours. All yours. A payment of which you can take receipt the moment I leave your ship – with your *other* cargo. Don't you understand, Captain?'

Halfhyde stared back at him, understanding only too well.

Archer-Caine's hypothesis had been accurate after all – and a total value, if as it now appeared he was being offered all of it, of a hundred thousand pounds could be more than enough to turn anyone's head in the required direction. He said, 'Yes, I believe I understand, Mr Smith. I believe also that I understand precisely why. You see, I have had words with a man called Archer-Caine.'

Smith's head jerked and the eyes narrowed. He had been thrown a little off balance, it seemed. He said, 'Ah – I see. But how does the Master of a ship come to be on speaking terms with a rogue convicted of fraud?'

'Perhaps,' Halfhyde said, 'the boot may soon be found to be on the other foot.'

'Which means?'

'It means that I believe Archer-Caine to be innocent – to have been framed so that other names could be protected, the names of the truly guilty men, Mr Smith.'

'Are you speaking personally, Captain?

'Of you? Perhaps I am.'

'Then I think you are very gullible. The silver tongue . . . it has spoken again, as so often in the past, and has managed to fool even a hard-bitten sea captain—'

'Who is well used to judging men, and telling who are the liars.'

'A hard thing to tell, and you are not very proficient it seems to me. However, that's not currently the point at issue, Captain. I have a request to make – to repeat, since I've made it already in effect – and that is, I wish Archer-Caine to be handed over to me without fuss, after which you may sail, a free man, the moment you have a wind for the Cape. With all your gold intact – a fortune, man, a fortune!'

'Indeed it is.'

'And in Liverpool you accepted some of it – as a bribe. You're already committed, Halfhyde.'

'Perhaps. That is my affair. But just one question, Mr Smith: what do you do if I accept your further offer, and later I talk?'

Smith laughed again. 'I doubt if you'll do that, somehow. It would hardly be logical, would it? Men who take bribes! Why ask?'

Halfhyde shrugged. 'I doesn't matter. Just my curiosity. I

have no intention whatsoever of accepting your offer, Mr Smith. Archer-Caine remains aboard my ship, and in due course, when his innocence is established, I believe you'll take his place in Dartmoor Gaol.'

Smith seemed mightily amused. He clapped his hands together as if in boundless mirth. A moment after he had done so a high scream, quickly stifled, came from the saloon alleyway.

FOURTEEN

'You little bitch,' Murchison said. Victoria, with the doctor's gun in her back, had bitten the hand with which he was holding her mouth shut. Murchison kneed her in the back and propelled her towards the saloon. He met Halfhyde in the doorway and before Halfhyde had a chance to speak Murchison said, 'One word, one move, and she dies.'

'And so do you, Captain,' Smith's voice said from behind. Halfhyde seethed; help was available immediately overhead on the poop, but he wouldn't risk calling for it now. Murchison's face was screwed up, the man himself was screwed up to what he had to do, but as usual he was shaking badly and his nerves were obviously raw. The girl's life was hanging on a sudden twitch in a drunk's fingers . . . and now there was no sound from the pantry. The steward had gone elsewhere, or had been silenced.

Smith spoke again. 'Well done, Doctor. A quick mind, I think. We didn't expect a woman, did we?'

Murchison said, 'No, no. That was luck.'

'And much more effective, I believe, than a gun directly in Halfhyde's back.'

Halfhyde said, 'Your advantage can't last. You've seen for yourself, I have armed guards on deck.'

'Yes. That, I expected, of course.' Smith pulled a turnip-shaped watch from a pocket and looked at it. 'Now, Captain, within four minutes a report will reach you, probably, I would think, down the companionway – a voice only, for no one on deck will be moving if they have any regard for their safety. When that report comes, you will answer that you will be on deck directly and that no action is to be taken in the meantime. Nothing else. You understand? Unless you do exactly as I tell you, Dr Murchison will shoot.'

Smith said no more; they waited. It was obvious to Halfhyde that before leaving the yacht Smith had given a time limit to his own crew, but so far that was all he could deduce. Murchison's bitten hand was still clamped around Victoria's mouth and she was breathing heavily through her nose. Sweat ran down her face, which had a white, pinched look; and she was staring at Halfhyde as though all her soul, all her hope, was there in her eyes. Halfhyde was very aware of one thing: he had four minutes' grace – a little less by now – and in that time he could call out to Edwards and Pendleton on the poop and soon after that the warders would go into action. Smith knew that too, of course; and Smith held the whip hand now – unless the girl was to become the sacrifice. His duty as Master was clear enough: his first responsibility was to the ship and the convict draft, and his orders from the Prison Commissioners and the Admiralty combined. His reserve commission as a lieutenant in Her Majesty's Fleet served only to underline all those responsibilities. Victoria Penn should not be permitted to count against them. She was something of a waif and stray, to put no finer point upon it, and she had no business to be aboard at all – if she hadn't been, then Smith's and Murchison's task would in fact have been the harder. She had asked for it, and in so doing had in effect put the ship in jeopardy.

But Halfhyde couldn't send her to certain death.

He clamped his mouth shut on any shout for help; and the seconds ticked away. Murchison's hand continued to shake; the doctor's whole body shook like a jelly and sweat poured down his hollow, shrunken cheeks, down the empurpled, whisky-sodden nose. In a low voice Halfhyde said, 'You sot. You vicious sot. The girl helped you attend the injured men . . . and this is how you repay. From now on, you're finished in your profession as of course you realize. But no doubt you're being well paid . . . a failure in your job, and now a potential murderer as well.'

It was Smith who spoke. He said warningly, 'Have a care. Do not upset Dr Murchison. There could be an accident, Captain.'

Once again Halfhyde set his teeth; his fingers itched to get themselves around the doctor's neck and squeeze the life out of him. Time passed and at last Smith said, 'Four minutes. Now remember, and keep cool.'

Ten more seconds ticked away; then Halfhyde heard the call down the companionway from the poop – the First Mate's urgent voice: 'Captain, sir . . . the yacht's mounted Gatlings, two of them, fore and aft!'

Gatlings . . . British Army machine-guns that could sweep the *Glen Halladale*'s decks from stem to stern, mowing down all hands, rendering the rifles virtually useless, cutting through the sails and rigging, the sound of them having God knew what effect on the crazed convicts below hatches in the hold. Smith hissed something at him and he called back, 'Thank you, Mr Edwards. I'll be up directly. Take no action in the meantime.'

'Well done,' Smith said softly behind him. 'In a few moments we shall go up on deck, all of us – no, wait. The purely fortuitous presence of the girl . . . you'll hold her here below, Doctor – in your cabin. You'll lock the door and await orders. You understand?'

Murchison said, 'Yes. If you have trouble—'

'If I have trouble, you will hear and interpret, Doctor. If that time comes, then you will make your own assessment of when to kill the girl.' Smith turned to Halfhyde. 'You, of course, will understand the implications of that, Captain.'

Halfhyde said, 'Kill her and you lose your hostage. People who hold hostages don't kill them.' He said it as much to give some comfort to Victoria as anything else.

'I wouldn't bank on that,' Smith said in a flat voice. 'Now, when we go up to the poop, you and I, we shall both be unarmed but my Gatlings will be fully in command, waiting for my order which I assure you will be given if needs be. You, for your part, will give your own orders to your First Mate and the warder in charge of the draft. The order will be to have Archer-Caine brought up on deck.'

'Easier said than done,' Halfhyde said.

'Why? A simple enough order, surely?'

'Not with convicts who are on the brink of mutiny.'

'Mutiny?' There was a sharpness in Smith's voice now. 'What do you mean?'

Halfhyde shrugged. 'Precisely what I say. Murder has been

done below already, and the prisoners are battened down in a stinking, floating hell. The moment I order the hatch covers removed, none of our lives will be safe. I repeat – none of them.'

Smith said, 'We shall see about that. All right, Doctor. Take the girl away. Come now, Captain – to the poop, and remember what may happen in the doctor's cabin.'

With Smith behind him, Halfhyde climbed the companion-way aft and emerged on to the poop. Looking across to the steam yacht he saw the snouts of the Gatlings, saw the hard-faced guns'-crews, men who looked like chunks of granite and about as unfeeling, men who had probably done time in gaol themselves. The First Mate came across.

'What do we do, sir? The warders—'

'They're to be held off, Mr Edwards. The rifles would be no more use than pea-shooters.' Halfhyde took a deep breath; he detested defeat but for the moment it seemed as though it had to be accepted. 'We've been outwitted, I'm sorry to say.' He indicated Smith. 'This person asks for the release of Archer-Caine, and his handing over. I may be powerless to prevent it . . . but I have explained the position in the hold. Be so good as to tell this person your own views, Mr Edwards.'

Edwards' face was a picture of horror. He said, 'We can't open up! It'll be wholesale murder. Every man aboard would be hacked to death, and the crew of the steam yacht would be no safer if they remained alongside.'

Smith was smiling, as calm, as collected as any gentleman strolling down Bond Street on a summer morning. 'As bad as that?' he asked.

'Every bit as bad,' Edwards answered. 'It would be sheer lunacy.'

'But you have warders with rifles.'

'Certainly,' Halfhyde said. 'But I shall not turn the rifles on men made into a mob by inhuman conditions – men who if they were not released would not need to die.'

'I see.' Smith turned away and paced the poop for a few moments before coming back to stand staring at Halfhyde. 'If you will not give the order, it will fall to me to do so – backed by my superior gun-power. You spoke of the convicts likely to commit wholesale slaughter. Well, my dear Halfhyde, others can play at that game as well as they!'

146

'Do you mean—'

Smith interrupted, 'I mean this: either you or I shall order the warders to stand by the hatch, and open it up, and do their best to control the convicts by rifle fire as they come out. When they reach the deck – if they storm the deck as you seem to suggest they will – why, then my Gatlings will take control of the situation—'

'You'd simply mow them down?'

Smith nodded coolly. 'As you or your Mate said they would mow down all of us – yes.'

'You're prepared for Archer-Caine to be amongst them?'

Smith said, 'Yes, certainly. I have no use for Archer-Caine other than dead—'

'Which suggests his innocence to me, I think.'

'You may think what you wish, Halfhyde, it's of no concern to me, but you should not allow yourself to be swayed and fooled by a man of easy speech and persuasive powers. The man is better dead . . . and what better way to kill him than as part of a mutinous convict mob?' Smith laughed, a sound that was beginning to grate on Halfhyde. 'Matters have come very nicely together in my favour – first the girl, and then the fact of discontented prisoners who deserve only to be shot. I think I can say that I hold all the trumps, my dear Halfhyde!'

'Until you are convicted in your turn, and of murder at that.'

'Ah, but I don't think anyone would call it murder. The simple restoration of discipline and obedience would be more like it, I rather think – a matter of my assisting the civil power, perhaps. You know as well as I do, Captain, all those men are ruffians and desperadoes.'

'Not all of them. Gatlings are indiscriminate. The prisoners have been led by the nose, by their ringleaders.'

'Then they shall suffer for their lack of spirit, for not resisting what they know to be wrong!' Smith reached again into his pocket and brought out his watch. Looking at it he went on, 'Two minutes, Captain. If you've not given the order for the hold to be cleared at the end of two minutes, I shall order my Gatlings into action against all men now on deck. Do as I ask, however, and you'll live, all of you. I shall be away in my yacht leaving you to wallow and wait for a wind – with the bullion still in your hold. Think carefully, Captain Halfhyde, think very carefully indeed.'

* * *

The hold by this time was a seething hell with most of the men driven now close to the point of madness. The very airlessness was torture both physical and mental. Archer-Caine was able to assess what was taking place on deck, at any rate to some extent. Sounds had penetrated below, the occasional touch of the steam yacht's hull against that of the *Glen Halladale* was clear evidence that at last contact had been made with the men who he was convinced were out to remove him from the windjammer. Whatever happened now, he believed he had little longer to live; if death didn't come in this stinking, foetid hold filled with murderous men, then it would come once he had been taken aboard the yacht and the *Glen Halladale* had been left behind on the glassy, windless South Atlantic wastes.

So far, curled away beneath the bunk, he had remained unremarked. He knew this would not last. Before long someone was going to start a hunt: over the days and weeks since he had first been removed to the saloon, and then held away from the others in the tween deck while his arm mended, there had been whispers and sometimes more than whispers: he was being favoured by the afterguard, treated as a privileged person, and of course the word about the following ship had gone round the convict mob like wildfire and a connection had been seen if for no very apparent reason beyond the fact that Archer-Caine was not one of themselves but was a refined man, a gentleman, the sort who would move in high circles where steam yachts were not so far removed from the ordinary.

If they turned on him now, he wouldn't have a chance. Like Sharp, he would be torn limb from limb.

But if he could get himself on deck . . .

Impossible! No use even thinking about that. There was no hope now. Yet Archer-Caine's mind insisted upon playing around the concept of getting clear of the hold. He believed Halfhyde would find a way of keeping him aboard his ship; Halfhyde, he believed, was not the man to give in to threats from any quarter. There was more hope in that than in the hold . . . and like the flicker of hope itself, the hold was still dimly lit by the flicker of the warder's lantern swinging from the cleat where it had been hung.

That lantern . . . and the first twitchings of an idea, a crazy enough one it was true, but it just might work if he could persuade enough of the convicts to listen to him. Archer-Caine was not without courage; had that not been so he could never have come through the nightmare of Dartmoor and his fall from grace, the cruel contrast of his previous life with hard labour alongside common men. He could also – he knew this – be persuasive; and as he had thought at the start of the voyage from Plymouth Sound, the voice of a gentleman carried weight, carried the sound of authority that might bring pause for just long enough to suit his purpose.

As a last hope it might be worth trying.

Archer-Caine came out from under the bunk and found himself in a moving mass of fighting men, men so inflamed that they struck out at anyone close to them. A mob was clustered at the foot of the ladder leading to the hatch, and the ladder itself was invisible behind more bodies clinging to it like flies while the monotonous sound of fists battering at the hatch cover continued to fill the hold with its hollow booming. Archer-Caine burrowed through the swaying, fighting figures like a mole, pushing past, taking blows to his head and body, sometimes going down on all fours to squirm between the legs. Reaching a bunk beneath the hanging lantern, he heaved himself up and got hold of the lantern and its flickering candle, and lifted it down from the cleat.

He raised his voice and shouted for silence. Sweat poured off him in a torrent and he felt weak with sheer terror in the moment of directing all attention towards himself; but his voice was steady enough and it had the effect he had hoped for.

He said, 'Listen to me, all of you. You want to get out of here and so do I. As I see it, there's just one way. I dare say you can all guess that the worst thing that could happen would be fire. Fire at sea – what every seaman dreads, and the more so in a wooden ship.'

Archer-Caine paused; he had his audience. Shouts were raised against him and there was a surge forward but the saner men spoke up for him: the gentleman convict was to have his say first.

Archer-Caine did. He said, 'All of you clear the ladder. Let me go up first – with the lantern. If I hold it close to the hatch cover, smoke will start to go through to the tween deck. The moment they smell that, they'll take the covers off, and we go through – and they won't stop us.'

FIFTEEN

The two minutes were coming to an end. Halfhyde said, 'You'd do well to bear some facts in mind, I fancy, Mr Smith.'

'Which?'

'That I hold the Queen's Commission in the Naval Reserve, and you are committing an act of piracy. For the rest of your life you'll be a hunted man – no matter what your connections are, you'll hang in the end – and so will the gentry behind you.'

Smith laughed: he was full of confidence, prey to no doubts at all. 'Oh, there are still salubrious places in the world where the extradition treaties don't apply and a gentleman can live very comfortably. You don't image I haven't made my preparations, do you?' He looked again at his watch. 'The time's nearly up, Captain. Don't forget the girl.'

'Why harm her now? You didn't expect to find her aboard. Isn't the threat to everyone else enough for you?'

'Perhaps. But is it not obvious that I can't afford to leave *anyone* alive if I'm forced to give the order to the Gatlings, Captain? Why not be reasonable? All I ask is for Archer-Caine to be handed over – that's all. Do that, and the girl will be saved along with the rest of you. I think you're merely being obstinate – you must realize you've no chance.'

It was true enough; Halfhyde looked across at the yacht, at the Gatlings, at the fingers ready on the triggers. There was no mercy, no humanity, in the hard-bitten faces of the gunners; they were going to enjoy their work. Had he the right, no matter what his duty as Master of the *Glen Halladale*, to put so many lives at risk for the sake of a convicted man, however innocent that man might prove to be? By any sensible reckoning he was beaten and would do well to accept the fact. But he was not the man to be beaten aboard his own ship. He had to play for time and see what use could be made of the warders. Probably very little; but they represented his only hope. He said, 'I think the time has come for a compromise.'

'How?'

'I shall allow you to talk to the convicts yourself. I've already told you, there'll be a riot the moment the hatch is opened, such an outpouring of men that even your Gatlings won't be able to control – even they can't fire everywhere at once and some desperate men will get away. Your own life will be at risk, as well as mine. But if you talk to them, through the hatch opened just enough not to—'

'How do you mean – talk to them, Captain?'

Halfhyde said, 'Ask for Archer-Caine to be sent up alone.'

'Damn likely they'll agree! From what you've said—'

'Yes. But you are a man of threats, Mr Smith.'

Halfhyde saw the beginnings of understanding glimmer in the man's eyes. 'You're saying, in effect, that you'd rather the threat was directed towards the convicts than against your crew?'

'Yes.'

'But you are a man of intelligence, Captain Halfhyde. Do you not still see the danger to yourself and your men before I leave the ship – the silencing of tongues—'

'I think not. You spoke of assisting the civil power, Mr Smith. As Master of the *Glen Halladale*, bound upon government service in time of war with the Boers, I am requesting your assistance in quelling a mutiny of the convicts. That will be official, and witnessed by my First and Second Mates and duly noted in the ship's log as my orders.'

'Well, well! You surprise me with your . . . understanding, Captain—'

'I repeat, I have the lives of my crew to consider.'

'Quite. And the tongues of all concerned will be held in check afterward by a hundred thousand pounds' worth of gold bullion to be distributed by the Master?'

'Exactly,' Halfhyde said, knowing full well that Smith wouldn't be leaving it there if matters went that far, which he had no intention they should. 'Now – shall we go together to the tween deck?'

* * *

'You're a lousy, drunken bum,' Victoria said to Dr Murchison.
'Don't come so bloody close to me, the bloody gun's enough,
right?'

The revolver shook in Murchison's hand as it pointed
towards Victoria, now sitting in the chair in the doctor's cabin.
Murchison said, 'It's force of circumstance. I'm not a criminal
. . . but you wouldn't understand.'

'Bloody right I wouldn't. Understand what?'

'What it's been like.'

'All the years on the bottle?'

'That didn't help. But it's too late now.'

'Been too late for a long while I shouldn't wonder.' She
stared at the haggard face, the bleary eyes, showing her disgust
at the waste of a medical education. 'What's the end going to
be, eh?'

'The end?'

'Yes, the end, mate! That bloke Smith, he's going to ditch
you once he's got his way, isn't he? You don't keep drunks on a
pension for life, not after you've finished with them. Too bloody
dangerous. Drunks talk too much, right?'

Murchison shook.

'He'll do you in. I reckon you'll be dead by bloody lunch
time. Just as soon as he's away with you in that bloody yacht.
Still, that's your affair. You know best, I s'pose. Reached the
end of the road and don't want to go on living anyway.'

'No . . .'

She asked, 'Why did you take it on, for God's sake?'

Murchison shrugged, his eyes straying for a second to the
bottle of whisky in its rack on the bulkhead, then back again
sharply as he remembered his duty. He said, 'I needed money.
I needed it badly. There was no hope . . .'

'That's just what I said. More or less, anyway. We used to
get no hopers in Australia. Easy to recognize at first sight. But
even no hopers don't have to be bastards. What have you got
against this Archer-Caine bloke anyway?'

'Nothing,' Murchison said, shaking.'

'Or my mate Captain Halfhyde?' She paused. 'Nothing

153

either, right? Look, do you know anything about Archer-Caine, eh?'

It was a shot in the dark really, uttered in response to some intuitive instinct that there could be more behind Dr Murchison than he had ever revealed. He was, after all, attached to the prison service. But whether or not he knew anything, Murchison was saying nothing. Archer-Caine was not his business.

She said, 'You're here because of him. Or is there something else?'

'You ask too many questions . . . no, there is nothing else.'

'What about that Colonel Bowler, eh? I reckon you probably know him, don't you?'

Murchison shrugged and muttered something indistinct and then said again she was asking too many questions and she had better stop for her own good. He was looking mighty sick, she thought, real white about the gills. Her words about what might happen to him once he was aboard the steam yacht could have penetrated his hazy mind, though in all conscience she'd have imagined he would have thought of that for himself a long while ago. Maybe he just didn't care so long as he had his whisky right up to the end.

* * *

As Halfhyde reached the tween deck with Smith he was all but knocked over by one of the fo'c'sle hands coming aft at the rush and a moment later he caught the smell of burning.

'Captain, sir, fire—'

'Where, man?'

'The hold, sir – there's twists of smoke coming up through the hatch cover—'

'Get the hatch opened up at once,' Halfhyde ordered. 'Where's the bosun?'

'Here, sir!' Patcham was running down from for'ard. Fire at sea was the ultimate enemy, more to be feared than free convicts, and he had already ordered the hands to get the hatch opened up; he reported as much to Halfhyde.

Halfhyde said, 'Right, Bosun. Hoses, as fast as you can!'

'Going for 'em now, sir.'

Halfhyde nodded and turned to Smith. 'In a few moments

there's going to be bedlam. I want all the warders down here at once. I warned you, your life would be in danger with the rest. If you've any sea sense at all, for God's sake use it now – get up top and warn your Gatlings' crews to lay off my ship's company's movements – and pass the word to the warders to double down to cover the tween deck companionways fore and aft.'

Smith said, 'You may have a use for my guns, Captain—'

'Yes, I may. But only on my order, not yours.'

There was fear in the man's face now and he was not disposed to argue. He turned back for the booby hatch, moving fast to get clear of the fire below as well as any convict emergence from the hatch. But as his hasty feet took the upper treads of the companionway his foot slipped on one of the polished brass bindings and he slid, arms scrabbling in an effort to save himself, down the ladder to the deck where he lay with a leg twisted beneath his body. As he tried to drag himself on to the ladder again there was an appalling racket from the fore end of the tween deck, yells and cries, followed by shots from the two warders stationed by the hatch. Still holding the lantern Archer-Caine came through, saw Halfhyde and called out to him that there was no fire below and that the hatch should be battened down again; but it was already too late for that. Right behind Archer-Caine the convicts were pouring up the ladder, determined now on their freedom, disregarding the warders' rifles and, once in the tween deck, running for the companionways. There was a stench of gunsmoke as the warders fired point blank into the mass, until they were taken by furious men and knocked senseless. Halfhyde, overwhelmed in the storming rush, went flat on the deck. Rolling his body, he managed to reach the ship's side and haul himself upright on the handrail, battered and bruised, torn flesh bleeding. Still the convicts were coming through, and once again Halfhyde was taken by the rush and sent aft willy-nilly as the men made for the booby hatch, yelling like animals, filled with blood-lust, crazed by the possibility of freedom. Halfhyde clung to the bottom of the companionway rail, aware of Smith now lying in a huddle behind the foot of the ladder. As the prisoners stormed up to the waist, Halfhyde dived behind the companionway towards Smith.

A moment later they heard the sudden stutter of the Gatlings followed by an eerie silence.

* * *

'It's the bloody cons,' Victoria said, dead scared; she had heard a rush of feet on the poop immediately overhead, and a shout from Edwards. Then came the sharp sound of the Gatlings from the steam yacht, and screams as the bullets found their targets. There was a series of thuds on the companionway and a body rolled from the ladder and fetched up in the alleyway outside Murchison's cabin. The doctor got to his feet, his hands shaking more than ever and a look of terror in his eyes.

Victoria said, 'Looks like they've got control, thanks to that mate of yours. Best give me that revolver, right? I reckon I can shoot straighter than you with that bloody whisky shake. Give it here.'

She reached out and took the revolver. Murchison, making no protests, slumped back against the cabin bulkhead, face working with fright. At any moment they could be torn limb from limb, unless the Gatlings made a clean sweep of the mutinous convicts, and it seemed, a moment after, that they hadn't. Filthy figures were crowding down the companionway from the poop, frenziedly putting safety between themselves and the guns. As a big, hairy man blundered past the doctor's doorway clutching a bloodstained fire-axe, Victoria aimed the revolver and fired, and the man gave a high scream and collapsed to the deck of the alleyway, blood pouring from his side. She got the next also; and then the rush below halted and she heard confused shouting from the deck. She was shaking like a leaf now, as badly as Murchison who had slumped into a chair and sat moaning with his head in his hands. But for the moment they seemed safe, and she remained in the cabin doorway, on guard, with the revolver ready still, her face tight and hard and determined.

Along the upper deck from poop to fo'c'sle a number of the convicts had been dropped. Men lay in pools of blood, those who had not been able to find cover behind the deckhouses or the masts or who had been unlucky in the sudden scramble to get below again. Now the Gatlings were in charge, with the yacht drawn off a little, away from the *Glen Halladale*'s side but still within close range. Halfhyde and Smith, behind the companion aft, saw the convicts milling down the ladders again, swearing viciously, out for what blood they could find. Halfhyde put his mouth close to Smith's ear,

'Out on deck,' he said. 'It's the best hope we have. Make it fast before we're seen.'

'My ankle—'

'All right. I'll carry you out,' Halfhyde said. 'The moment we clear the hatch I'll make for the port side of the sail locker – that'll give us cover from your guns until you've passed them the order to hold their fire. Understand?'

Smith nodded.

'Now,' Halfhyde said. He got to his feet, and bent his body. Smith heaved himself onto his back and hung on tight. Halfhyde reached out for the rail and swung himself and Smith on to the companion ladder and started climbing fast. As the two men were seen there was a howl of anger from the convicts and a surge towards the after end of the tween deck; Halfhyde was saved by a warder, one of those on deck who had not managed to get below before the convicts had erupted, who risked the Gatlings, emerged from cover and fired his rifle down, working the bolt fast. As the press of men fell back, Halfhyde reached the deck and set Smith on his feet to hobble after him to the lee offered by the sail locker.

'Orders,' Halfhyde said briefly. 'Orders to your gunners.'

Hoarsely, Smith gave the yacht a shout. Peering round the sail locker, Halfhyde saw the answering wave. 'It'll be safe now,' he said. They came out from cover; no convicts appeared from below and they made the poop without interference, to be met by the First Mate, while the Gatlings continued to cover the waist.

Halfhyde's first question was for Victoria. Edwards reported that she was safe and sound and had got the revolver away from Murchison. Pendleton, the Second Mate, had been hit by the first burst from the Gatlings and his body had gone over the bulwarks. Archer-Caine, Edwards said, had reached the poop ahead of the rush and when the Gatlings had opened had flung himself into the lee of the wheel casing at the after end of the poop and was there still, unhurt. As Edwards was reporting this, Archer-Caine emerged from cover and came up to

Halfhyde.

Halfhyde asked. 'Do you know this man?' He indicated Smith.

Archer-Caine shook his head. 'No, I don't, Captain.'

'You've never seen him before?'

'No.'

Halfhyde looked from one to the other. The answer had been very pat, almost too swift . . . and Halfhyde could have sworn there was a sudden look of relief in Smith's face, some relaxation of tautened nerves and apprehensions. *Why*? It must have been obvious to Smith all along that he was going to be brought face to face with Archer-Caine in the end, and most probably in Halfhyde's presence; and if Archer-Caine was an innocent man, why should he not be telling the truth as to the man who called himself Smith? So far as Smith was concerned, part at least of the answer could lie in the fact that when he had boarded the *Glen Halladale* he had been very much in charge of the situation and revelations as to his identity wouldn't have mattered a row of beans . . . whereas now he was in the middle of a mutinous situation and was largely in Halfhyde's hands. Except, that was, for the continuing threat of the Gatlings so close along the windjammer's starboard side, guns that were still manned and trained on Halfhyde's decks fore and aft.

The situation was on a tightrope. For the moment the convicts were keeping their heads down, remaining below out of respect for the Gatlings. But Halfhyde didn't believe that would last. The terrible humid heat of the Doldrums, the aroused passions, that sudden freedom from the hold and from their chains, would be bound to erupt however foolishly, and there would be a concerted attempt to seize control of the ship, perhaps to force Halfhyde and his officers and crew to sail the *Glen Halladale* to the further and final freedom of some outlandish river on the African continent.

Halfhyde himself was in a cleft stick: he had an urgent need of the steam yacht's presence, of her guns, until the mutiny had been overcome. A deal with the man who called himself Smith began to seem inevitable, however much Halfhyde detested any such thought, the more so as any such deal must obviously include the handing over of Archer-Caine. But, of course, even that would be abortive. Smith would merely steam away with his guns, and, the last sanction gone, the mutineers would storm up on deck to bring the final tragedy, which would suit Smith's book well enough. The further bloodshed would not have been of his own making and to that extent his hands would be clean.

Halfhyde blew out his cheeks, a prey to an unusual lack of decision. He believed that further probing of Archer-Caine would prove unfruitful – unless perhaps he used the threat of a handover to Smith; that might loosen the man's tongue. On the other hand the true identity of Smith was not of first importance at this moment and it could wait. Halfhyde had a strong inner conviction that for a while developments must be left to unfold themselves and give him a pointer: it was in his view the time for that touch of masterly inactivity that had served him well enough in past crises. There were moments, and this was one, where to force events would be only to invite worse trouble . . .

Suddenly over the yells and cries from the tween deck a single revolver was heard, coming from below in the saloon accommodation to echo up the companionway and the saloon skylight.

SIXTEEN

Disregarding the Gatlings, Halfhyde ran for the companion-way: his first thought was for the girl. It was with immense relief that he saw her coming up the ladder, white-faced, obviously shaken, but otherwise all right.

She said, 'It's Murchison . . .'

'What about him?'

'Got the gun back. Shot himself.'

'Dead?'

'No. But bad, I reckon, not long to go. I just . . . came up to tell you, mate. He seems to be trying to say something but I can't get it.'

'Where's the revolver?'

She said, 'Still in his hand. I wasn't worried so I left it . . . held bloody tight, it was, but he's in no state to use it any more.'

'Get below again,' Halfhyde said briefly. The girl turned away down the ladder and Halfhyde followed. He went into the doctor's cabin. The place was like a slaughterhouse, blood everywhere, with Murchison lying on the deck, spreadeagled, still clutching the revolver. Halfhyde knelt by his side; he seemed to have made a botch of the job. Half the face was shot away and one eye had gone; Murchison was moaning and breathing stertorously and there was froth bubbling from his lips, which were slack and bloodless and moving in a pathetic attempt at speech.

Halfhyde bent close. There was a curious clacking noise as of false teeth or of some constriction in the throat, and more bubbling froth. Halfhyde said, 'Do you want to tell me anything, Doctor?'

The remaining eye had a glazed look but there was some intelligence remaining it; the lips seemed to be trying to frame a word but Halfhyde could make nothing of it. He tried again. He said, 'Tell me. I'm listening, Doctor. Take it easy, take your time.'

Victoria said, 'Look, mate, time's just what the poor bugger hasn't got—'

'Shut up, Victoria.'

'Sorry,' she said. Halfhyde listened hard, watched the movement of the lips. They came out in a round, framing, he believed, an O . . . *Bowler*? He took a chance and said, 'Are you telling me something about Bowler, Doctor? Colonel Bowler?' He looked up and caught the girl's eye: he read a look of I-told-you-so when Murchison gave a faint nod, no more than a tiny affirmative movement of what remained of the face and chin.

'What about Bowler?'

There was a reaction from the dying man, a kind of rally. The eye came round to stare into Halfhyde's face; a great effort was being made. The lips moved spasmodically and the body began to jerk and then for a brief time the words came clearly: 'I heard things . . . in the prison service, before I . . . I can't be sure . . .' After that the words slurred together without discernible meaning and the staring eye glazed over again and dulled with a look of finality and the head fell sideways.

Halfhyde removed the revolver from the doctor's grip and got to his feet. 'That's it,' he said.

'Gone, has he?'

Halfhyde nodded. 'And we, I think, are no farther ahead – except that I fancy doubt's been cast on Bowler for what it's worth. Murchison was a—'

'Bum,' the girl said. 'But maybe he was trying to make amends before it was too late.'

'Yes, perhaps.' Halfhyde, suddenly finding time to wonder why the man Smith hadn't followed him down the companion ladder to monitor anything Murchison might have said, was making along the saloon alleyway to go back to the poop when there was a rattle of fire from the Gatlings and the First Mate appeared at the head of the ladder.

'What is it, Edwards?'

'They're taking Archer-Caine, sir!'

'The devil they are!' Halfhyde continued up the companion ladder and with Edwards remained for a moment hidden in the lee of the hatch covering. Looking cautiously round he saw that the steam yacht had approached more closely and was once again hard alongside the *Glen Halladale*'s starboard quarter. Smith was standing by the bulwarks ready to jump across. Already contact had been made, apparently: another man had jumped the gap and was holding a revolver in Archer-Caine's back. Halfhyde took a swift all-round glance over his decks; he could hear the sounds of menace from the tween deck but believed that the threat of more firing from the Gatlings would keep the convicts below for a while yet. For the time being they were no longer in action: the recent bursts had sent all hands into such cover as they could find along the upper deck. The bosun, Patcham, was crouched with three of the warders beneath the port bulkhead of the midship deckhouse; more warders, all of them still with their rifles, and some of the fo'c'sle hands were scattered about having taken cover in the lee of the boats or the thickness of the masts where they drove down through the deck, or behind the capstan, even crouched down in the lee of the main hatch coaming ... Halfhyde wondered briefly why Smith had not disarmed the warders, and came to the conclusion that he was understandably reluctant, for as long as he was aboard, to reduce any force that might be needed against the mutinous convicts below. As for any counter attack, the rifles would be useless against the rapid fire of the Gatlings.

With Murchison's revolver in his hand Halfhyde moved out from his own cover. The steam yacht was now ready to embark Smith and Archer-Caine. He called out, 'Hold it, Smith! Take your man away from Archer-Caine or I'll drop you.'

Smith turned round, cool and smiling. 'No use, Captain.' You're beaten. You haven't a chance. Do I need to tell you that?'

'If I'm beaten,' Halfhyde said, 'then so are you. I am a man of my word. I tell you once again: let Archer-Caine go at once.'

'Come, Captain Halfhyde, you spoke earlier of murder—'

'To shoot you will not be murder,' Halfhyde said. From the corner of his eye he had noted a small movement along the port side of the deckhouse, two of the armed warders inching along fore and aft. They could not be seen from the steam yacht's bridge or decks. If they could get their rifle barrels round the angles of the deckhouse, still unseen . . . currently all attention was aft on the poop, on Smith and Halfhyde. There was a need now to gain a little time; Halfhyde proceeded to do this. He called out, 'Dr Murchison is dead. Before he died, he was able to speak. What he said was interesting.'

Smith was smiling still. 'To you, perhaps. Not to me. It's too late now. For reasons you'll soon find out, Captain Halfhyde.'

The two warders were coming close now to the angles of the deckhouse. Just a few more moments . . . Halfhyde said, 'He mentioned Colonel Bowler. What do you know of Bowler, Smith?'

There was a shrug. 'Only that he's a rogue. That's something else you'll—' He broke off suddenly; the warders, now in their firing stations, had opened with their rifles and their aim had been good. Both the men manning the steam yacht's forward Gatling collapsed in heaps on the deck. As Smith made a leap for the yacht, Halfhyde used Murchison's revolver and caught the man in mid-air. Smith dropped, right between the hulls of the two vessels, and a scream came back as the yacht ground his body against the windjammer. The moment he had fired Halfhyde was on the move, running across the poop towards Archer-Caine who was being thrust at gun-point towards the ship's side and a jump across to the yacht. By now more of the warders had come out from cover and were firing towards the yacht; there was a brief burst of fire from the second Gatling, and then, very abruptly, it stopped. Halfhyde gave a grin of relief as he reached Archer-Caine and grabbed the shoulder of the man with the revolver: Gatlings had a habit of jamming at unpropitious moments. Halfhyde swung the gunman round bodily and sent a fist slamming into the face; the man staggered backwards, fell across the bulwarks and disappeared, a flurry of arms and legs dropping to the deck of the yacht. As the two men from the jammed Gatling ran for the remaining gun, they were caught by the warders' rifles and went overboard. Then Halfhyde saw the man on the yacht's bridge taking aim with a rifle at Archer-Caine. He shouted a warning and at the same time threw himself on the convict, sending him down to the deck. Just in time: he felt the wind of bullets zipping across above his head. By now the First Mate was down in the waist, taking charge of the hands and the armed warders and sustained firing was starting, a fight back against the yacht's crew, who were now getting the worst of it – and indeed looked like pulling off from the windjammer's side. With Smith gone, the tables had been turned against them; they were giving up.

But they were not going to get away.

Halfhyde cupped his hands and shouted for'ard. 'Mr Edwards! Grapnels, with heavy ropes – fast as you can!'

Edwards waved an acknowledgement. Patcham had heard the order and didn't wait for the First Mate. He shouted for the hands and the first two grapnels were ready within seconds and being hurled through the air to take the yacht's rails and anchor cables with their barbed spikes. The moment they had gripped the lines were hauled taut and belayed around the bitts along the *Glen Halladale*'s deck. With her way checked, the steam yacht remained firmly against the windjammer's starboard side while the warders' rifles covered her crew.

Halfhyde roared out the next order exultantly: 'Boarding party away! All hands to board!'

With ex-Leading Seaman Patcham in the lead it was done with the precision of a fleet exercise. The yacht's crew was heavily outnumbered and there was virtually no opposition; and within a matter of minutes the yacht, gripped against the *Glen Halladale*'s side with more grapnel lines, had been taken and was under Halfhyde's command. Heavier lines were sent across and made fast and fenders were lowered to protect the windjammer's side planking. With a block and tackle rigged from the main yard the two Gatlings were lifted clear of the yacht and lowered to the poop, where they were mounted to face for'ard along the waist in a commanding position. Patcham, trained in the fleet as a seaman gunner, began stripping down the Gatling that had jammed.

The first Mate came aft to join Halfhyde on the poop. Halfhyde asked, 'How is the situation below, Mr Edwards?'

'Touchy, sir, very touchy. Tinder's not in it.'

Halfhyde smiled. 'As I expected, but they'll see sense now.' He indicated the Gatlings. 'As for the ship . . .'

'Not a sign of any wind, sir.'

'No. But now we have motive power hard alongside us, Mr

Edwards, at least until the steam yacht runs short of coal! Once the Doldrums are behind us we shall reverse our roles and tow the yacht into Simon's Town – under arrest.' He paused. 'In the meantime there's still some mysteries to be solved in regard to Archer-Caine – and Colonel Bowler.'

* * *

Working in watches two warders at a time were stationed aboard the steam yacht with their rifles, ready for any trouble from the crew as the engine turned over and transmitted movement to the *Glen Halladale*. With a due regard for his wooden sides Halfhyde ordered the speed to be kept slow as they made progress south. When squalls came it would be necessary to cast off the yacht and leave her in the hands of the armed warders. With Pendleton dead, Halfhyde and Edwards would need to work watch-and-watch all the rest of the way through to Simon's Town; and once the ships were out of the Doldrums and had picked up the south-east Trades and had the steam yacht under tow it would be necessary to put more warders aboard to ensure that Halfhyde's edict still ran and to prevent any attempt by the crew to cast off the tow. The shortage of warders aboard his own ship didn't worry Halfhyde unduly; he could rely on the Gatlings to keep the convicts below decks. He had had further words from the top of the booby hatch companion: the prisoners would not be returned to the hold and no attempt would be made to put back the chains; but they would not be allowed on deck again and any emergence from the companions fore and aft would be met with the Gatlings, fired on the instant of any man appearing, and no questions asked first. Food and water would be provided from the galley as usual, but would be left at the booby hatch where four men would be permitted to collect it and see to its distribution.

When all his arrangements had been made, Halfhyde left Edwards in charge on deck and went below to the after accommodation, where by his order Archer-Caine had been locked into the cabin previously occupied by Murchison, whose body had been sent overboard once all details had been noted in the ship's log. Halfhyde went first to the saloon, where Victoria was sitting listlessly, the urchin face white and drawn.

'Well, mate?' she asked.

'Very well – except for Archer-Caine. I've a lot to find out from that quarter.'

'I thought he'd told you.'

'Not everything, I think.' Halfhyde was remembering the convict's too-swift answer when he'd been asked if he knew the real identity of Smith. And there was still the question of the gold beneath his hold. That, it was now clear, had been put aboard by Smith and his confederates; but Halfhyde had an instinctive feeling that it was there for more than just a bribe, more also than a means of discommoding himself on arrival in South Africa – the angle of threat. What the further reason could be, he had no idea. Archer-Caine had earlier denied all knowledge of it; and where – if he was indeed a rogue – did Colonel Bowler fit into the scene?

Victoria, hunched on the settee with her hands around her knees, said, 'Penny for 'em, mate?'

'What?'

'Worried again, aren't you?'

He said, 'Yes.'

'It'll come out in the wash now. When we get to Simon's Town. Won't it?' She looked up at him. 'Why not just get there and let someone else do the worrying, eh?'

'We've still a long way to go,' he answered broodingly. He moved out into the alleyway before the girl could find anything further to say, went to his cabin, opened the safe and brought out the key of the late doctor's cabin. Opening the door, he found Archer-Caine sitting on the bunk, his head in his hands. Archer-Caine's face held a defensive look as the hands came away.

He said, 'Questions, I suppose?'

Halfhyde nodded. 'I'm not entirely satisfied.'

'I'm sorry. As for me . . . I'm grateful to you, Captain.'

'For keeping you out of Smith's hands?'

'Yes—'

'Then why did you deny any knowledge of his identity when I asked you?'

Archer-Caine said quietly, 'That was the truth as it so happens. I've no idea who he was. The attempt to shanghai me from the prison draft couldn't have been made by anyone who could have been known, could have been identified—'

'But Smith's intention was to shoot down everyone aboard, in which case it wouldn't have mattered.'

'Perhaps not. But the real principals never do the dirty work themselves, Captain. I swear to you, I've genuinely no idea who Smith was. I can only ask you to believe that. It's something I can't prove.'

'Very well,' Halfhyde said after a moment. 'I shall accept your statement unless and until events prove otherwise – I am, and always have been, disposed to believe you and I think your story's been corroborated rather than the opposite. But tell me this: do you know anything about Colonel Bowler, other than as regards his official standing in the prison service?'

'I know nothing of him personally. Only that . . .'

'Yes?'

'When he was governor of Dartmoor – I've told you this – he seemed determined not to give me a proper hearing, that's all.' Archer-Caine smiled rather wearily. 'He was definitely not on my side!'

'You heard the man Smith refer to him as a rogue?'

Archer-Caine nodded.

'Did that surprise you?'

'Yes, I think it did.'

'You've no reason yourself to think of Bowler in that light?'

'None at all.'

Halfhyde said, 'I'm intrigued as to why one rogue should call another a rogue – if the second one *is* a rogue, that is! To put it more simply, I'm wondering if there's been some collusion between Smith and Bowler, and rogues have fallen out. How does that strike you, Archer-Caine?'

'It seems unlikely, that's my first reaction. May I ask your reasons, Captain?'

Halfhyde laughed. 'You may, and I answer that I have none beyond what I've already said. Call it an instinctive feeling with no basis, or a thought bred in a mind that is seeking a little light in the darkness, a mind that has been busy pondering all the alternatives – the unlikelihoods as well as the likelihoods.' Almost as a non sequitur he added, 'And there is, of course, the bullion.'

'Which Bowler knew about . . .'

'Yes. But I'd not go so far as to suggest that he's in this for the bullion!'

'What you're saying, then, is this: he's one of the men who want to see me off the scene. But I've no reason to connect him with any of my erstwhile fellow directors.'

'Or with Sir Humphrey Tallerman – his Under-Secretary of State at the Home Office?'

'No.'

Halfhyde rocked backwards and forwards on the balls of his feet, his face sombre and troubled. He was making no headway; and he was convinced that more trouble was yet to plague his voyage south. Colonel Bowler remained on his mind; those dying words of Murchison's hadn't amounted to much, it was true, but they had been a pointer to what Murchison might have added had he lived a little longer, and dying men didn't waste their last words. Murchison, in whose appointment as medical man to a prison ship Bowler would naturally have been concerned . . . it all smelled higher and higher in Halfhyde's mind. But Archer-Caine, as a source of any further information, appeared useless, a waste of time except perhaps as someone to try out Halfhyde's theories on.

Locking the man back in the cabin, Halfhyde made his way along towards the companion ladder, to be met on the poop by the First Mate with a report.

'Smoke astern, sir, – I was about to call you.'

'Thank you, Mr Edwards.' Halfhyde brought up his telescope and levelled it on the patch of thick, black smoke billowing up over the horizon to the north. As yet the steamer beneath it was still hull down, but it was not long before it hove into sight: a big ship, three masts and tiered decks. The decks were crowded, and before long khaki-clad figures were brought up by Halfhyde's telescope as the steamer closed, overhauling fast. She came up on the *Glen Halladale*'s starboard quarter, steering close to give the war-bound troops a good view of a square-rigged ship. As the soldiers moved across the steamer's decks she took a list to port under their weight. When the gap narrowed further a megaphone boomed out from her high bridge.

'What ship?'

'*Glen Halladale* out of Devonport for Simon's Town,' Halfhyde called back. 'What ship are you?'

'The hired transport *Tintagel Castle*, out of Southampton, for Simon's Town also.' The megaphone was lowered as the liner came up closer, then it was lifted again. 'The steam yacht made fast alongside you . . . are you in difficulty, Captain?'

Tongue in cheek Halfhyde answered, 'I'm being assisted through the Doldrums, just until I can find a wind. I thank you for the enquiry, Captain.'

There was an answering wave, and as the ships began to draw apart again cheering came from the massed infantrymen lining the decks of the transport, the friendly gesture of men who were bound for war towards other men enduring a hard and dangerous life.

'Seems they appreciate real sailoring, sir,' Edwards remarked. A return cheer went up from the *Glen Halladale*, but Halfhyde was scarcely aware of it. Scanning the transport's decks as she pulled ahead he had noticed a solitary figure standing half in the lee of a lifeboat, high up aft on the boat deck, which would be reserved for the officers of the embarked battalion. A figure in plain clothes . . . a moment later, as though aware he was under scrutiny, the man turned his back sharply and moved deeper into the lifeboat's lee, but not before Halfhyde's telescope had identified him positively as Colonel Bowler of Her Majesty's Prison Commissioners.

SEVENTEEN

'I'm far from mistaken, Mr Edwards,' Halfhyde said. 'I know Colonel Bowler when I see him, and he'll have had the time to embark and overtake us easily enough.' The *Tintagel Castle* would have been making fifteen knots consistently through storm and calm, while the *Glen Halladale* had been losing time. 'My only doubt is what he's embarked for! I'll take any wager it's not the war that brings him far from home – he's well retired, and too old to be of use to his regiment.'

He snapped his telescope shut and paced the poop, his thoughts running this way and that. Bowler had seemed anxious not to be recognized and that in itself was ominous. The natural thing to do when passing the *Glen Halladale* at sea would be for him to go to the bridge and seek the hospitality of the Captain's megaphone to exchange greetings.

Surely, in all the circumstances, an honest man would have done that?

Victoria, who had come up to the poop soon after the transport had been sighted, was equally suspicious and concerned. 'It's what I said a long while ago, mate. That Bowler, he's not on the square. Bloody twister, I reckon. Murchison—'

'Yes, I know. Archer-Caine doesn't believe it but I'm beginning to. More than beginning to.'

'What's he up to? Any ideas?'

'None,' Halfhyde answered shortly. 'No doubt events will show me which way the wind's blowing, in a metaphorical sense – we can certainly assume that Bowler will be waiting for us in Simon's Town, even if he doesn't show himself immediately.'

The urchin face was turned up towards him with an expectant look. 'See any connection now with the bloody bullion, eh?'

* * *

Within an hour the *Tintagel Castle* was hull down ahead of the windjammer's track and soon after that she was no more than a lingering smudge of smoke. Halfhyde, having taken over the watch from Edwards and pacing the poop as he waited for a wind to fill his sails, wondered what Bowler's thoughts would be now: if he was the twister that Victoria believed him to be, then he would surely be highly agitated at the sight of the steam yacht alongside the *Glen Halladale*. If he had noted the presence of the armed warders on the yacht's bridge he might well conclude that matters had gone awry for his nefarious schemes . . . and what would be his reaction to that?

The future was full of imponderables.

Halfhyde, pacing across the poop to starboard, looked down thoughtfully at the steam yacht, taking him through the flat sea and the stifling heat at between two and three knots and rubbing gently against the fenders as the securing ropes alternately strained bar taut from the bollards or fell slack. Some of the imponderables might well be resolved by words with her crew; and the present was as good a time as any other. Halfhyde was about to call down for her Master to come aboard when there was a shout from the man posted as lookout in the foretopmast cross-trees, and Halfhyde, looking for'ard, saw the sudden black line of cloud forming right along the horizon ahead, with fingers reaching out towards the *Glen Halladale* and, as the temperature dropped with terrifying suddenness, coming north with tremendous speed and starting to obliterate the sun.

Halfhyde, with no more than minutes in hand, reacted fast. He shouted down the saloon companion: 'Mr Edwards, on deck immediately!' Then he turned for the fore rail as the bosun appeared from the midship deckhouse. 'Patcham, two more armed warders to be sent across to the yacht at once, then she's to be given a grass line for a tow and the securing ropes cast off.'

'Aye, aye, sir.' Patcham was already shouting for the hands

as the First Mate reached the poop.

'Mr Edwards, get the men aloft without delay – take off all sail except for the lower tops'ls. This looks like being the great-grandfather of all the squalls I've ever seen!'

Edwards went down the starboard ladder to the waist and doubled for'ard, shouting all hands to the shrouds except for those who were dealing with the steam yacht. For a while, as the sky darkened and the temperature continued to drop, there was a curious lull, a time entirely without sound other than that made by the hands themselves. But this did not last; the yacht, cast off with the grass line passed in the nick of time, was standing just clear astern of the *Glen Halladale* when there was a high whine like an artillery shell passing overhead and the wind struck with hurricane force, taking the square-rigger on the port bow and sending her heavily over to starboard with her head seemingly thrust down into a sea that had suddenly become a boiling cauldron of foam and steep waves. The masts themselves bent under the sudden onslaught. The upper sails, taken before the hands aloft could pass the reefs, slammed against their masts with sounds like rifle shots and then, one by one, were ripped from the boltropes to fly away into what was fast becoming night rather than day. Seas swept along the decks from stem to stern, filling the waist with water that built up against the raised poop, water that was too much for the wash-ports to cope with, water that rose arm-pit high as the hands on deck clung fast to the lifelines. The very air was filled with spray; the tops of the waves were cut off as though by a scythe, flattened to spindrift that lay like a carpet over the sea, bringing the visibility down to virtually nil.

The steam yacht was by now invisible astern; and within little more than half a minute after the first blow had struck the ship, Halfhyde saw the grass line, leading from the bitts at an angle of some forty-five degrees from the *Glen Halladale*'s starboard quarter, fall suddenly slack. The tow had parted; the sudden strain on the tow-rope had been too much, the jar as the stern had been thrown over to port the last straw. But for now the steam yacht must watch out for herself and if she took the opportunity, as no doubt she would, warders or no warders, to put distance between herself and the sailing ship, then so be it. There was now nothing to be done about that; and Halfhyde had his own command to worry about – that, and the convicts, below in the tween deck. Water was swilling down in huge quantities; there had been no time to seal off the companion-ways fore and aft. There was another worry: the opened hold would be taking ton after ton of water as the sea rushed along the tween deck and spilled down through the hatch. Halfhyde's mind was on the convicts and the warders guarding them when he saw men emerging from the fore companion, like drowned rats, men who were soon taken by the seas dropping, pounding down from the break of the fo'c'sle, and flung on the water's surface along the waist, a tumble of arms and legs smashing into deck gear and bulwarks with no chance to grab for the lifelines and no skill to save themselves as the ship lurched and laboured to the shrieking wind, convicts whose thoughts of mutiny were now submerged in sheer survival.

In the middle of the battle against the elements Halfhyde spared a fleeting moment to reflect that this was just as well: although the Gatlings had both been secured with ropes against just such a possibility as this current squall, both had been wrenched from their lashings by the surging waves and both had gone overboard; and Halfhyde's last sanction against mutiny had gone with them.

Edwards was fighting his way aft.

Reaching the poop he reported the lower topsails holding up, shouting the words with his lips close against Halfhyde's ear. He added, 'We're all right up top, sir. If we can keep head to the wind and sea, we shall come through. We've only to ride it out now.'

* * *

The squall passed as suddenly as it had come and once again the tropic sun shone down. Astern, away to the north, the line of black cloud moved towards the horizon, leaving a sea already showing signs of returning to an oily calm. The temperature rose again, and the decks began to steam as the wetness was drawn away by the blistering sun.

There was no sign of the steam yacht. Halfhyde searched astern with his telescope. The vessel seemed to have vanished from the sea's surface – surprisingly, for the squall had lasted a bare half-hour from start to finish and with her engine the yacht should have been able to maintain steerage way and not drift too far astern. But for the moment other worries took precedence: the pumps were hard at work, once again manned by the convicts under Patcham's orders, and they had an unconscionable amount of water to shift; in the meantime the *Glen Halladale* stood well down in the water. The carpenter and sailmaker were busy along the deck making running repairs and overhauling the rigging, under the supervision of the First Mate.

From the poop, Halfhyde watched closely, sensing incipient trouble. All the remaining warders were on guard with their rifles, and for the present the Dartmoor draft, itself also depleted by losses overboard, was working hard enough to make the ship seaworthy in case another squall should come. But the docility might not last: the warders were by now much reduced in numbers, partly because of the men detached to the steam yacht, partly on account of the casualties already sustained and fresh casualties resulting from the squall – two had gone overboard, three had been badly injured when taken and hurled along by the sea and were now being looked after by Victoria in the saloon. The convicts might be seeing their chance, while the ship's company was fully occupied; and the absence of the Gatlings would certainly not have gone unnoticed.

Some lunatic ringleader could yet emerge and take a chance . . .

Halfhyde called for'ard. 'Mr Edwards, lay aft, if you please.'

'Aye, aye, sir.' The First Mate made his way along the deck and joined Halfhyde on the poop. Halfhyde asked him how he assessed the mood of the convicts.

'Nasty, I'd say, sir.'

'Likely to break out, d'you suppose?'

Edwards blew out his cheeks. 'Wouldn't get them anywhere, sir, would it?'

'It could get them control of the ship. If that happened the crew would continue working under convict orders if only to save their own lives and make port – that's something we've faced all along since they left the hold. And that hasn't changed.'

'No, sir—'

'I want you to speak to each of the warders, Edwards. I don't want to have to call out orders . . . they're to withdraw towards the poop, mustering below the fore rail where they'll form a line of defence. If there's any general move aft on the part of the convicts, I'll order them up to the poop where they'll have a clear field of fire covering the whole of the upper deck. It's all we can do. And as soon as they can be spared, all crew hands are to come aft and man the poop.'

'Fight it out from here, sir?'

Halfhyde nodded. 'Exactly. In the old days the poop was the after castle – that's what we shall make it if we're forced to. I can only hope we won't be.'

The First Mate left the poop to carry out the orders. Halfhyde watched him circulate, looking as casual as possible as he spoke to the warders and the fo'c'sle hands. In the meantime the ship lay motionless on the still water; the sun, by contrast with the squall, seemed more ferocious than ever. The deck, so recently beneath the rushing onslaught of the sea, was starting to bubble with blobs of tar as the caulking of the seams melted in the terrible, inescapable heat. Dirty water from the hold and bilges was spewed out to run away down the scuppers and wash-ports as the convicts slaved away at the pumps, backs bent to the heavy task, a task that would go on for hours yet until the carpenter was satisfied that the ship was dry below.

It was as the first of the warders was moving back towards the break of the poop that the trouble started. It started with an argument between the two convicts on either handle of one of the pumps: one was accused of not bearing down with his full weight, and in seconds the two men had left the pump and fists were being slung. Edwards moved in fast and tried to separate the prisoners, getting for his pains a heavy blow to the chin that sent him sprawling. He fetched up against the port bulwarks and lay stunned.

That did it. The fighting became general, convict against convict and convict against the ship's company, a vicious business of fists and marline-spikes. Halfhyde roared out from the poop for all the warders to come aft as fast as possible and stand ready to open fire the moment any convicts could be isolated from the crew. Within the next half minute the ship was in pandemonium, with blood along the decks as heads were split open by the marline-spikes or any other handy weapon that offered itself. Whenever a clear field of fire could be found, the rifles were used; but the convicts' blood was up and the rifles had little damping effect. There was a roar from the convicts when one of them hurled a marline-spike through the air towards the poop: thrown with immense force, it took a warder full in the face; the point entered the man's mouth and went through the back of the throat. There was a gurgling sound, a bubbling scream, and he fell. His rifle went over the fore rail of the poop to take the deck on the port side of the sail locker.

At once a convict darted forward, seized the rifle and ran back with it. As the warders rallied, Halfhyde passed the order to fire a volley point blank into the milling mob. His own crew had now mostly reached the temporary safety of the poop; those who had not had been trampled underfoot by the mass of prisoners. The concerted fire from the warders' rifles brought a pause in what would have been a rush aft. As it happened, the lull was just long enough.

* * *

Aboard the *Tintagel Castle*, which had been not so far ahead of the *Glen Halladale*, there had been concern on the bridge for the safety of the windjammer and the steam yacht that had been alongside her. The weight of the squall, the screaming wind, could have caused damage: and there was a camaraderie amongst seafarers that overrode schedules and even the delivery of troops to a battle zone. The Master of the *Tintagel Castle*, himself trained in the square-riggers, had taken little time to reach a decision.

'We'll turn and steam back,' he said to his Chief Officer. 'Just to make sure.'

The wheel had been put over and the transport turned through one hundred and eighty degrees on to a reciprocal of her course. It was not long before the lookouts had raised the *Glen Halladale*; and for Halfhyde the first distant sight of the big ship bearing down from ahead came in the nick of time. When his shout from the poop cut through the sounds of mayhem and murder a sudden silence fell. The convicts stared across the water at the approaching liner, coming down fast: a battalion of British infantry, once its assistance was sought, would be every bit as keen to put down mutineers as to fight Brother Boer in South Africa. The *Glen Halladale*'s decks could be raked by the rifles and the Maxims at a word from Halfhyde.

There was an instinctive rush below as the soldiers were seen crowding the high decks. As the *Tintagel Castle* came down the windjammer's starboard side a hail came from her bridge.

'Do you require assistance, Captain?'

Halfhyde called back his thanks. 'I'm seaworthy enough and I can reach Simon's Town when I get a wind, Captain. But I'd much appreciate military assistance. I'm carrying convicts from Dartmoor prison, to form a labour battalion in South Africa . . . they've mutinied and I'm short of guards and arms. I'd appreciate a half-company of infantry sent across, to come with me to Simon's Town, Captain.'

There was a pause; the officer commanding the troops would have to be consulted, naturally. Halfhyde called across again. 'Have you a Colonel Bowler aboard . . . Colonel Bowler of the Prison Commissioners?'

The answer was affirmative. Halfhyde called back, 'I am under his orders in regard to the convict draft. As a matter of first importance to me, I ask that he be put aboard my ship. There are matters to be discussed – urgently.'

* * *

Halfhyde's request for military assistance was answered after some delay and two boats crammed with soldiers were lowered from the davits on the transport's embarkation deck. Fifty men with two corporals and a colour-sergeant were pulled across with their rifles and ammunition. The guard would be a strong one and the discipline would be that of Her Majesty's Army.

Bowler was not with the boats. Halfhyde asked why.

The colour-sergeant reported, 'Colonel Bowler was not disposed to come, sir.'

'I see,' Halfhyde said crisply. 'In that case I shall board the *Tintagel Castle* myself.' He called down to the transport's Second Officer in charge of the boats. 'I'd be obliged if you'd remain alongside for a few moments, and then take me and one other across to your ship.'

'I'm under orders not to delay overlong, sir—'

'Yes, I appreciate that, but I, too, am on government service and I must ask that your captain renders assistance as required by Her Majesty the Queen.' Tongue slightly in cheek at his own pomposity, Halfhyde turned away before the young officer could respond. He went down the companion to the saloon alleyway and opened up the doctor's cabin.

'You'll come with me,' he said to Archer-Caine.

'Where to?'

'To the *Tintagel Castle* — to confront Colonel Bowler,' Halfhyde answered. 'My patience is at an end and there are answers that I intend to force to the surface before the next half-hour is out.'

EIGHTEEN

As the boat's crew pulled towards the *Tintagel Castle's* falls to be hooked on and hoisted to the embarkation deck, Halfhyde watched Archer-Caine covertly. The man seemed ill at ease, had seemed so from the moment Halfhyde had told him of his intentions. Perhaps it was a natural reaction; Archer-Caine was, after all, a convicted criminal for whom Bowler was known to have no sympathy, no belief in his protestations of innocence; and Archer-Caine had made some very pointed accusations against Bowler's chief, Sir Humphrey Tallerman. To be forced to repeat those accusations to Colonel Bowler might well be embarrassing even to an innocent man. If Bowler was after all on the square – and Archer-Caine himself had never suggested the opposite – then in the absence of hard, factual proof Archer-Caine might very well find more charges brought against him . . .

As he stepped from the boat to the embarkation deck Halfhyde was met by the transport's Chief Officer and Master-at-Arms. He said, 'I wish words with one of your passengers – Colonel Bowler, under whose orders—'

'Yes, Captain. I'm aware of the position. Colonel Bowler—'

'Would not come to my ship. Therefore Mahomet has come to the mountain.' Halfhyde's face was formidable now, not disposed for any argument. 'I insist upon seeing him immediately – in the name of the Admiralty in London.'

* * *

After words with the liner's captain, who passed the information that the colonel had embarked without prior notice at

Southampton only minutes before the *Tintagel Castle* had been hauled off by the harbour tugs, Halfhyde and Archer-Caine were taken to Bowler's B Deck stateroom. They were accompanied by the Master-at-Arms, who knocked. There was no reply. When the Master-at-Arms tried the handle, the door was found to be locked.

'Then where the devil is he?' Halfhyde demanded.

The Master-at-Arms shrugged. 'Might be anywhere in the passenger accommodation, sir, on deck maybe.'

'Have him looked for, if you please. I shall wait.'

'Aye, aye, sir.' The Master-at-Arms called up a steward and sent him off on his errand. They waited, Halfhyde growing more and more impatient. After some ten minutes Bowler appeared at the end of the alleyway, portly, militarily trim. He walked along towards his stateroom, eyebrows raised as he saw and recognized Archer-Caine.

'Well now, Halfhyde, what's the meaning of this, pray?'

'The meaning of what, Colonel?'

'The presence of this convict, of course! Upon what authority do you—'

'My own, Colonel. There are matters to be discussed, and we shall discuss them. Kindly unlock your stateroom, and we shall go in.'

'The devil I will! Look here, Halfhyde, this really is damnably rude behaviour—'

'Never mind that, Colonel. Just do as I say. Unless you wish the affairs of Sir Humphrey Tallerman to be discussed in public.'

'Sir Humphrey—' Bowler's face had gone suddenly white beneath its tan and there was a perceptible shake in the plump body. 'Very well, then, but I promise you your attitude will be reported to the Admiralty the moment I'm able to send word from Simon's Town.' There was no reaction from Halfhyde, and Bowler opened the door of the stateroom and led the way in. Then, seeming to vibrate with anger, he turned on Halfhyde. 'Now, what the devil's all this, man? And how is it that you managed to lose control of the convicts? Damn it, that's no way to command a ship!'

'One thing at a time, Colonel,' Halfhyde said evenly. 'And first, Archer-Caine. As a result of certain things he has told me —'

'A damn convict!

'I believe him to be innocent of the charges brought against him. I believe him because what he said—'

'Even to listen to—'

'Kindly listen yourself, Colonel. What he told me has been largely borne out by subsequent events. An attempt was made to seize him from my ship, an attempt in which men died. One of them was a man who called himself Smith.'

'Really.'

'From the steam yacht which you no doubt saw alongside me earlier – and which has now vanished somewhere astern, with four of your Dartmoor warders, who by this time may well have found out more of the yacht's intentions. That is, if the vessel hasn't foundered. I doubt if it has, so I am expecting further evidence to emerge.'

'Evidence of what?'

Halfhyde shrugged. 'Obviously, Colonel, evidence as to who it is who is so determined to silence Archer-Caine. The names of those involved in perversion of justice.'

'Perversion of justice. I see.' Bowler's voice was icy; but Halfhyde believed he detected some manifestation of fear in it. 'Anything else while you're about it?'

Halfhyde said, 'Attempted kidnap. Murder on the high seas. Bribery by the stowage of gold bullion—'

'Which you yourself accepted. *You* took a bribe, Halfhyde.'

Halfhyde smiled acidly. 'Unction ill becomes you, Colonel. But now we have some of the truth, I fancy. I think you're losing your nerve, .Colonel Bowler. Either that or you're somewhat too sure of yourself for your own good.'

'What d'you mean by that?'

'Simply that both you and I know that you've just made an admission of a sort, an admission that you were told about the gold – an admission made in front of a third party—'

'A convict, Halfhyde, a man who would tell any lies to a willing ear in his own interest. No one would call that evidence, I fancy! As to the rest, well, that will be taken care of in due course.'

'Another attack at sea – or false evidence in Simon's Town, an official denial of any knowledge of the bullion, and myself arrested and given no chance to offer a defence, after a submission by Colonel Bowler of the Prison Commission in London? Is that to be it?' Halfhyde remembered Victoria's warning aboard the *Glen Halladale*; many things were now coming home to roost, it seemed. And Bowler was no fool; he had many strings to pull in the right quarters and was in a fine position to get away with anything he chose to do. Yet there was still Archer-Caine, listening to every word; and Halfhyde did not believe that his testimony would be entirely disregarded simply because he was a person convicted of fraud.

What game was Bowler playing now? Archer-Caine, when Halfhyde returned aboard his ship, would go with him, and be a constant danger to Bowler . . . or would Bowler use his authority as one of Her Majesty's Prison Commissioners to have the man held in custody aboard, to be landed independently in Simon's Town and then conveniently disposed of through the agency of persons in Bowler's pocket? It was reasonably obvious now that Bowler was in league with the men who had offered a bribe to Halfhyde, in league with the men who wished Archer-Caine finally silenced – and it began to look as though Bowler felt himself close to his objective.

Halfhyde glanced at Archer-Caine, wondering what the man's thoughts and fears might be now; and he was in time to see the odd look that flashed between Archer-Caine and Bowler, no more really than a meeting of eyes very momentarily. Bowler was about to speak again when there was a knock at the door of the stateroom and the Master-at-Arms entered holding a canvas bag wet with seawater.

'Beg pardon, sir. Recovered from the sea, this was. Galley hand saw it floating and put a fishing line out from a lower port and caught it on his hook, like. A military gentleman on deck said he'd seen it go overboard . . . thrown by Colonel Bowler.'

* * *

Bloodstained as to his uniform, Halfhyde was pulled back to the *Glen Halladale*; the blood was Archer-Caine's. Halfhyde returned the First Mate's salute as he came over the bulwarks; the tranport's boat returned across the water, ruffled now by the beginnings of a breeze, and the *Tintagel Castle*'s screws turned over as soon as the boat had been hooked on to the falls, resuming her interrupted passage to the Cape. Taking advantage of the breeze to carry the ship as far as possible down to the south-east Trades and a steady blow, Edwards called out the hands to trim the sails and send up more canvas. As soon as the *Glen Halladale* was moving Halfhyde had a word with the First Mate and then went below to the saloon where Victoria was waiting.

She said, 'Archer-Caine?'

'Dead. Bowler went berserk when a bag was produced . . . he drew a revolver and shot Archer-Caine. I don't know if he meant to – he could have been aiming for me for all I know. He wasn't in control of himself. Anyway, he's under arrest now and a full report will be made in Simon's Town. He'll be charged with murder.'

Bewildered, the girl asked, 'What was it all about, then? Who was telling the bloody truth, for God's sake?'

Halfhyde said, 'Neither of them. That bag . . . it contained all the evidence. Full transcriptions of Archer-Caine's trial plus a confession made later and obviously extorted by Bowler or another of the gang. Names – the lot. Tallerman included – a lot of heads are going to roll, Victoria. It was Bowler's method of keeping his hands on the reins of power, of putting the squeeze on when he needed to. I suppose, when I embarked aboard the *Tintagel Castle* he panicked and decided to get rid of the evidence.'

'But where did Archer-Caine fit in?'

'They were hand-in-glove. Archer-Caine was in fact inno-cent of the charge – he'd been framed all right, and as I said the "confession" made after the trial was extorted – and those men were out to get him before he could persuade someone in authority of his innocence. But that was just as far as the innocence went, Victoria. He and Bowler had cooked up a scheme when Bowler was governor of Dartmoor . . . Bowler was a poor man and hadn't long to go for a small pension – like Murchison. They were going to get out to South Africa – the prison draft was sheer luck – and share the loot.'

'The bloody bullion, d'you mean?'

He nodded. 'Bowler would've fixed the army authorities. Bowler was in a position to fix everything his way. If I hadn't allowed the discharge of the bullion, I'd have been charged with accepting a bribe whilst on government service.'

Victoria gave a long whistle. 'Bloody lucky escape for you, mate! Don't take any more risks, eh? Take my advice, all right? I always said, I didn't like it. Too bloody trusting . . . I reckon women have more insight than men.' She paused, looking up at him quizzically. Fondly too, and anxiously. 'You've had a lot on your plate, haven't you? What happens next?'

He said, 'A safe delivery of the convicts at Simon's Town, God willing.'

'How about that steam yacht?'

'A search will be made once the *Tintagel Castle* berths in Simon's Town and makes a report. By this time I'd not be surprised to hear the yacht's used up her bunkers and any woodwork they can feed into the boiler, and she may be drifting, as useless as I am without a wind – but she'll be picked up in due course.'

'Suppose they've reached land, mate?'

'They'll still be picked up one day.'

She said, 'It's the warders I'm worried about.'

'So am I. But we all face danger when serving the Queen, Victoria. She's a hard taskmistress!'

'A woman,' Victoria said. She stood with the light breeze ruffling her hair, a hand on the poop rail, watching Halfhyde as he stared aloft at the set of his sails. The sun was strong now, burning down like the fire of a furnace. She fancied the breeze was becoming a little stronger; the sails were starting to belly out from their yards and there was a slight ruffle on the water. Victoria wanted to ask Halfhyde if he was glad he'd taken a woman with him, but she thought better of it. She would probably have got a dusty answer. As it was, she felt content enough. She was part of the fittings and that was all she wanted as little by little the breeze grew into a fresh wind and the *Glen Halladale* started the last haul south into the Trades for the arrival off the Cape.